LIGHT OF EXILE

LIGHT OF EXILE

CHRISTOPHER FARRAR

Lingua
Franca

Book design and production by Columbus Publishing Lab
www.ColumbusPublishingLab.com

Reference maps drawn by Dr. Steven Fink.

Hebrew Bible translations by Dr. Christopher Farrar.

Cover image:

James Jacques Joseph Tissot (French, 1836–1902). *The Flight of the Prisoners,* c. 1896–1902, gouache on board. Gift of the heirs of Jacob Schiff. X1952-366. Courtesy of the Jewish Museum, New York.

Paperback ISBN: 978-1-63337-670-0
E-book ISBN: 978-1-63337-671-7

LCCN: 9781633376700

1 3 5 7 9 10 8 6 4 2

How do we get to thank the teachers who've been important in our lives? One way is to go on and build a life for ourselves with the foundation they've given us. And I did do that. I earned a doctorate in Linguistics. I honed my writing skills, becoming known for that in my professional circles. Later, much later, I became a novelist. All of that would have been a sufficient tribute to Rita. But when she was 96, six decades after I had left her classroom and just before she died, I was able to meet with her and let her know, or rather show her in person, the profound influence she had had on me. For that, I'm very grateful.

Some Terms Used in the Novel

In order to enhance the reader's immersion in the time and culture of the novel, some terms and names are presented in forms that might not be familiar. Here are some to get started with. There's a complete list at the back of the book.

Bavel, Bab-ili: Babylon in Hebrew and Babylonian, respectively

Yehudah: Judah, in Hebrew

Yerushalayim: Jerusalem in Hebrew

Mitzrayim: Egypt in Hebrew

Yahweh: the name of the God of Israel

If you are unfaithful, I will scatter you among the peoples; but if you return to Me, and guard My commandments and do them, even if your dispersed are at the ends of the earth, I will gather them and bring them to the place where I have chosen that My name should dwell.

NEHEMIAH 1:8–9

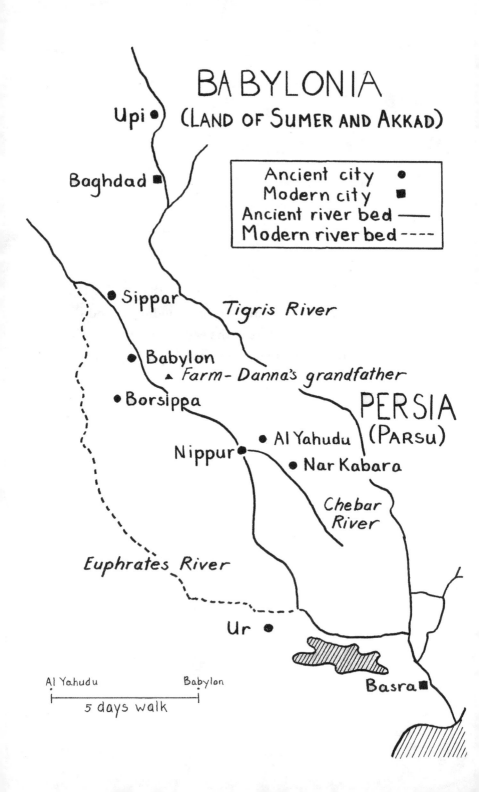

PART I

Late Spring, Year 17 of King Nabu-na'id

> I am weary with groaning;
> > every night I drench my bed,
> > I melt my couch in tears.
> My eyes are wasted by vexation,
> > worn out because of all my foes.

PSALM 6:7–8

Village of Nar Kabara

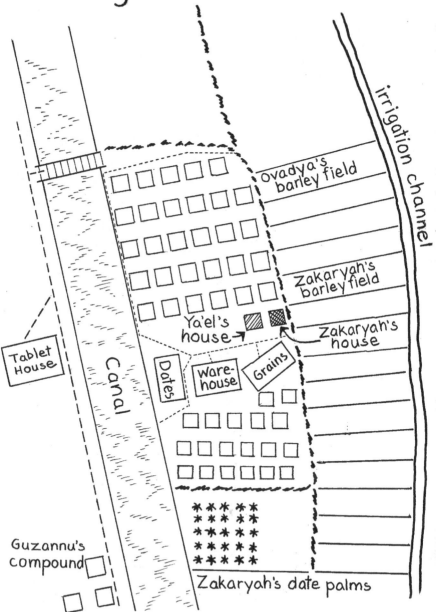

Tablet House

Canal

Guzannu's compound

irrigation channel

Ovadya's barley field

Zakaryah's barley field

Ya'el's house

Zakaryah's house

Dates

Ware-house

Grains

Zakaryah's date palms

CHAPTER I

ZAKARYAH SHUFFLED ALONG the road after his father's burial, sandals kicking up dust in small clouds. He tugged at the gap in his sleeve where the stitches had been pulled apart for the mourning period. He stifled a sob but couldn't stop his head from sagging forward. A small cloud of ash spilled from it. Curls hung heavy and damp in front of his face, rust-colored underneath but gray with the ash on top.

The townspeople trailed well back, giving him and Hannah space. He was still numb. Two days earlier, Shillemyah had been alive, laughing and joking with him at the end of the day's labors in the fields. Today he was in a hole in the earth, covered with the dry dirt of Nar Kabara.

He looked back to see Hannah walking a pace or so behind him, her head swiveling from side to side. She glanced at the barley fields they were passing through, at the distant hills, at the mud-brick homes that dotted the landscape. What was there to look at that she hadn't already seen? Didn't she understand what had happened? Six was old enough to care, wasn't it? To acknowledge in some way the loss of their father?

"Hannah!" he snapped. She turned toward him. "Father is dead. We just buried him."

"Yes," she answered. "There's smoke."

"What?"

"Smoke. There." Without thinking he looked to see where she was pointing. She wasn't pointing. Right. She never pointed. He kept forgetting. Instead he followed her gaze. A delicate ribbon of smoke rose into the air, barely visible against the washed-out blue of the warming day.

"But Father's dead. Don't you care?"

"Look at the smoke."

The column was thicker still, white mixed with brown.

"So what?" he answered. "Someone's burning field stubble."

"It's our barley."

"That's stupid. You can't possibly know that." But his knees began to weaken and his stomach started to knot because he suspected that in fact she did know.

His apprehension mounting, he grabbed her hand and pulled her into a run. She let him tug her along, not resisting, increasing her pace as much as her short legs would allow.

Ahead, brown smoke swirled up into the sky, a pillar to guide him like his grandmother had told him about, when the people escaped from Mitzrayim. But he feared this pillar was leading them toward disaster, not salvation.

They arrived gasping for breath at the small vegetable garden between the house and the barley field. The flames whispered and snapped as they consumed the stalks with their full ears of grain.

Zakaryah sat on the ground to catch his breath, unable to do anything to stop the raging fire. A bush went up like a torch along the edge of the field, then another and another. A leaf snapped off one of the bushes and was swirled up into the sky on the column of smoke. In his mind he was flung skyward with the leaf, tumbling and twisting with it as it disappeared into the emptiness of the west.

He shook the vision out of his head and looked closely at Hannah for some sign, any sign, that she understood this new catastrophe that was happening right in front of them. Nothing.

"He's there," she said.

He roused himself from the dark place his thoughts had taken him. "Who's there?"

"Him. The fire-starter." She stared at the far side of the field, now obscured, now visible through the shifting bands of flame and smoke.

Was someone standing there? Impossible to tell through the inferno. But he didn't doubt her, not now.

The townspeople who had been following behind drifted in around them. They stood silently, watching as the flames devoured the last of the barley. His father's friend Ovadyah laid a hand on Zakaryah's shoulder and went off to look after his own field.

The fire was slowing, having consumed all it could and run up against the irrigation ditches that bordered the field.

Embers glowed here and there around the edges where the woody bushes of the windbreak had been burned.

Tears welled up in his eyes and ran down his cheeks. The king's taxes were due at the end of the month.

He thanked Yahweh that they still had their dates.

ZAKARYAH ROCKED back and forth in the deepening gloom of the house, head in his hands, elbows planted on his knees. It would be dark soon. He should light the lamp.

Soon, he would light it soon.

He didn't get up from his seat.

Hannah's words as they watched the field burn haunted him. Someone had burned the field, she was sure. He didn't doubt her. She knew. Hannah always knew.

Who hated them enough to do this? There was nobody. Everyone had loved his father. And Hannah was too young to have enemies, strange as she might be. There was only one person he had ever fought with, but this was too extreme even for Gimillu, wasn't it?

In the courtyard between the pillars of the house, Hannah was working on the evening meal. He stared at her for a long moment. She was squatting on the ground, stirring the pot of barley stew. Why had he expected her to cry over their father? She had never cried, not as long as he could remember. What would happen to her if the king's tax collector took him away? Would she cry then? He was all she had, and she was all he had. Who would look after such a strange child when he was gone?

She ladled the stew into two clay bowls sitting next to her on the ground. She picked one up without looking at him and moved it a hand's breadth in his direction, the signal for him to come eat.

The day before, when the ox killed his father, the townspeople stoned it to death as Yahweh's law required. He himself had thrown the first stone. They had put it in his hand and pushed him forward. "Throw it!" they told him. It was the snake, he insisted. He was there. He saw. The ox reared because of the snake. "Throw the stone," they told him. And he had. After that everyone had thrown stones.

When it was over they dragged the dead animal off and buried it. He looked outside again where his bowl of porridge was cooling on the ground. They couldn't even use the carcass for meat. It was forbidden.

And the ox could have saved them. He could have sold it for silver, real silver, to pay the taxes.

Too late for that, too late for the barley.

The king didn't care that he was an orphan, didn't care that he was only twelve years old. The king wanted his taxes, that was what mattered. He couldn't even pay them by joining the army. Too young, too small. And who would take care of Hannah? His grandmother was dead, his mother was dead, his uncles were all dead. There were no relatives to take care of two orphan children. They were on their own.

But there were the dates. The date harvest wouldn't begin for three to four months, but he could borrow against it for the taxes. That's how he would pay them. And rents were due from Aqara, the tenant farmer who worked the date trees. There should be enough from that to feed them until a new barley crop came in. But how would he pay for the seed? And who would help him in the field? It had taken all he could do, and all his father could do, to manage the field even with the ox. Now the ox was gone, along with the payments he could have earned from renting it out. He would need to hire workers, but all he could pay them with would be a portion of the harvest. People did that, of course they did. Would it leave enough to pay next year's taxes and living costs? He would need to work the ciphers to figure it out. Not now, though. Tomorrow. Tomorrow he would be able to think better. Today it was just too much.

CHAPTER 2

GIMILLU KNEW HE SHOULDN'T GLOAT, but he couldn't wipe the smirk from his face. Payback, finally.

Instead of heading directly to his uncle's house just across the river, he stopped by the home of Uqupu. The boy was sitting in the dirt in front of the house biting his lip as he copied a passage of *Enuma Elish*. He studied the tablet he was copying, pressed the stylus into the wax of his practice tablet with rapid, nervous gestures, then stopped to look at the result and compare it with the original.

Even at work on the text he looked like the monkey he was named for: small, thin, twitchy.

"I can't believe you're still working on that," Gimillu said.

Uqupu squinted up at him from the wax board, eyes watering in the strong sunlight at the older boy's back. "You're doing it again," he said.

"Doing what?"

"Standing where the sun will blind me. And if you're so smart why does Master keep boxing your ears?"

"Where's Shulmu? I left him with you."

Uqupu dropped his eyes. "He's your dog. Why did you dump him on me?"

Without answering, Gimillu yelled "Shulmu! Shulmu!" There was no response, but soon he heard the rapid scrabbling of paws on dirt. The dog rounded the corner of the building at speed, jumping up on his owner and smearing brown dust all over his robe.

When the dog had received enough pats on the head to calm him down, Gimillu dropped to the ground next to the other boy. He patted the ground by his feet and the dog plopped itself down, tongue out, panting with the heat.

"Where have you been?" Uqupu asked, looking sideways at him after resuming his copying. "Why did you leave that dog with me?"

"Is that how you talk to your best friend?" He stared until Uqupu averted his eyes, murmuring, "Sorry, sorry."

His pique at Uqupu wasn't going to dissuade him from sharing his triumph. "I did it," he said. "I paid him back."

"Who? Who did you pay back?"

"That Yahudu boy, Zakar-yama," he said, chin high. "I showed him. He put that snake in my lunch two days ago."

"Yes, you peed all over yourself," Uqupu said. "In front of everyone in the tablet-house. But wasn't that after you tried to catch him at the bridge and beat him up?"

"He's always showing me up in front of the master. What

if my father hears about it?"

"And then he swam to the middle of the canal and shouted insults at you with half the students watching. They're still laughing about it."

Gimillu scowled at Uqupu, who snapped his mouth shut and muttered, "I need to work on this text."

"Well don't you want to know what I did?" He rushed on without waiting for an answer. "I set fire to his barley!"

The stylus halted a finger's breadth above the wax. Uqupu carefully set stylus and tablet on the ground and stared straight at Gimillu for the first time. "You did what?"

"I . . . I burned his field." Somehow this didn't come out as triumphant as he thought it should.

"But they'll see you here and think I helped you! And you smell like smoke. It'll get on me." He grabbed his board and stylus, jumped up and ran into his house.

The boy's fear touched a little spot of worry that Gimillu had successfully ignored until now. Of course, Uqupu was always nervous about something. There was no reason to be concerned just because the boy ran away.

Anyway, Zakar-yama deserved it. The snake had been black, just like the deadly ones. He had been sure he was going to die. When Zakar-yama had laughed out loud, when the other students had laughed with him, that was when Gimillu had decided.

Revenge.

Maybe Uqupu was right. Maybe it hadn't been such a good idea, but it was only one season's crop. They would plant another one in a few months. And the family had a whole date orchard. The boy had boasted about it often enough. It's not like they would starve to death.

When the boy had insulted him, he had insulted Gimillu's father, hadn't he? His father would understand, he was sure of it. It was a matter of family honor, of his father's honor.

And really, nobody had seen him. There was no possible way he could be connected to the fire. He reached up to his neck to finger his mother's Pazuzu amulet.

It wasn't there.

GIMILLU STOOD in the doorway shifting his weight from foot to foot as he waited to be noticed. His uncle Guzannu was sitting at a low table studying a tablet. Even from across the room Gimillu could see that it was upside down.

Eventually his uncle looked up and said, "Oh. It's you. Come here. I just got this tablet from your father. And leave that animal outside."

Gimillu shuffled over to the table after signaling to Shulmu to stay behind.

"Here." Guzannu pushed the tablet toward him. "What does it say?"

This wasn't why he had come here. "Can't you send for a scribe?"

"Why should I pay for a scribe when you've been getting this expensive tablet-house education? Now read!"

"You aren't paying for it," he muttered. He dropped his

eyes before his uncle's glare and began silently studying the tablet. The silence dragged on. Guzannu started tapping his foot. "I'm just a student," Gimillu complained. His uncle said nothing. The tapping continued.

"Father sends his greetings," he began after a moment. "There's family news. My brother Kudurru has secured a position at court as an apprentice scribe. Father says it will force him to tame his temper."

"Hmm," Guzannu murmured. "Who will your father use to terrorize people who cross him, with your brother in the palace?"

Gimillu hurried on, not wanting to revisit his own terror at the hands of that same brother. "M-my sister Nidintu remains unmarried."

"Still smarting over her joke about poisoning you for your inheritance? She couldn't inherit anyway unless the two of you and your father were all dead. But maybe she was going to poison you for the fun of it."

His face heated. It definitely hadn't sounded like a joke when she said it. For a month he had refused to eat at home, much to Nidintu's amusement. Still, she was the only one in the family who was occasionally kind to him.

He summarized the rest. Guzannu was to collect the taxes from his district a week early this month. The festival of Nabu was coming up and the temple priests wanted to honor the god to compensate for the king's neglect of Marduk, Nabu's father-god.

Guzannu scowled. "The Yahudus will scream at that," he said. "The barley won't ripen fully for another week. They'll have to cut the grain in the middle of the month when the moon is full. It will mean working all night."

Gimillu shrugged and wrapped up his summary. "At the end my father says that the rumors you've heard about the advance of the army of Kurush of Parsu are completely false. Crown prince Bel-shar-utsur has stopped them on the border at Upi. There's no need for alarm." He looked up from the tablet. "Uncle, do we need to be concerned?"

"No, no, if your father says Kurush has been stopped then there's no problem." But to himself he muttered, "Why is he telling me there's nothing to worry about?" He stared out the window without speaking.

When the silence had dragged on as long as he could stand, Gimillu whispered, "Uncle?"

No answer.

"Uncle?" Gimillu repeated.

Guzannu wrenched his eyes from their distant focus. He looked up at Gimillu, who was still standing next to him. "Well?"

"I . . . I was standing next to a barley field when it caught fire."

Guzannu looked hard into Gimillu's eyes. "You were standing there. And it caught fire."

"Y-yes. It just caught fire."

"I see. And whose field was it?"

"Some Yahudu family's."

"This wouldn't be the family of that boy, would it? The one in the tablet-house that you're always having trouble with?"

"He put a snake in my lunch!"

"So you set the family's field on fire," Guzannu stated softly, still staring. "Do you know the penalty for that under the king's code?"

"He deserved it! He's always mocking me. He makes me look bad in front of the others."

"So the answer is no. You didn't think at all about penalties."

Gimillu thought hard, trying to remember what he had heard about penalties under the code.

"Fines!" he announced. "The judges assess fines."

"That's if it's considered property damage. But what you did stole the food out of the family's mouth. And you stole their tax payment. The penalty for theft is death."

As he let that hang in the air, Gimillu's knees began to shake and sweat broke out all over his face.

"And for endangering a free man's life, also death."

"But they're Yahudus."

"You're the only one who cares about that. As far as the king is concerned, they're tax-paying subjects under his protection. Like everyone else."

As Gimillu opened his mouth to speak, his uncle shouted, "Shut up, idiot. I need to think."

He started pacing back and forth in the small room, scowling and periodically shooting looks of deep disgust at the trembling boy.

Eventually he stopped his pacing and turned to face Gimillu, his eyes hard. "You've put all of us in jeopardy. Yourself, me, your father. You think your father will be able to hold his position at court if you're charged with stealing the king's taxes?

He might be able to save you from being executed. I don't know why he should bother, though. Whether he does or doesn't, his enemies will use it to get him expelled from court, along with your brother Kudurru. And I have my position from your father, so then I'm gone too." He glared, chest heaving.

"But we must be able to do something!"

"If it were just your neck on the line I'd drag you to the judges myself. You didn't mention this boy's name. What is it?"

"Zakar-yama."

"No, stupid. His full name."

"Oh. Zakar-yama, son of . . . son of . . ." Then he remembered seeing the boy write his name at the bottom of a lesson tablet. "Son of Shillim-yama."

"In their language, Zakaryah ben Shillemyah. What I was afraid of. Did anyone see you?"

"No," Gimillu said, "the fields were completely empty."

"And you didn't wonder why? Never mind, I can see it never crossed your mind. I'll tell you why the fields were empty. Everyone in the village was at his father's burial. The man was killed yesterday when his ox reared back and crushed him. So you burned the field of an orphan. Two orphans. He has a sister."

Gimillu collapsed onto the edge of the table, knocking off two tablets that broke as they hit the floor. Orphans! Would that call for the harshest penalty? He wasn't sure and wasn't about to ask. He buried his head in his hands, not knowing what to say, not able to say anything. His uncle was silent too, and when Gimillu eventually looked up to see why, Guzannu was staring at him.

He reached for the amulet on his chest and jerked his hand away when he remembered it wasn't there.

"Lost your Pazuzu at the scene, did you?" Guzannu said, lip curling. "This is what you're going to do. His father owns—owned—a date orchard. Tomorrow you'll go to the village and find out how many trees there are. Now get out of my sight."

CHAPTER 3

ZAKARYAH KNEW IT WAS A DREAM. This time he almost saw his grandmother's face. She was walking through the doorway of her house. Maybe she turned toward him slightly, as if suggesting that he follow. But that was the only thing that was different. Just like all the other times, he drifted after her into the dim interior of her home. *Talk to me*, he thought. *Say something. Please.* But just like the other times, she ignored him, picking up her reed broom, sweeping the floor of the far corner past the pillars of the little courtyard. Then she was silhouetted within the door frame in the corner, facing out, gazing west, in the direction of the setting sun. Beyond her he glimpsed a city, its walls and buildings glowing softly in the golden light. Her pain and her yearning pulled him as she stared at the dream city of her youth. Yerushalayim, destroyed now this half a hundred years.

He woke, the sense of longing constricting his chest even as he opened his eyes. The dream-door bothered him for some reason. Of course it was a dream, but there had been no such door in that corner of her house. Even if there had been, the view of the western sun would have been blocked by the impenetrable solidity of his own house.

And why hadn't she spoken? She used to talk to him all the time. They studied the scrolls together, the sacred writings. She taught him to read them, how to think about them, how to ask questions.

She hadn't turned toward him either. Now more than ever he wished he could see more than just the back of her head. Was he beginning to forget what she looked like?

He ran his eyes over his body and sleeping pallet to make sure no rats or scorpions had fallen on him from the fronds above. Once a few months ago he had awakened to a slapping thud and found a snake squirming on top of him. He had shouted and his father had wakened immediately, reached over from his pallet, swept the thing off him, jumped up and crushed its head with the heel of his foot. It had turned out to be a harmless brown snake from the fields, the kind that kept down the rodents, and he felt bad that it had been killed. But how had it gotten up into the palm fronds anyway? He never did figure that out.

He pulled on his over-robe, then stood and looked down at his sandals. No scorpions. He slid his feet in. Next to him on the floor was his father's sleeping pallet. Empty, now and for-ever. He stood by the foot of the pallet, eyes brimming, unable for the moment to take another step. To the side of his father's bed, Hannah's lay. Empty too, but only because she had risen earlier to prepare the morning meal.

He stepped over both mats to the basket in the corner that held his mother's things. The neighbors had told his father to get rid of them when his mother died. They'll only make you sad, they told him, and your next wife won't like it. But Shillemyah hadn't been able to part with them, and anyway there was no next wife.

He rooted around in the basket. Got it! He pulled out a copper mirror his grandmother had given his mother as a wedding gift. You look so much like your grandmother, people had told him. He had shrugged it off. He didn't look a bit like her, he was sure. But since he couldn't see her face in his dreams, maybe looking at himself was the closest he could come.

He moved into the light from the courtyard and peered into the mirror. And now he saw it. The same curly hair, the color of rusty iron. The same brown eyes, spaced just a tiny bit wide in his face. The same serious expression she always wore when she was thinking about a verse in the scrolls or was about to demolish some man's ignorant statement about the sacred writings. Nose a little bent, though. That wasn't like her. It was more like his father. And his ears stuck out some. *Mine were like that too*, his father had told him. *You'll grow into them eventually.*

His grandmother would have known what to do in the face of this catastrophe, he was certain. But whatever of her lingered in his mirror-face, it offered him no clues.

He put the mirror back in the basket.

There was a clattering of clay vessels from the narrow courtyard as his sister prepared to warm over the previous night's porridge. "Hannah," he yelled. "Put in some dates. And take out the pits this time." She didn't acknowledge that she had heard him, but he made out a grating sound as she removed the clay lid of the date jar. Hannah didn't care much about the food she ate. The meals she prepared were usually pretty bland. This morning, though, he needed a bit of sweetness.

The day itself was going to be very bitter.

AS HE WALKED OUT through the courtyard, Hannah was scooping a handful of starter dough from its jar. She brushed off most of the fruit flies that had gotten in overnight and began to knead it together with the flour and water for the day's bread, reciting the proper protective blessings as she worked the dough.

He jerked to a stop, palms sweating. "Be careful," he admonished her. "Don't use too much." How much flour did they actually have? How would he replace what she used up?

"We'll have flour," she answered without looking up from her kneading.

"But our barley. It's all burned."

"They'll give us some."

"Who? Who'll give us some?"

But she just kept on kneading, saying nothing more. He almost yelled at her, clamping his jaws only with difficulty. What good would it do? Hannah was Hannah. She would ignore him. She always did. And there wasn't time for an argument. No, today was going to be about their survival.

He gulped hard and stepped through the door leading out to the narrow path in front of the house.

CHRISTOPHER FARRAR

The path ended to the left at the near edge of his barley field, just beyond the little garden from which he had watched the grain crop burn. He walked the few paces to the border of the field. To his right was the house of his neighbor Achiyah and next to that, the man's field. The barley was golden brown, almost ready to harvest. And to the left was Neriyah's field with its ripe stalks.

In between, the charred remains of his own crop.

The waning moon, two days past full, hovered low in the west. How often had he wished he could follow it? Out beyond the fields, out beyond the marshes, out into the endless burning desert. He could leave behind the burned barley, the unpaid taxes, the grasping hands of Banayahu, who he would now have to beg for a loan. He blinked the tears from his eyes. The fantasy was only a fantasy, for a hundred practical reasons. But the biggest reason was that he couldn't leave Hannah behind, and that was that.

At the far end of his field he could see the vegetation lining the main trench that brought water from the reservoir to the irrigation ditches that separated the fields. Whoever started the fire must have stood out there to do it. The flames had simply burned from plant to plant until they had consumed the entire length of his long, narrow field. His neighbors' fields hadn't burned. Lucky for them, disastrous for him.

His anguished question from the night before came back to him. Who had done this? Maybe there would be clues at the far end where the blaze had been started.

He headed down the middle of the blackened field. Within three paces black dust covered his feet, working its way under the straps of his sandals. The smell of smoke filled his nostrils and made him cough, even though nothing was actively burning.

At the far edge of the field, he stepped onto the maintenance path that ran along the edge of the water trench, glad to be out of the blackened earth. This was where the person must have been, somewhere around here. But there was nothing on the path.

He sat abruptly in the dirt of the path, feet in the blackened remains of his harvest. His throat was tight, his eyes once again filling with tears.

What had he expected? A clay tablet inscribed with the fire-starter's name?

But Hannah had been sure that someone had been here. How had she known? He had long ago given up trying to understand how she knew what she knew. Maybe her eyes were better, or her hearing, or something. It was pointless to ask her. But more often than not, she was right. So someone had been here.

He took a few deep breaths to calm himself, to push down the fear and the anger.

When he felt more under control, he let his eyes wander over the near edge of the field. Maybe he would see something.

And he did. Lying in the blackened stubble, just a few paces away, was a small patch of sand. He rose and stepped off the path for a closer look. It was so ordinary that it took him a moment to realize why it had caught his eye. Then he got it. Sand didn't belong in the dirt fields of Nar Kabara. It would sometimes wash up along the riverbank after a big storm, but even when the river flooded in late spring it wasn't to be found here.

Someone had carried an ember on sand, probably in a pouch where he could blow on it to keep it alive. And in fact, now that he was looking closely he could see the burned remnants of a pocket woven from palm fronds.

With a live ember it would be easy to set the ripe barley on fire.

As he stood staring at the spot where the sand lay, something metallic glinted at him from the ashes. He picked it up, felt the weight of it in his hand. It was a bronze amulet with the raised shape of the Chaldean demon Pazuzu. No Yehudi from the village would wear it.

But Gimillu wore one.

CHAPTER 4

BACK IN FRONT OF HIS HOUSE, Zakaryah sat down on a bench of mud bricks that was off the path just to the side of the door. He removed his sandals and slapped them together sole to sole to knock off the clinging barley ash. His feet he cleaned on the inside of his robe.

Hannah poked her head out the doorway and locked her grey eyes on his. "They're coming," she said. She almost never made eye contact, and he found his own eyes sliding away from the intensity of her gaze.

"What do you mean? Who's coming?"

She shrugged, adding, "And Kashaya brought flour."

Ah. That was how she knew there would be flour. Ever since Kashaya's illness, when Hannah sent their father over with warm porridge, Ovadyah and Kashaya had been particularly kind. Zakaryah still couldn't figure out how Hannah had known the woman was sick. That was another matter that wasn't worth pursuing.

But what did she mean about someone coming? Why did she always need to be so mysterious?

Before he could get the question out she asked, "Where are you going?"

"Never mind. Just get back to your work." Surely there was wool to be spun, water to be fetched or pots to be made. And what difference did it make if she knew where he was going?

She pulled her head back inside without another word. He heard her sandals slapping across the courtyard toward the back of the house. Then he felt bad. True, she likely hadn't noticed his rudeness. But still. There was no need.

Cheeks burning, he stepped into the doorway and shouted, "I'm going to talk to Aqara!"

All he heard back from inside was a sneeze. Then he was angry at himself for chasing after her. She could be so bossy. He was the one in charge. He was the one who had lost all his friends to the responsibility of caring for her, this strange unappreciative misfit of a sister. Only now he was carrying the additional crushing weight of the taxes and the burned field and keeping them fed through the coming year.

But there was really no time for this. He needed to ask Aqara about the date harvest.

He walked past the crumbling foundation of his grandmother's house and deeper into the town, turning left around the grain storage building and toward their date orchard.

Most of the villagers were in their fields. He did pass a few women hurrying on errands. He scrutinized each person he passed. There was Bosmat, whose husband had died last year from a fever somewhere north in Ashur where he had been stationed. There was old Elnatan, too feeble now to work in the fields, hobbling through the town, gossiping with whoever would stop. He stared as Zakaryah came near, dropping his walking stick. When Zakaryah picked it up and handed it to him the man lowered his eyes and said nothing. And there were a few others. He glared at them, lips thin, eyes narrowed. They could at least acknowledge the disaster, offer a few words of comfort or help.

Where the houses ended he stopped and scanned the orchard. There were twenty-five trees, well-spaced for irrigation and ease of weed control. He eventually spotted Aqara at the far corner, the one closest to the river. He was high in a tree. As he watched, Aqara plucked a bud and dropped it to the ground, then another, and another.

Zakaryah wove his way through the palms, careful not to trip in the little watering ditches that circled each trunk.

At the base of the tree he yelled up, "Aqara!"

The man answered without looking. "Zakar-yama," he said in Chaldean, "I've been expecting you. I'm sorry I couldn't make it to the burial. The trees won't wait, and without your father to help—"

His father. A tremor shook Zakaryah and his throat tightened. Would he even be able to speak? But he pushed the pain down and managed to force out the words. "It's what I need to talk about," he responded in Chaldean.

"I'll be down." With that, there was a rapid patter of quiet thuds as a volley of buds hit the ground around Zakaryah.

Aqara followed them down, though, more slowly and carefully as he worked the raffia belt that went around both him and the trunk of the palm. At the bottom he left it circling the tree and stepped out of the loop.

Zakaryah stared at the buds on the ground and thought of all the dates he would have been able to sell if they had been left to mature. "I wish they didn't have to come off."

The man shrugged. "If they're not thinned the crop will suffer. I heard about the barley. That's why you're here?"

"Will the crop be good this year?"

Aqara shrugged again. "It's in the hands of the gods. Or in your case, the hands of your Yahweh. But the trees are healthy, the pests are no worse than usual and there are plenty of buds. Each tree should give us about three hundred ka. That would be maybe three of those large baskets I keep in the house. When you fill one it weighs almost as much as you."

"So about seventy-five of those from the whole orchard."

"Yes. You're worried about the taxes?"

"They're due at the end of the month."

The farmer bent down, picked up a bud and placed it gently in Zakaryah's palm, closing his fingers around it. "That's your crop right now."

"I know. I'll need a loan."

"Ah. At the usual interest of one part in five you should just be able to make it after I take my share. If the crop is good."

"But that interest is for the whole year. We're talking half a year at most until all the crop is in."

"Right. Well in that case, my guess is that you'll make it and have some to spare for food, and maybe even for barley seed."

Zakaryah raised his eyes to the sky, knees weak with the sudden release of tension. He mumbled a prayer of thanksgiving to Yahweh.

"You know," Aqara added, "you'll need to help me like your father did. I can't do it all myself and I can't hire anyone, not if you'll be using part of the crop to pay off a loan."

"Yes, yes, fine," Zakaryah answered, his mind already turning to the problem of the loan. He turned to leave.

"Oh," said Aqara. "I almost forgot. There was a boy here earlier. He was counting the trees."

"A boy?"

"Your age, or maybe a little older. With a dog. His uncle is the local tax collector for the king. That's what he said. The uncle wanted to know how many palms the village has. Maybe he wants an estimate of the year's taxes?"

Zakaryah's breath caught. He reached into the pocket hidden inside his robe and fingered the small bronze medallion he had collected from the barley field. "Was he . . . do you remember . . . was he wearing an amulet?"

Aqara's brows creased. "I'm not sure. Why?"

Zakaryah didn't answer. No surprise that Aqara wouldn't notice the amulet. Who would? But only one Chaldean boy kept a dog.

His nostrils flared, his hands clenched and unclenched. It was Gimillu after all. Gimillu had burned his field.

He began to shake.

He left the orchard at a run, leaving Aqara staring after him.

He raced through the village, drawing angry comments as he rushed past people without seeing them. He arrived panting at Ovadyah's house, not knowing where else to go. Ovadyah's wife Kashaya directed him to the far end of their field, where the irrigation trough came off the main water trench. "He's clearing the weeds from the water gate," she told him. "This is the second time in a little over a week. They grow so fast in the spring, don't they?"

Zakaryah nodded, mumbled his thanks and dashed out on the little path along the length of the field that paralleled the irrigation ditch.

"You're sure it was this Gimillu?" Ovadyah asked him after hearing the story.

"Who else?" he got out, still gasping from the run through the town. He managed to control his breathing a bit and continued more normally. "How many Chaldean boys keep a dog? None, that's how many. Just Gimillu. And," he continued, pulling the amulet from its pouch in the robe, "I found this where the fire began."

Ovadyah took the bronze medallion that Zakaryah held out to him. He felt its heft and looked carefully at both sides. "It's an ordinary Pazuzu charm," he offered. "It could be anybody's. Any Chaldean's, that is."

"And Gimillu wears one. I've seen it."

"He did this for no reason?" Ovadyah asked.

Zakaryah dropped his eyes but said nothing.

"Well," Ovadyah sighed, "reason or not, it's serious. You need to go to one of the king's judges. The nearest is in Al Yahudu."

"The king has a judge in a Yehudi town?"

"His name is Bel-shunu. You'll go to him and make a complaint."

"I need to go anyway to talk to Banayahu about a loan for the taxes. He was going to be my next visit after Aqara."

"It's a good half day to get there. You'll need to wait until tomorrow. But as soon as you're there, make your complaint to the judge. For now, go to your house and get Hannah. She can help Kashaya prepare the evening meal. You can eat with us tonight. Then come out and help me clear these weeds."

As the boy turned to leave, Ovadyah said suddenly, "You know, the Chaldeans settled your grandmother in Al Yahudu after the rebellion of King Zidkiyahu."

Zakaryah frowned slightly. Of course he knew this. Why was Ovadyah mentioning it?

"From what I've heard," Ovadyah added, "the town hasn't been the same since."

THE NEXT MORNING before dawn Zakaryah ate, got some food ready for the journey and prepared to leave.

As he stepped through the door and onto the path that would take him to the river and the road to Al Yahudu, he noticed that Hannah had come out to see him off. He hadn't expected that. It made him feel good.

"I'm coming with you," she announced without looking at him.

"What? Don't be ridiculous. You can't come. You have

work to do. And you'll slow me down."

"I'm coming. You'll need me. And I have to meet her."

"Meet her? Meet who?" He took a deep breath and let it out slowly, a trick he had learned from his grandmother. More calmly, he told her, "You don't know anyone outside Nar Kabara."

And what made her so sure he would need her? Didn't she think he could take care of himself? What possible use could a six-year-old girl be on a trip like this?

"Anyway," he continued, "you aren't coming. Stay here and bake bread or spin more wool. You're growing and you'll need a new robe. You might as well get started on it."

With that, he set off toward the river, glad to be leaving the matter behind. He didn't like to argue with her. Sometimes, though, you just had to be firm.

When he arrived at the river road she was waiting for him.

CHAPTER 5

THEY ENTERED Al Yahudu late in the morning.

Zakaryah had remonstrated with her at the start, had physically picked her up and turned her around, had pushed her in the direction of the village and begun walking, pretending to ignore her. But when he looked back she was following him at a distance of fifty paces.

He had tried speeding up, counting on his longer legs to carry him faster. It worked, too. Soon she was a hundred paces behind, then a hundred and fifty.

Still following.

He went around a bend obscured by bushes and lost sight of her. Finally. Now she would get the message and turn back. Unless there was someone hiding in the bushes, waiting to attack her. Or maybe there would be a snake, not the harmless kind he had slipped into Gimillu's lunch, but one of the other black ones, the kind that could kill a grown man almost instantly. And didn't the road there cross a low bluff above the river? What if she fell in?

He turned back and ran, heart pounding, faster and faster, heedless of the irregular surface of the dirt road, stumbling many times but never quite falling. He stopped finally in front of her and bent over with his hands on his knees to support the weight of his upper body. When his breathing had slowed he straightened up. She took hold of his hand and together they resumed their walk to Al Yahudu.

As they entered the town his heart sped up. He let go of Hannah and wiped both hands on his robe. But he was the victim here, wasn't he? Why should he be nervous about lodging his complaint? He forced himself to picture his charred crop, to recall his despair about paying the taxes. No, he would go there; he would state his case and demand justice.

But did it really have to be the first stop? Wouldn't it be a good idea to learn something about Al Yahudu before that? His grandmother had lived here for many years. What harm would it do to see where her house had been? Of course the house itself wouldn't still be there. It had been almost five decades, after all. The mud bricks would either have decayed or been taken for other buildings. Still, if he saw the place, maybe some sense of her would come through. That would be a comfort.

And anyway it wasn't like the judge would be going anywhere.

As Zakaryah walked through narrow streets and alleyways, Hannah's hand once again in his, he was stunned by the town's size. A thousand households, two maybe, or three? It was hard to tell, but big, very big. He could get lost here and never find his way out. That's how it seemed.

What had Ovadyah meant that the town hadn't been the same since his grandmother lived there? He had needed to ask several people before he found even one, an old lady, who remembered her.

"You know," she told him, glancing with a frown at Hannah, "it was a long bitter road, when the Chaldeans dragged us out of Yerushalayim. We all hated her, your grandmother."

He took a step back, blinking rapidly. Hated her? Hated his grandmother? "How? Why?" he demanded.

"Of course, she was just a girl then. But so smart with the reading and the writing, and proud of it. All she wanted to do was study the sacred scrolls with that priest of hers. What was his name? Azaryah? Something like that. Anyway, she never had a good word for any of the rest of us."

After the initial shock, he realized it wasn't all that surprising, knowing his grandmother. She had been literate, quick-witted, with no patience for ignorance or sloppy thinking. He had watched her leave would-be challengers gasping for breath as she tore apart their foolishness and fallacies in study gatherings during Shabbat. It hadn't made her popular, especially with some of the more self-important men. He had learned to keep his grin to himself when she did this, but inside he was always smiling.

But the woman was talking again. "Of course that all changed the day she sang to us." She grew very still, looking off into the distance, moisture glistening in the corners of her eyes.

The moment dragged on. He began shifting his weight from foot to foot, curious to learn more but regretting that he had decided on this little side trip. He was keenly aware of the sun's trajectory through the sky, of Hannah standing silently beside him. He had visits to make, important visits. Was there some way to escape without being hideously rude? He looked around at the alleys, the houses, the storage buildings here near the canal.

He realized that the old lady had his upper arm in a claw-like grip and was looking intently at his face.

"Come with me!" she ordered, and began dragging him deeper into the town. To Hannah she said, "You come too."

THE WOMAN WHO GREETED THEM at the door was covered in flour up to her elbows. She might have been in the middle twenties of her life. Ancient. Of course, not nearly as ancient as the old lady whose hand was still clamped around his arm.

The younger woman's eyes took in the three of them. "Ginat," she said, wiping her hands on her robe. "What brings you here? And who is this young man you're holding onto so fiercely? And this little girl?"

"Oh," Ginat laughed, releasing him. "He looked so lost. And he was about to run off. I didn't want him escaping." She smiled.

He rubbed his arm to restore the circulation. How could such an old lady have such a strong grip?

"Michal, this is—" She scratched her head and smiled at him. "I don't know your name, young man."

"Zakaryah."

"And your sister?"

"Hannah."

"Zakaryah here says that Ya'el bat Matanyah was their grandmother."

Michal smiled broadly, suddenly looking not so ancient. And she still had all her teeth. "Come in," she invited them, stepping back so they could pass through.

She led them into the courtyard, where a grinding stone, a mortar and a bowl of barley grain had been set aside. In the narrow side room to the left six girls and three boys sat at a low table, scrolls spread out in front of them.

"Danna!"

One of the girls looked up. She was the oldest of the students, maybe about his own age. Black hair tight with curls peeked out from under her scarf, but what really surprised him was the color of her skin. It was almost as black as that ebony wood that traders brought from Mitzrayim. A Kushite! Like in his grandmother's scrolls. He stared.

"Danna," Michal said with a sidewise glance at him, "go finish the grinding or there'll be no bread tonight."

The girl aimed a curious glance at Zakaryah and Hannah, then nodded and stood up, straightening her robe. She went over to the grinding area, arranged herself on the kneeling pad, and whispered the requisite blessings. She dumped a handful of grain on the flat surface of the stone and began pushing the mortar rhythmically across it.

Michal was looking at him severely. "Danna is our most

37

advanced student. She can spare a bit of time from studying."

"So this is like a tablet-house," he blurted, ears reddening. "Only with girls."

Michal looked at Ginat, eyebrows raised. "You say he's Ya'el's grandson?"

"So he says."

The tips of his ears grew even warmer. He dropped his eyes.

"Well, Zakaryah," Michal said, smiling finally, "in this house we teach boys *and* girls to read and write. They study the scrolls too. And of course we have to teach them other things." She nodded in the direction of a niche in which a large bowl held a shapeless lump of damp clay. Next to it, a loom leaned against the wall of the house.

But girls! Really, he shouldn't have been surprised. His grandmother had been a girl once. At least, he assumed she had. And she had learned, had in fact been the one to teach him.

Michal looked down at Hannah and said, "Maybe you'd like to study here one day." But Hannah was studying the girl Danna and didn't respond.

"What brings you to Al Yahudu?" Ginat asked him when the moment dragged on.

He told them then about their father's death, the fire, why he was certain who had set it, his need for a loan and his determination to demand justice under the king's code.

As he spoke he realized that the sound of grinding had stopped, had in fact been absent for some time. He looked over at the Kushite girl who had been grinding the grain—Danna,

Michal had called her—and saw that she was following the conversation closely.

Michal noticed too and told her to get back to work. To Zakaryah she said, "So I understand why you came to Al Yahudu, but why did you come here?"

"I asked this lady—Ginat—about my grandmother and she brought us here. I wanted to see where she lived. I didn't think the house would still be here. I just wanted to see. And Ovadyah, that's my father's friend, he said Al Yahudu was never the same after her. So I wondered what that meant."

"I don't know about that," she said. "But your grand-mother started teaching as soon as she was settled here by the Chaldeans. And now this is the only town where girls can study and learn just like boys. She did that. My mother was one of her first students. When Ya'el married, her father Matanyah was all alone. He rented the lands and the house to my father and followed Ya'el to Nar Kabara. After Matanyah's death my father bought it from Ya'el's husband, your grandfather. I inherited it. And here we are." She smiled.

"You're not married?"

"My husband died two years ago."

"Do your children study here too?"

The smile vanished and he kicked himself. But how could he have known she was childless?

She sighed. A small wave of her hand took in the students watching by their scrolls. "These are my children."

No husband, no children. Who was looking after her? Who was managing the school's business? Who would find her a new husband? Who would take care of her when she was old?

Well, it was sad but it wasn't his problem. He had enough of his own.

After that she told him where to find the judge Bel-shunu, and then Banayahu, who he was going to ask for the loan.

She offered him food, so he and Hannah ate with them all—Ginat, Michal, the nine students. During the meal the younger students chatted and asked him questions about his exotic village of Nar Kabara.

Only the girl Danna held herself apart. She followed the conversation closely, eyes going from face to face but always coming back to him and Hannah. She never spoke. It made him a little uncomfortable, but he was too caught up answering the children's questions to think about it much.

As he and Hannah left he turned and waved to them all.

Danna was staring at him.

CHAPTER 6

ZAKARYAH FOLLOWED Michal and Ginat's directions to the center of the town. Hannah walked at his side, eyes taking in the strange new city. She hadn't spoken while they were at Michal's school and didn't talk now.

The sun wasn't yet at its zenith but the heat this far from the river was intense. He wiped his face with his woolen sleeve, wishing as he did so that his father had been able to afford lighter linen clothing for the hot weather.

The house they stopped in front of didn't look like a king's judge would be living in it. There was no sign either in Yehudit or Chaldean. The mud bricks were cracked and weathered. The layer of rushes in the mud of the roof seemed to have been hollowed out by nesting sparrows, a sure indication of neglect. But it was right where they told him, just opposite the tax collection warehouse.

The robe of the servant who answered the door was also

in need of repair, with thin patches at the elbows and a slightly ragged hem. The man glanced briefly at Hannah, then looked him up and down. "What do you want?" he asked.

"Is this the house of King's Judge Bel-shunu?"

The man nodded minutely.

"Then I've come to make a complaint."

The man peered to the left and right along the street. "Where's your father?"

"My father died. Three days ago."

"Older brother?"

"There's just me. Us," he amended, indicating Hannah.

The servant hesitated, frowning, then stepped aside, motioning to them to enter.

He stepped through into the relative gloom of the interior, Hannah a half step behind him. He looked around the room as his eyes slowly adjusted. There was a low table with eating vessels stacked at one corner. A tablet of moist clay lay at the near edge of the table, half filled with writing. A stylus lay next to it.

The man stood silently, eyeing him with an unreadable expression.

"Well," Zakaryah said, returning his gaze to the silent servant, "can I talk to the king's judge?"

"I'm Bel-shunu. You mentioned a complaint?"

Zakaryah opened his mouth, snapped it shut again. This ragged man was the king's judge?

"Gimillu burned my field!" He kicked himself as soon as he blurted it out, but by then it was too late. He hadn't given any thought to what he would say to the judge when he stood in front of him.

"The same Gimillu whose uncle is Guzannu the tax aggregator?" At Zakaryah's silence, Bel-shunu's frown turned to a scowl. "This is a serious charge against the family of an important official. You have proof?"

Zakaryah reached into the inner pocket of his robe. He retrieved the amulet and wetted his lips, extending his hand slowly toward the judge.

Bel-shunu plucked the amulet out of Zakaryah's palm. He took a step toward the door, holding the object in the bright light that streamed through the joins between the planks.

"A Pazuzu amulet," he said, examining it closely. "Every third person has one."

"I found it where the fire was started. And Gimillu wears one."

The judge turned to confront Zakaryah. "He wears a Pazuzu," he said, lip curling. Instead of replacing the amulet in Zakaryah's outstretched hand he tossed it onto the table where it landed with a clatter. "You're young so I'm not going to charge you with lodging a false complaint. But I'm keeping the amulet in case I change my mind."

At that moment Hannah trained her piercing grey eyes on the judge. He took an abrupt step back. Without taking her eyes off him she pointed to something. She pointed! It was on the table, a pouch with gathers at the top, secured by a drawstring. It was the kind of pouch people used for carrying silver.

The judge's face darkened and he jerked the door open. "Out!" he shouted. "Now!" He shoved them both out with such force that they tripped over the threshold, staggering out into the bright sunlight.

Eyes welling, Zakaryah sagged against the judge's house, slowly sliding down the wall. The bricks scraped his back as he slid. He barely noticed. He fetched up in the dirt, curled over with his arms wrapped around his knees, face buried. Why hadn't he thought it through? Gimillu was from a family with connections at court. He should have waited until he had more evidence. He had lost the closest thing he had to proof. Nobody would believe him now. Gimillu would get away with it. There was nothing he could do. What would happen to him? He looked at Hannah, standing impassively a couple paces away. What would happen to her? Would she be sold into slavery to pay the taxes? Or maybe they'd starve to death between now and when the dates could be harvested.

"Feeling sorry for yourself?" a girl's voice asked.

He jerked up his head, but the girl's face was hidden by her hood. He couldn't make it out.

"You never had a chance, you know," she continued.

"What? What do you mean? Who are you? How do you know?"

She didn't answer, saying instead, "You're very naive."

He looked hard at her. Ebony skin. Aha! "You're that Danna. What are you doing here? Won't you be in trouble with Michal?"

She shrugged. "My grandfather pays her plenty to keep me in the school," she told him. "He bribed the judge."

"Your grandfather?" he asked.

"No, dummy. Your Gimillu."

"He's not my Gimillu!"

She ignored this, sweeping her arm in a broad gesture that took in the judge's entire house. "Does this look like the house of a rich man? How much silver do you think it would take to turn his head?"

Hannah spoke up then, her high child's voice sounding surprisingly adult. "Ten shekels," she answered. "I pointed at the bag. He was sooo mad." And she giggled.

He stared at her, mouth falling open. Danna was staring at her too. Hannah never laughed. Of course she was just guessing about the weight of the silver, but even so, what in her limited experience allowed her even to guess?

Danna stepped forward, grabbed his arm and pulled him to his feet. "I'm going to take you to this Banayahu. But he won't give you a loan. They'll have gotten to him too."

"Why are you doing this?"

But she didn't answer, just pulled him and Hannah along deeper into the town.

THE HOUSE they stood in front of was clearly that of a wealthy man. Zakaryah marveled at the size of the building, at the rich wooden door with real iron hinges, at the second story. There was a small pavilion on top, shaded by a woven cloth. It would be where the man and his family took their meals during the summer months, up high to catch whatever breeze there was. They probably slept there too. Such a contrast with the judge's house.

Maybe Danna was wrong. This man's wealth made him famous even in Nar Kabara. He owned multiple ox teams that he rented out during the plowing seasons. He had orchards and orchards of date palms. He owned lands in Al Yahudu and beyond, lands he had acquired as surety when farmers couldn't repay loans he made them. Rumor had it that he had marriage ties to a family highly placed in the king's administration.

What could Gimillu offer him that he didn't already own?

They were greeted at the door by a slave woman. Another sign of the man's riches. How many of the households in the Yehudah community were wealthy enough to own slaves?

The woman led them to an open room just off the court-yard. There they found a man kneeling at a low table. He looked up as Zakaryah, Hannah and Danna entered. He motioned them closer until they stood less than an arm's length away.

The slave bowed to the man and left. Danna leaned next to Zakaryah's ear and murmured, "Banayahu."

"You're Banayahu?" he asked the man with a quick glance at Danna.

"And who are you?" the man responded.

"I'm Zakaryah ben Shillemyah. This is my sister Hannah."

"Zakaryah ben Shillemyah. Yes, yes. From Nar Kabara, right?"

"You know me?"

"Your father. And this girl?" He took in Danna's raven-colored skin, black eyes, and black curly hair, then reached out and rubbed his fingers along the skin of her arm. She recoiled and he examined his fingertips.

"Uh, a guide," Zakaryah answered, glancing at Danna. She regarded him without expression, moving her arm behind her back. "I don't know my way around here."

"So, Zakaryah ben Shillemyah," he said, rubbing his hand on his robe. "About your father. Such an unfortunate accident. And the ox too. So sad. But what brings you here?"

The ox? He was sad about the ox?

Zakaryah ran a hand through his hair. He closed his eyes briefly and took a deep, calming breath. His and Hannah's future was hanging on this. "I need a loan. For the taxes."

"A loan. I see. For taxes. But don't you have barley?"

He responded hesitantly, the encounter with Bel-shunu very fresh in his mind. "The field . . . burned."

"Such misfortune! I would like to help if I can. At standard interest rates, of course."

Zakaryah let out a breath he didn't realize he was holding. He looked again at Danna, searching her face for signs that she regretted her pessimism. She continued to regard him without expression. Why? This was going well, wasn't it?

He turned back as Banayahu asked him, "What do you propose for the collateral?"

"I have twenty-five date palms that have just flowered. My farmer tells me there'll be a good crop in four or five months. They'll fetch a high price at market. I'll have enough to repay the loan and the interest, with some left over for the next barley planting."

"Then you don't know," Banayahu said with a deep sigh. "Your father already took a loan. The ox was the collateral. This is the contract." He picked up the clay tablet on the table and held it briefly in front of Zakaryah before whisking it away. "The date palms were the secondary surety. The ox is dead, I understand? The palms belong to me."

CHAPTER 7

ZAKARYAH barely remembered the walk back to Nar Kabara, lost as he was in his rage and his distress. The tablet was forged. There was no proof, no proof at all, but he was sure of it. The glimpse he had gotten was brief, but it was long enough for him to see the irregular depth of the wedge marks, the indifferent attention to the spacing of the signs pressed into the clay. Master Nabu-ushabshi didn't tolerate such sloppiness in his tablet-house, but there was one student who never got the message no matter how many times the master cuffed him.

How could Gimillu do this to him, to Hannah? It wasn't right, it was evil. He would take revenge. Gimillu would suffer. The next snake would be a venomous one, it would bite him and he would lie writhing in the dirt. Or a scorpion in the sandal, unnoticed until Gimillu slipped his foot onto it. Or maybe poison that would convulse him in agony, sending waves of disgusting excrement erupting from his body.

One time he broke through the desperate whirl of his thoughts to become aware of his surroundings, realizing when he did that Hannah had hold of his hand and was pulling him down the road toward home. What would he have done if she hadn't been there? He didn't know.

Another time he surfaced enough to wonder when that Danna girl had left them. He had a vague recollection of Hannah hugging her and knew he must have been lost in his nightmare. His sister never hugged anyone.

He fell again into the swirl of his grief and fear and anger.

As they neared Nar Kabara, Hannah pushed him hard off the side of the road, falling down on top of him. Just as he opened his mouth to yell at her, four horsemen in priests' robes thundered past at great speed, heading in the same direction they were.

They crossed the river and entered Nar Kabara a short while later. There was no sign of the horsemen. He decided they must have been heading for Karkara or some other town along the Kabara river. It was just as well. After the day he'd had he would probably have screamed at them for running him and Hannah off the road. That would surely not have gone well.

The sun was low in the west, casting lengthening shadows everywhere. A few people were moving about on late errands. The doors of the houses they passed were closed in anticipation of the evening, but the homey smell of baking bread and cooking stews filled the air, reminding Zakaryah of just how exhausted and hungry he was. He regarded Hannah as she walked beside him. She gave no sign that she shared his fatigue and despair, though certainly she must. He would need to help her prepare the meal given how late it was getting.

Their house looked just as they had left it that morning, but more precious somehow after the catastrophic events of the day. How long would they be able to live there? Would the king's tax agents come to get them first, or would Banayahu show up with his forged contract to claim the house along with the date orchard?

Because he was preoccupied with these thoughts, it took him a moment to notice that Hannah had stopped a few steps from their home. She was looking at the remains of their grandmother's house, just a foundation now, the bricks of the walls having been taken by his father and others for their own building needs.

For once he wasn't feeling impatient with her. "Hannah," he told her, reaching for her hand to tug her gently along. "We need to light the fire in the oven so we can make our evening meal. I'll help you." In truth, though, he didn't know if he had the strength. Maybe they would just go without food tonight, as they did on fast days.

"Look," she told him, not moving.

Just in time he stopped himself from trying to see where she was pointing. She wouldn't be pointing anywhere. Instead he studied her face to determine where her attention was directed.

"What should I look at?" he asked, giving up.

"Over there in the corner. Like your dreams."

His dreams? Oh, when he dreamed of his grandmother. She was always sweeping the floor, and yes, just in that corner.

He didn't remember telling Hannah about the dreams. But he had told his father once. "I still dream of her too," Shillemyah had responded. Hannah had obviously overheard.

He looked again where she indicated. Nothing. Now he was in fact becoming impatient. He turned to go but Hannah stepped over the ruins of the foundation and went to squat by the corner. He sighed and followed her.

Was there a slight depression there? Maybe it was just a trick of the slanting sunlight, but the more he looked the more he was convinced.

He ran the few steps to the house and returned with the iron pick his father had purchased after a particularly good crop year.

With Hannah watching intently, he scored the earth around the depression, careful not to go too deep with the pointed end. A couple more circles, and there was a light scraping noise as the tool head encountered what sounded like pottery of some sort.

It was getting hard to see. Hannah went back into their house and returned with an oil lamp. The light it cast was dim but sufficient to finish the job. What emerged was an earthen jar as tall as his forearm and a quarter of that across. It was covered with a lid that was sealed with pitch. There was nothing else buried with it.

He refilled the hole, scraping together loose dirt to make up for the space that had been taken up by the jar. No sense giving anyone the idea that something precious had been hidden there. Though in fact he was hoping that it was something precious. Silver, maybe? That would solve all of their tax problems!

Perhaps there would even be enough to take Banayahu and Gimillu before a judge—an honest one.

Happy for the first time during this terrible day, Zakaryah carried the jar to the house. Hannah started laying out a cold meal of bread, dates and beer while he scraped away at the pitch seal with a knife.

After eating he scratched away the last of the pitch, barely aware that he was holding his breath. Hannah watched, silent as usual.

He pried off the lid.

Inside was an old scroll of papyrus.

He drew it out and set it in front of them on the low table. He picked up the jar and angled it so that the meager light from the oil lamp penetrated to the bottom.

Empty.

He stared at the jar in disbelief, struggling to grasp this latest disaster, a sob catching in his throat. The enormity of the day crashed down on him. He buried his head in his hands then and cried, his hopes as empty as the jar.

When the crying eased he wiped his eyes on the sleeve of his robe and raised his head, remembering belatedly that Hannah was depending on him, that he needed to be strong for her.

She was staring at the scroll. As he watched she slowly extended her arm.

With one tentative finger, she touched it.

ZAKARYAH SPENT THE NEXT DAY slumped silently on the mud-brick bench by the door of his house, staring into the distance or down at his hands. His thoughts were jumbled, chaotic. Gimillu. The judge. Banayahu. His father. The ox. The burial. Gimillu. The fire. The taxes. They whirled and swirled like the embers and burning leaves that whipped into the sky the other day. He thought of the one leaf he had watched, of how he had wanted to follow it, to fly after it far into the western distance, far from people, from obligations, from pain.

The roots that held him anchored to this soil were being wrenched from the earth one by one. But they had been shallow to begin with. Some of that had been Ya'el. She had told him how she had been cut from her own family, her own place, like the suckers of the date palms that were cut off to be planted in a different field. Some of it was Hannah, who had cost him any chance at a normal childhood. But it wasn't only her. He had seen what happened to his uncles when their land was confiscated by lenders for non-payment of debt. It wasn't their fault that the fields they inherited were too small to sustain them and pay their taxes.

He sat motionless as his pocket of shade dwindled with the advancing day, diminished slowly by the relentless transit of the sun. The shadows of the afternoon lengthened and still he didn't move.

He finally roused himself when Hannah called him into the little courtyard for their evening meal.

Afterward she wanted him to read from the scroll.

He refused. Their last hope had been crushed the night before. Instead of the silver hoard of his fantasy, all they had was a worthless piece of papyrus. Some incomprehensible note left by his grandmother, surely. Normally he would have been eager to read it, to have even this poor memento from her. But that was before their whole world had collapsed.

No, he told her, he was not going to read it.

She went into the house and returned with the scroll. She set it down in front of him. She unrolled it a bit and weighted the loose edge with stones. Then she unrolled it further and placed another stone to prevent it from curling back up.

She sat down in the dirt, crossed her legs and waited, eyes on the papyrus.

He glared at her, then lifted the scroll, dumping the rocks off. He rolled it and put it back in its jar.

The next night Hannah again brought the scroll out. He took it back inside without reading it.

During the day he worked with Ovadyah, earning enough to keep them fed without depleting their own limited supply of grain and beer. As they worked he told Ovadyah in halting terms about the trip, the visit to the school, the disastrous outcome of the whole thing.

On the third night after they discovered the scroll, Hannah once again brought it out. Such a tiring game! Why wouldn't she give up?

This time, though, she rolled it all the way to its end. He reached out to roll it up. She intercepted his hand and guided it down to the surface of the papyrus. What was she doing?

"Read!" she commanded him.

He shook his head and tried to withdraw his hand. She held it there with surprising strength.

The moment dragged on and she still didn't release him. He felt his cheeks warming. What was he doing, getting into a power struggle with a six-year-old? It was true, there was no silver in the jar and the scroll did nothing to improve their situation. Still, what harm would it cause to read to her? Perhaps she would get some comfort from hearing their grandmother's words. Maybe even he would.

He nodded at her and she released him.

He looked down at the writing that had been partially covered by his hand.

It was a poem.

By the waters of Bavel, he read to her, *there we sat, sat and wept, remembering Yerushalayim.*

Other verses followed, but he skipped over them. It was the lines at the end that jumped out at him, that struck him with the unbearable yearning of his dream as his grandmother stared out a door that never existed toward a city that existed no longer.

If I forget you, Yerushalayim, let my right hand wither, let my tongue stick to my palate, if I cease to think of you, if I do not keep you in memory, even at my happiest hour.

"We forgot Yerushalayim," Hannah whispered. "We have to go back."

PART II

Late Spring, Year 17 of King Nabu-na'id

Open for me the gates of justice.

PSALM 118:19

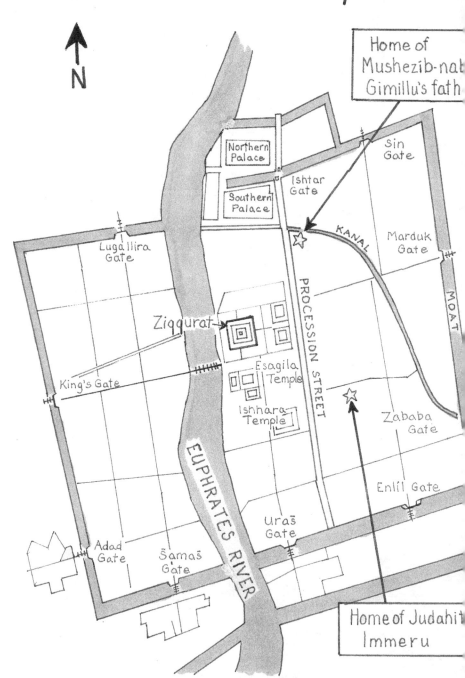

Bab-ili/Bavel/Babylon

N

Home of
Mushezib-nab
Gimillu's fath

Northern
Palace

Ishtar
Gate

Sin
Gate

Southern
Palace

KANAL

Marduk
Gate

Lugalira
Gate

MOAT

Ziqqurat

PROCESSION STREET

King's Gate

Esagila
Temple

Ishhara
Temple

Zababa
Gate

EUPHRATES RIVER

Enlil
Gate

Uras
Gate

Adad
Gate

Šamaš
Gate

Home of Judahit
Immeru

CHAPTER 8

GIMILLU STOOD WAITING for his uncle to stop talking to the servant, to look at him directly. He shifted his weight from foot to foot. Why couldn't he bring Shulmu inside with him? It would feel good right now just to have the dog at his side, looking up at him with those loving eyes.

He had done well, hadn't he? Had done just what his uncle demanded? Then why was he so nervous?

Finally Guzannu dismissed the servant and turned his attention to Gimillu. "Well?" he demanded.

"I did what you said. All of it."

"The judge?"

"Ten shekels of silver."

"Bana-yama?"

"I wrote out the false contract for the loan against the ox, just as you said. We added the names of some witnesses to make it legal. He fired it while I was there."

"Witnesses? Does anyone else know about this?"

"No. He gave me the names to write. If anyone asks them afterward he'll pay them and they'll say whatever he tells them to."

"Very well," Guzannu said. He gave Gimillu a long searching look. The boy chewed his lower lip. He looked toward the door, wishing that he could call in Shulmu.

"This is what you'll do," his uncle declared. "You'll write a letter to your father. I'll dictate it. He needs to know the jeopardy you've put him in. We'll fire it and seal it in a clay case."

There was another long silence. As it dragged on, Gimillu had time to think about the likely reaction in his family. Thank goodness he was here, far away from his father and from his brother's temper.

"Then," his uncle told him, "you'll carry it to Bab-ili and deliver it to your father in person."

"What? Why not a messenger?"

"We can't risk this being intercepted and delivered to one of his enemies at court. You will carry it. However, I'll have a messenger ride ahead of you. He'll tell your father to expect you no later than three days from tomorrow, and that if you fail to arrive, or if the seal is broken on the case, he's to denounce you immediately to the king's justice."

Guzannu called to a servant for a tablet of fresh wet clay. When it arrived he placed it on the table in front of Gimillu. He handed him a stylus. "Now write," he ordered and began dictating the letter.

GIMILLU PRESSED THE POUCH he carried under his robe, wincing at the pain where the heavy case of the tablet had rubbed his skin raw right where his mother's amulet would have been. Would she have thought it a fair trade, the clay case for her amulet?

The woolen pocket was the last thing he touched at night when he lay down at the side of the road and the first thing he touched in the morning. Had his uncle deliberately chosen that rough weave when he had told Gimillu to carry it next to his chest?

He reached down and scratched the panting Shulmu behind his ears as they waited for the ferry that would take them over the first of the two reeking moats they needed to cross to enter Bab-ili. He had briefly considered leaving Shulmu behind. His father hated the dog and would probably not allow the animal into the house. But Shulmu had proven his worth. On both nights of this journey his angry barking had woken Gimillu in time to see strange men slinking away into the darkness.

When the small boat pulled up to the bank in front of him he started forward, the dog following on his heels. He pulled a slim piece of silver out of the purse his uncle had given him, held it out for the ferryman. At a fortieth of a shekel it was generous. But the man pointed to the dog and shook his head.

"You have to take us both," Gimillu told him.

"I don't take wild animals," the man responded.

Gimillu scowled and said, "Sit, Shulmu." When the dog promptly sat, he told the ferryman, "Not wild. Now let us in."

But the man shook his head.

"My father is Mushezib-nabu. You've heard of him? You'll hear more when I tell him you refused to ferry me across." What he didn't say, of course, was that his father would surely side with the ferryman. In the end, he added a bit more silver to the fare and the man grudgingly agreed to take them.

The ferry dropped him and the dog off on the Litamu side. He hadn't been to this quarter in years. What reason would he have had for visiting here? It was a desperately poor area, situated as it was between the two moats. They were supposed to be defensive barriers, the moats, and maybe they had been once, but their real function now was to carry off the effluent of the entire city. The underground waste tunnels from the wealthy areas and the cesspits from the others all ended up in this warm, slow-flowing water.

He hurried along the narrow street to the bridge that would take him across the second moat and through the Urash gate in the southern wall. It was three hundred paces through air steamy with the smell of the waste fermenting in the moats. He breathed through his mouth the whole way because holding his breath wasn't possible. Tasting the air wasn't any better than smelling it. He envied Shulmu, who swung his head from side to side, raising his nose to sniff the air and then lowering it to sniff the ground. The dog, at least, was clearly enjoying the wealth of new odors.

Once through the gate the smell of the moats faded quickly, giving way rapidly to the odors of sweat, cooking fires, sheep and goats and pigs. He found himself in a mass of rushing, jostling people. There were soldiers on foot and on horseback. Merchants plowed their way to market squares, bundles on their backs: sticks, wood and dung for fires; boxes of small animals; bags of grain; and much, much more. Women wound their way in and out of the moving crowd offering water from jugs, a cool respite for those suffering from the heat. Gimillu was briefly tempted but thought about the moats he had just crossed. Was that where they had drawn the water? He decided to find a beer vendor at a market square.

Shulmu wove around beside him, dashing here and there to sniff at peoples' legs, collecting more than a few kicks before he figured out to dodge away as soon as the leg drew back. The ownerless dogs of the city attracted his attention too, until their snarls and growls sent him racing back to Gimillu's side.

As he walked, Gimillu patted reflexively at the heavy tablet dangling against his chest. He shuddered, his ears heating at the thought of facing his father and the humiliation that would bring. His pace slowed, his sandals dragging up small puffs of dust. People bumped into him, cursing when they realized he wasn't moving with the crowd.

It was all because of that Zakar-yama showing him up, mocking him, making him look foolish and stupid, just because he wasn't as quick with the lessons as the other boys. Worse, making him look like a coward, screaming and wetting himself in front of the whole tablet-house as the snake's head poked up through the opening of his lunch sack.

His father would surely see that Zakar-yama had left him no choice, had humiliated not only Gimillu, but also

Mushezib-nabu himself. Of course he would see that. He would finally side with his son, would even be proud of him for protecting his father's name and reputation. He would strike back at the Yahudu with the full might of his office and would write to his uncle, telling him that he had been wrong to treat Gimillu the way he had. In the end, this journey, intended as a punishment, would be a good thing, ushering in new respect for him in his father's eyes. It would surely be that way. It would.

The heat in his ears subsided. He straightened up, aware as he did so that he had been slumping, curling in on himself. He resumed walking, eyes ahead, gait steadying as he turned left onto the procession way, the main thoroughfare that would lead him to his father's house near the northern gate.

He glanced down at the dog trotting by his side, worried about what he would do with him when they reached the house. But Shulmu's ears were standing up, their tips leaning forward. As they came nearer to the Ishtar Gate he became aware of the sound of shouting and of a great grinding noise that went on and on. There were sounds of the same sort coming from other parts of the city, fainter with the distance. The street began filling with armed soldiers rushing toward the gate, shoving people aside in their haste.

When Gimillu drew into view of the Ishtar Gate he realized that the grinding noise was the groaning of the gate hinges. For the first time in six decades, masses of grunting soldiers were pulling the gates slowly inward. Through the narrowing gap in the huge doors, just before they slammed shut, he spied a group of cavalrymen in a distant phalanx, watching intently as the doors swung closed.

Even at this distance, it was obvious.

They weren't the king's soldiers.

CHAPTER 9

IT WAS THE DARKEST PART of the night when his father and his brother Kudurru finally came home from the palace, faces hard and etched with exhaustion.

Gimillu was squatting in the far corner of the room where the feeble light of the oil lamps barely reached. The sight of Kudurru, squat and powerful, had him cringing back as far as the corner would let him.

Shulmu lay curled on the floor next to him, his head on his paws.

His sister Nidintu had admitted him to the house earlier that day. "So you're finally here," was all her greeting when Gimillu showed up at the door. But she had stepped aside to let him enter. When Shulmu trotted in behind she raised an eyebrow but said nothing.

Nidintu greeted the two men and tilted her head at Gimillu. He scrambled to his feet and bowed. His father scowled at him. "We'll talk in the morning," he said.

"What news do you have?" Nidintu asked.

It was their father who answered. "The other counselors thought Kurush would stop at Upi. It's in the borderlands. They argued that he just wanted to create a buffer area. I told the king that after the slaughter there he would keep coming all the way to Bab-ili. The king listened to the other counselors. And here we are."

Kudurru added, "The priests suspected something like this. Esagila temple sent horse messengers out three days ago to warn the other temples."

"All the temples?" Mushezib-nabu asked with a smile.

"Marduk first, then the others. But they might have forgotten to warn the temples of Sin," his son answered, also smiling. "I'm guessing that the king will soon be too busy to worry about his precious moon god."

"Soon we will all have more than enough to worry about," his father answered, yawning.

IN THE MORNING, while the family was still together after their meal of lamb, dates and wine, Gimillu's father said to him, "This tablet you're carrying. Give it to me."

Gimillu drew the clay case from inside his robe, the physical weight on his chest finally going away, only to be replaced by a different kind of weight. He handed it over.

Mushezib-nabu broke the seal, slipped the tablet out and began reading. From time to time he paused, raised his eyes, and regarded the boy before resuming.

Gimillu chewed on his knuckles, squirming on his seat as his sister and brother stared silently at him. He glanced over at the dark corner from last night, where Shulmu was currently sleeping. If only he could be there now.

When his father finished he set the tablet down and addressed Gimillu's siblings. "Our boy here burned the barley field of a Yahudu child who taunted him in the tablet-house."

"I was defending your honor!"

"My honor had nothing to do with it. You were thinking only of your humiliation. Guzannu was right to send you here. You put us all in jeopardy."

Kudurru said, "The wrong one died when he was born."

His father turned to him. "It's not the boy's fault that your mother died. You know that."

Kudurru nodded minutely and Gimillu felt his whole body sag with relief. His father didn't hate him.

"Still," Mushezib-nabu continued, regarding him without expression, "it was about what we would expect of you."

He addressed the others. "Fortunately Guzannu was able to contain the damage." He described the actions his brother-in-law had taken to blur the trail leading back to the family. To Gimillu: "Does the Yahudu boy suspect you?"

"No! Nobody saw me."

"That judge Bel-shunu saw you. So did that rich man in Al Yahudu."

"They won't say anything."

"And how did you find out the number of date palms the boy owned?" When there was no answer he said, "So. And I notice you're not wearing your mother's amulet."

Gimillu turned bright red, raised his hand toward his chest, immediately dropped it.

"The one thing she desperately wanted you to have, that she made us promise to give you when you were old enough to wear it. To protect you from evil influences, she said. Too bad it couldn't protect you from your own stupidity. Fortunately for you, Bab-ili is now under siege by Kurush of Parsu. This," he tapped the tablet, "is not our biggest problem."

He and Gimillu's siblings began quietly discussing plans for dealing with the situation while Gimillu himself slipped away into the same corner where Shulmu was curled up. The others didn't notice. Shulmu licked his hand when he squatted down.

As the conversation went on he began hearing his name mentioned in low tones. Nidintu was facing him. He caught her studying him and shuddered.

When the discussion ended they all turned to look at him.

"Gimillu," his father said, "we have a job for you."

CHAPTER 10

ZAKARYAH TRIED HIS BEST to explain it. We can't go back to Yerushalayim, he told Hannah. We're too young. It will take three and a half months, maybe more. What will we eat? Where will we sleep? There'll be brigands. We'll be robbed or killed. We'll need provisions. How will we pay for them? There's nothing there, Nevuchadnetsar destroyed it, destroyed all of Yehudah. We'd be going back to a ruin.

No, it was clearly impossible.

She listened to him without speaking. When he was done she went off to prepare their evening meal.

Was she offended? He hoped not. It was a silly idea. She had to hear that, but he didn't want her to feel bad.

It did help him clarify his own thoughts, though. He had made a mistake following Ovadyah's advice. The judge in Al Yahudu was too poor, too susceptible to being bribed. That wouldn't be true in Bavel. The Chaldean name, Bab-ili, meant gate of the gods. The king would never permit corrupt judges there, with all his gods looking over his shoulder. Never mind that they were all false gods. The king believed in them. Zakaryah would seek justice there. Gimillu would be punished, punished severely. At the least, he would be heavily fined.

And maybe he would be condemned to death.

Zakaryah could even hear in his mind the speech he would make to the judge, the speech that would seal Gimillu's fate. We're orphans, he would say. Gimillu burned the food of orphans and condemned us to starvation or slavery on account of the taxes.

He broached the decision to Hannah, sure that she would object. "I need to go to Bavel. There'll be honest judges there. I'll get our dates back, and maybe there'll be a fine that I can use to pay our taxes and replant our barley field."

But instead of arguing, she just said, "I'll come too."

This time he knew better than to refuse her outright. He had never been to Bavel but he had heard it was a huge and frightening place. She could get lost in the crowds. Some of the people could be dangerous. And there were all those temples with their gods and goddesses. She was just a child. What if her head was turned? He didn't want to be looking after her constantly and worrying about her.

He did have a plan, though. They would pass by Al Yahudu and he would leave her with Michal at the school. Maybe she would even begin learning something. He would continue on by himself to Bavel. Hannah would remain safe with Michal.

Outside, the remaining purple of dusk was fading away,

signaling the start of Shabbat. Tomorrow they would rest, as Yahweh commanded, and the day after that they would leave.

Justice, justice shall you pursue. Hadn't he read that during one of the lessons from his grandmother? Well, he would pursue justice. He would pursue it all the way to Bavel.

Gimillu would pay for what he had done.

HE SLEPT POORLY that night, dozing fitfully and waking in the morning without feeling refreshed. He chafed at the delay that Shabbat would impose on his plans, but in the end he was glad of it, glad for one brief day to be out of the whirlwind. Not that it was enough. Nothing would ever be enough.

In the morning the community gathered at one of the storehouses that fronted the river, empty now of the grains and other products that would shortly be stored there for the tax collector. They broke apart loaves of Shabbat bread, said the blessings, and shared them around. One of the priests opened a scroll, pulled out a small hand-like pointer, and began reading the story of the peoples' escape centuries before from Mitzrayim. Zakaryah had heard the story many times. What did it have to do with him?

He looked around the room. Here and there boys his age clustered together, talking and laughing. Occasionally one or another would glance over at him, out of pity no doubt. Did they remember being friends, playing with him? But that was before his mother died, leaving him to take care of the strange little girl who was his sister.

He turned his thoughts away. It didn't hurt, not anymore. He didn't have much in common with them anyway, especially not now. They had fields and a future. He had neither.

Then Hannah squeezed his hand. The priest was talking about their father. A good man, he said, a wonderful father, loved by everyone in Nar Kabara. After that, Zakaryah heard nothing. His head was buried in his arms, his back shook and the tears spilled down his face in a torrent that wouldn't abate. He knew without looking that everyone was staring at him in pity. Not able to take it any longer, he staggered to his feet and stumbled outside. Back in his house he flung himself onto his father's sleeping pallet and stayed there until later in the day when Hannah returned from the assembly hall.

That evening Hannah packed provisions. There wasn't enough in the house for him and her both for the five days it would take to walk to Bavel. There would be enough for him alone, though. He was grateful that she didn't notice. That feeling ended abruptly when she told him that Michal in Al Yahudu would supply them with the rest.

Zakaryah slipped his grandmother's scroll into the sack with the provisions. Maybe Michal would like to see it, or perhaps Ginat, that old woman with the fierce grip.

The next day at around noon he banged on the door of the scribal school.

Michal opened the door and smiled at them.

"Come in," she said. "We've been expecting you."

CHAPTER 11

THE WATER WAS WARM and the night dark. Even so, Gimillu shivered as he floated through the city on the slow current, looking at the walls of the houses that backed up against the canal. Occasional torches lit the roof pavilions of the homes he passed, but the light barely reached to the edge of the canal, let alone to its middle. There were so many people up there after the heat of the day. It would only take one to spot him.

He had pointed that out to them when they told him what he would need to do. The answer had been that he would be covered by bushes, that there would be no moon until much later, that there was a huge enemy army camped north of the city. Did he really think anyone would be looking at the canal?

He had told them he couldn't swim.

They would tie a section of palm trunk to his back. It would keep him afloat.

If a guard saw him he'd be killed.

If Kurush were to take the city by force he'd be dead anyway. Had he forgotten the massacre at Upi, up north on the border?

What if the priests at the Esagila Temple didn't go along?

They'd go along. His father had contacts there. He knew their feelings about the king.

What about Shulmu?

The dog would be there when he got back. Unspoken: *If in fact he did get back.*

In the end, they had given him no choice. He was the only one of the males slim enough to slip through the iron bars where the canal passed below the city wall and into the moat beyond. He would do as they told him or they would push him into the canal where it passed by the back of the house. He could learn to swim right there. Or not.

His father watched as Kudurru tied the section of palm trunk to his back with a cord that went full around his chest. Kudurru then sealed the newly fired tablet into the same clay case he had carried all the way from the Yahudu area, hanging it around his neck with another cord. Nidintu brandished a small dagger in Gimillu's face, grinning as he drew back in alarm. No, stupid, it's not to stab you with. You'll use it to cut the log loose on the other side of the moat. And if you're caught before you get there, you'll use it to sever the cord holding the tablet so it sinks straight to the bottom of the canal. Got that?

They had marched him to the water then, lashing the bushes to him as a disguise. Kudurru cut a reed from a patch growing at the water's edge. He spied along the inside, declaring it to be hollow. He handed it to Gimillu and pushed him in.

He whimpered as he floated in the warm water, unable to wrench his gaze from the houses lining the canal.

His terror abated a bit as the current moved him gently along. He drew some comfort from the knife he clutched in one hand and the reed in the other. It would be all right. His father wouldn't send him to certain death. They had as much at stake as he did. It was a good plan. He would do what they needed. When he returned, the mission successfully accomplished, they would look at him with new affection and respect.

He thought through his instructions. The canal ahead would make a lazy curve to the right in its course from the palace area in the northwestern part of the city. After that a wide curve to the left would signal its approach to the point where it passed under the three city walls just before flowing into the moat. This was where the danger would be greatest. There would be soldiers at the adjacent Zababa gate and all along the three closely spaced walls that defended the city. He would pass right under them.

Suddenly the inner wall of the city was in front of him. It was just a dark shadow in the moonless night, but Gimillu could make out the top by the faint light of the small oil lamps placed along it at regular intervals. He wondered about them but decided they must mark the stairs the soldiers used to ascend and descend.

The Zababa gate would be in the third, outermost wall, perhaps thirty or forty paces beyond that. This was where he would need to be absolutely quiet, they had told him. There would be more soldiers and they'd be more alert—much more. Their attention would be directed outward, though, not toward the inside of the city.

But won't I be outside the walls when I'm in the moat? Won't they see me then?

You'll float beneath the surface of the water. Why do you think I cut the reed? his brother had retorted.

He trembled even more as the current quickened. The wall loomed higher in the darkness. He started hearing the subdued voices of the soldiers on top. The voices grew louder, the conversations clearer.

He cursed the Yahudu boy who had landed him in this peril. In his head, though, he heard his friend Uqupu taunting him. *Who burned the barley? What about all those times you went after him with fists and sticks because he was a better student, because you thought he didn't respect you? Did you think the boy would just take it, wouldn't find a way to get revenge? Did you think he would be like me?*

The canal narrowed to less than two arm spans across. He was spun forward as the water sped him toward a patch of deeper darkness at the base of the wall. A tunnel! He started slashing wildly around with the knife to cut the bushes loose, moaning as the rushing water swept him into the pitch-black maw of the underground channel.

IT WAS THE IRON BARS that almost drowned him. They covered the far opening of the tunnel from top to bottom, spaced closely so that an enemy soldier would be unable to squeeze through from outside and gain access to the interior of the city. For him, though, smaller, slimmer, it should just be possible. That's what his father had counted on.

What his father hadn't counted on was the rushing pressure of the water and the way the bushes with him had been caught in the current, pressing him hard against the bars; the near impossibility of slashing himself loose from them with water pouring over, under and around him; and finally, when he somehow managed that, the way that the palm trunk keeping him afloat twisted sideways in the flow, catching on the bars he was trying to squeeze through. In the end he severed the cord holding it to his back, then grabbed it desperately as he and it were spit through the barrier and into the sewage-laden waters of the moat.

He dragged himself out on the far bank, burying his mouth in the crook of his elbow to suppress the coughs that were convulsing him.

As the coughing subsided he raised his head. Had he been heard? Spotted? But the tumbling of the canal's waters as they spilled from the channel helped to drown out the noises that he had been unable to suppress. He imagined the trunk section he had clung to floating away in the night and felt for his knife. Gone. The reed too had disappeared. The tablet! He jerked his hand to his chest, sighing with both relief and dismay when he pressed its rough weight against his skin. There was no excuse now. He would have to go forward.

He knew that a path led directly east through the farm fields that surrounded the city in the buffer zone outside the main walls. It had to be near to where he had landed on the bank.

He found it several paces to his left, a lighter patch of earth that was just discernible in the faint light of the stars. He groped his way along it, surprised to find that the smell of the moat was following him even as the distance grew. He shuddered as he realized it was his robe, still drenched with sewage. With sudden horror, he pulled some strands of his hair down to his nose and smelled them. Awful! But nothing to do about it now. He tried to put it out of his mind and it wasn't that hard. He had enough other things to worry about.

He crossed a small canal on a footbridge and shortly found himself in front of a gate, silent and sealed shut.

The far wall.

NIDINTU HAD TOLD HIM that the wall wasn't maintained. The king had wanted to spend his resources on the temple of his favorite god, Sin.

Gimillu wasn't surprised, then, when he found a break a few hundred paces to the north. An access road running the length of the wall made his passage relatively easy, even in the dense darkness of the night. It was a surprise then when he tripped over a section of the road that had been eroded through. A shallow runnel had undermined both the road surface and the wall next to it, causing the mudbricks to shift randomly about. He was able to grope his way to the top.

From there he scanned the countryside. The moon was just rising above the eastern horizon, but the land spread out before him was still deep in darkness. The singing of crickets filled the night, fading out to the far distance. Apart from that, he detected no signs that anything was stirring in his immediate vicinity.

Well to the north, though, he could make out the glow of the watch fires of the enemy army. They stretched an impossible distance across the steppe. He realized with a shock that his father was wrong, dead wrong. The plan would never work. So many soldiers! What was he supposed to do? Just walk into their camp? They'd impale him for sure.

He squeezed his eyes shut, his whole body rigid.

To the south and east there were no fires. That was it. That's where he would go. He would put some distance behind him and then turn to the southeast, toward the Yahudu country he was familiar with. He would find his way from there to the mouth of the sea that he had heard about, down beyond the city of Ur. He would get on a trading boat and sail off to somewhere else, it didn't matter where. What was he leaving behind? His family hated him, had sent him to certain death. He had no friends, no close relatives who would care. Then he thought of Shulmu, trusting, loving Shulmu. Tears began flowing down his cheeks. But Shulmu would be fine, someone would take care of him. They wouldn't just throw him out into the street, to starve to death or eat whatever leavings he could find. Would they?

But there was no choice, just death if he didn't escape.

He looked again at the fires to the north, then back at the city behind him. Shulmu would be there waiting, ears drooping, eyes heavy and sad.

Vision blurred by tears, he clambered carefully down the tumbled blocks and began heading in the direction of a road he had seen from the top of the wall. He walked in the center of a moving circle of quiet as the crickets around him fell silent with his passage. Beyond the edge of this invisible boundary, the insects' singing continued unabated.

His thoughts turned to the long trip ahead. He would get water from the irrigation ditches along the way. Food would be harder. He would need to stay out of sight of people, walking along the edges of the permanent fields of grain. There would be marshy areas beyond many of these, left over from last year's spring floods. Birds and other animals would be abundant there. Of course there would be lions as well, attracted to the marshes for the same reasons. He would need to be careful. Even so he should be able to catch some of the waterfowl, and that would keep him going until he was far enough away that there was no chance anyone would think to stop him. He would need to replace the knife he had lost in the moat. He would steal one somewhere. A bow and some arrows would be essential too. But he could make those, cut them from branches with the knife. And bows were strung with gut, that's what he'd heard. He'd get that from the animals he caught.

As he rounded a dense thicket, the crickets' chirping stopped entirely. At the same moment a dozen men in strange robes materialized in front of him, spears leveled. He screamed and turned to run. There was a sharp crack as a spear struck his chest. He crumpled to the ground.

CHAPTER 12

DURING THE MIDDAY MEAL at the school, Zakaryah asked Michal how she knew that he and Hannah would be coming.

"Danna," she answered, "would you like to say something?"

Danna shook her head and kept eating.

"All right. Well, Danna told me that sooner or later you would think of trying to find an honest judge and that you'd be stopping here on the way to Bavel."

He just glared at the girl. It wasn't fair. She had told him that Banayahu had been bribed and she was right about that too. And there she sat not even looking at him as she ate. So smug. Such a know-it-all.

He looked back at Michal. Thank goodness she didn't know what he was thinking. Then he saw the faint trace of a smile as she regarded him.

Danna spoke up for the first time. "You won't find an

honest judge in Bavel either."

"That's not true! The king is there. He would never allow dishonest judges."

She shrugged. "I used to spend summers there with my relatives. They're merchants. They know all about bribing government officials." She paused, looked him up and down, then added, "But don't let me stop you."

Horrible girl.

But Michal was speaking to him. "Why don't you and Hannah spend the night here? It's late in the day to be starting a trip to Bavel."

Hannah addressed her. "He wants to leave me here with you."

Danna asked Hannah, "But you're going, aren't you?"

"Yes," Hannah responded.

"Good," the older girl said. "I'll go too."

"What? What?" Zakaryah looked from Hannah to Danna and back again.

"Poor Zakaryah," Michal murmured. "You're always a step or two behind the girls, aren't you?"

He addressed Danna in desperation. "You can't come. You're a girl."

"And?"

"But what if someone tries to . . . bother you?"

"I'm still as flat as you," she answered. "And anyway, who would want to touch a Kushite girl?"

He turned to Michal. "You can't let her go. It's dangerous."

"It's up to her grandfather, not me," the woman answered.

"And he's not here. He has a farm along the way. Maybe he'll be so glad to see her that he'll forget to be furious. But Danna, why do you want to go? You'll miss at least half a month of instruction."

"I need to ask my relatives something."

He barely heard her. His mind was racing. Travel with a girl who wasn't his sister? Impossible. And how would he protect her and Hannah? Anything could happen. This Danna was infuriating. Four and a half days on the road with her? And back again?

He snuck a glance at her. She caught him looking and raised an eyebrow. He shuddered.

Michal said, "Good. So you'll all stay here tonight. I have some things to take care of in the town. Hannah, you'll make the bread and the porridge for tonight's meal. Zakaryah, you'll have to help out too. Danna will teach half of the children while I'm away. You'll teach the other half. I'm not mistaken, am I? You do read and write?"

He sat up straighter. "Of course. My grandmother was Ya'el."

"And you also read Chaldean, don't you? I've never heard of the scribal guild allowing one of us to learn."

"Master Nabu-ushabshi has a tablet-house across the canal from Nar Kabara. There's a rumor he lost some political fight at court. He needed the tuition. My father thought we should have someone to read the letters and contracts they write for us. To keep them honest, he said."

"Interesting. Danna, show Zakaryah the material we're studying now and help him get started."

His heart sank. Bad enough that Danna was coming with him to Bavel. Now he had to be instructed by her? But he knew better than to say anything.

That evening they took their meal in the courtyard. As they were finishing, Danna began clearing the eating bowls. The younger students were talking among themselves. Michal was busy polishing off the last loaf of bread.

Hannah nudged Zakaryah in the ribs.

"What?" he demanded.

"The scroll," she answered. "You need to leave it with Michal."

"Scroll?" Michal asked, her hand stopping halfway to her mouth. "What scroll?"

Zakaryah turned around and retrieved the scroll from the sack behind him. "This one," he told her, holding it up. "We found it buried in the foundation of my grandmother's house. Hannah's right. We should leave it with you until we come back."

"May I see it?" Michal asked.

He handed it to her.

She unrolled it and began reading. After a moment she stopped and asked, voice catching, "Ya'el wrote this?"

He found himself choking up, able to manage only a nod.

"Ginat will want to see this," Michal said. "You remember Ginat, Zakaryah? She brought you here last week."

He nodded.

Michal told one of the boys to run and fetch Ginat. While they waited she skipped through the scroll, smiling at some points, sucking in her breath at others. Once she stopped and looked up, eyes picking out each of the young people in turn. "She met Yirmeyahu the prophet," she whispered, shaking her head. "She wasn't very nice to him."

She advanced the scroll a bit. "Hmm. Here she writes about a Chaldean guard, a young man."

Danna was suddenly standing next to her. "His name!" she demanded. "What was his name?"

Michal searched forward and backward in the scroll. "She doesn't say. Why?"

"Keep looking. Please."

Eventually she found something. "It's hard to read. The ink is smeared. But it seems to start with 'Ab.' I can't make it out."

"Never mind," Danna told her, eyes wide. "It's Abir-ilu. That's his name." She took a deep breath.

"My grandfather."

CHAPTER 13

A SOLDIER WAS LOOMING over Gimillu as he came to, spear in his hand, pointing directly at his chest. The man was shouting at him in an unfamiliar language, his voice loud and angry.

"I don't understand Parsaya," Gimillu said, shaking all over. He tried to scoot backward on his rear. The soldier followed him, still shouting, shaking the spear at his face, then at his chest. His rearward progress stopped when he backed up against something that didn't move.

There was a shout from behind him and the soldier abruptly stepped back, lowering the point of the spear to the ground.

"You, boy," a voice behind him said in Akkadu. "You're not hurt. Get up."

Not hurt? He felt his chest. It was tender where the spearhead struck him, but there was no wound. And the message tablet was gone.

"Yes," said the voice. "You ran straight into my spear. The point snapped on that clay case you were wearing. Then you fainted. Now get up."

He'd fainted! He stood slowly and turned around, cheeks burning.

The soldier who had been talking wrinkled his nose, said "Phew!" and took a hasty step backward. The other soldiers encircling him stepped back a few paces as well. The man gestured at the guard who had been shaking the spear and said, "Marduniya here is sure you're a spy. He says we should kill you. I think you might be a spy, but then you're just a boy. Who would send a boy as a spy? And why were you heading away from our army? If you were a spy wouldn't you be heading toward it? He said what better way to fool us. Then I told him it seems strange that a spy would be carrying some kind of message. He said it's probably a trap. I said that if it's a trap it's a poor one, since you're all alone and blundered straight into us. I suggested that maybe we should learn more, and he agreed. He wasn't happy about it, but he said we could always kill you later. And I agreed. We can always kill you later. So now you know your situation. It's your turn to talk."

What would keep these terrible men from killing him? "The m . . . m . . . message," he stammered. "It's for the king. Kurush."

"I know who the king is."

"It's a plan for taking the city without attacking it."

"Ah. I see. And who is sending us this wondrous plan, and why?"

The words flooded out of Gimillu, unstoppable as a desert storm. He told them about his father's position at court, about the current king's neglect of Marduk, about the priesthood's disdain for the king, about the plan for taking over the city. There was more, and he babbled on, unable to stop, until the soldier held up his hand, staring at him for a long moment during which Gimillu fought to keep his bladder from loosening.

The man shook his head and spoke to the other soldiers in Parsaya. Translating? There were comments, questions maybe. Deciding whether to kill him? He studied them for clues to his fate. Hard faces, glances thrown his way. The soldier Marduniya was listening and nodding, but never took his eyes off Gimillu.

The discussion came to an end. The soldier who had been talking to him said, "We're taking you to King Kurush." He held his hand out behind him and someone placed the broken case in it. He handed it to Gimillu. The message tablet was still inside. "You'll give this to the king. He'll decide what to do with you. What's your name?"

"Gimillu."

"Well, Gimillu, I'm Manu. You're about the age of my own son. Let's hope the king wants you alive."

The patrol closed in around him, herding him toward the distant fires of the enemy camp.

The crickets resumed their chirping.

HIS PASSAGE THROUGH the Parsu host was terrifying. His captors formed a phalanx around him and plowed through. The plain where the army was encamped was filled with tents and fire rings. It was the light from all these fires he had seen the night before that had persuaded him to flee rather than face this fearsome army. How many soldiers did this King Kurush have? He soon gave up trying to count them all. They grinned at him and sharpened their swords as he was herded past them.

They shoved him into a tub and forced him to bathe. They wouldn't bring him into the presence of the king smelling like a cesspit, they told him. He protested that it had been less than a year since his last bath. They told him that he could bathe himself or they'd do it and take him to the king naked.

It was well after dawn when they brought him into the king's tent.

Gimillu was wearing a fresh robe, one reluctantly given to him by a soldier in the patrol that captured him. It was too long. It dragged on the ground, turning the hem into a brown mess with the dirt it collected.

The first thing Gimillu noticed about King Kurush was how short he was, just a head taller than Gimillu himself. His face was lined and darkened by the sun, his hair and beard black streaked with grey. His robe was striking, a rich golden color with sunburst designs, all trimmed in deep elegant blue. A spear and sword leaned casually against his chair. He looked to be in perhaps the fifth decade of his life.

His presence filled the tent. There was no question who was in charge. Everyone entering his presence bowed low.

Manu, next to Gimillu, knelt on the ground, his forehead

pressed to the earthen floor of the tent, awaiting the pleasure of the king.

Gimillu did the same.

At a command, Manu stood and faced the king. He nudged Gimillu with his foot and he stood too.

The soldier spoke at length in Parsaya. The king and the other soldiers around him listened closely, turning their heads from time to time to study the trembling Gimillu.

When Manu finished, the king snapped his fingers. Manu took the clay case from Gimillu and bowed deeply, handing it to Kurush. The king inspected it. The tablet was intact inside, visible through the crack in the case. He set it on a stool next to him, saying something to an attendant that set the man running from the tent. He turned his full attention to Gimillu.

"So," he said in clear Akkadu, "you've come to help us take the city."

"Yes. No. It's my father. He made me come."

"What's your name?"

"Gimillu."

"And your father?"

"Mu . . . Mushezib-nabu."

The king turned to the man next to him. "Gaubaruva?"

Gaubaruva? The governor of Upi? He wasn't killed when the city fell?

The man spoke to the king in a low voice, regarding Gimillu closely as he did so. "A high counselor to King Nabuna'id. Started as a scribe and rose in the king's service. May I see the case, my lord?" At a nod he picked it up and inspected it, putting his finger below a spot on the top. "His seal, my lord."

Kurush nodded, turned back to Gimillu, studying him with a steady gaze and a furrowed brow. "Not a spy, I think," addressing Gaubaruva. "Or if so a very bad one. It could be a trap though. What's keeping that scribe?"

Footsteps approached at a run and a man came rushing through the tent entrance, bowing deeply to the king as he paused to catch his breath. At a gesture from Kurush, Gaubaruva handed the case to the new arrival. "Read it," the king ordered. The man inserted his fingers into the crack and broke off enough of the case to extract the tablet. While he was reading to himself, the king spoke to Gimillu. "Why did your father send you and not someone more suitable?"

"The bars. Where the canal joins the moat. I'm small enough to get through them. My brother and father aren't."

"So he sent his least-valued son." He again addressed Gaubaruva. "No use as a hostage, then. It has to be a trap."

"It's not a trap!" Gimillu blurted, knees weakening. "My lord," he added hastily.

By then the scribe had finished reading the tablet. He cleared his throat. In response to the king's nod, he said, "It's a plan for taking the city. It depends on treachery from within, led by this boy's father. You will proclaim your reverence for Marduk, chief among their gods. It appears that the current king is widely hated by priests and people because of his neglect of this god. If the plan works it will cost very few lives. The father asks for a high position in my lord's new administration. He says that he can greatly smooth your takeover of all the land, both in the land of the two rivers and beyond the river to the western sea, all the way to the nation of Pharaoh. He adds that if possible he would appreciate his son here being returned alive." He glanced a moment at Gimillu. "That, however, isn't a major demand. If you agree to the proposal we're to raise a red flag where it can be seen from the Ishtar Gate."

"Read the whole letter through," Kurush ordered.

The scribe read in a steady voice, but Gimillu didn't hear any of it. What he did hear was that his father didn't care if he came back alive. He managed to stifle the sobs, but he couldn't stop the tears from flooding his eyes and rolling down his cheeks.

When the scribe finished reading, the king said to Gaubaruva, "An interesting plan. Or a trap, but one we can spring with little risk."

He studied Gimillu, now wiping his eyes and nose with the sleeve of the robe. "You think the soldier who gave you that will be happy to have your snot all over it?"

"I miss my dog."

The king's expression lightened. "I was a shepherd when I was your age. I loved my dogs. Yours has a name?"

"Shulmu."

Kurush addressed the soldier Manu, still standing silently next to Gimillu. "Take him to your tent, feed him and bind him there."

To Gimillu the king said, "Tomorrow we'll do as your father proposes. If it goes well, I'll return you to your Shulmu. If it doesn't, I'll kill you myself."

CHAPTER 14

AS THEY STEPPED OUT OF THE SCHOOL in the morning, Michal told Zakaryah, "Remember, you're traveling with your two sisters. You're going to join your father in Bavel."

Danna said, "They won't believe I'm his sister."

"Half-sister, then. And anyone who hears how you talk to each other will have no problem believing you're siblings."

They said goodbye to Michal and started for the river. After only a few paces Danna stopped. She pulled the top of her bag open and looked inside, shaking her head. Then she shoved the bag into Zakaryah's hands. "Hold this!" She ran back into the house, emerging a short time later carrying what looked like a small coil of woven cord in the palm of her hand. She grabbed the bag back from Zakaryah without a word and dropped the thing inside, closing the sack.

"What was that?" he asked her.

"Let's go," she said.

Insufferable girl.

They joined the river road and headed to the northwest, the direction of Bavel.

Even this early the day was hot. Hannah and Danna already had their heads covered. Zakaryah reached into the bag he was carrying and extracted a large square cloth, which he folded in half from corner to corner. He placed it on his head and wrapped a length of rope around his temples. He fumbled with the cord behind his head, trying to knot it so the cloth would stay put.

Danna stepped up and tied it from behind.

"Too tight!" he complained.

"You do it then," she snapped. But she loosened it.

The road began to fill with foot traffic, donkey carts, and even the occasional rider on horseback. Once they passed a man resting his camels by the side of the road. Part of a caravan from the desert? But the animals carried no burdens. Perhaps he was taking them to market to be sold or rented out.

The day continued to warm up. Flies buzzed around his face, landing on his cheeks, lips and nose. They were especially bad on the bridges over the irrigation ditches that branched from the river. He brushed them off, but they returned as soon as his attention wandered. He noticed Danna brushing away flies as well and felt a brief moment of satisfaction that she was suffering as much as he was. Then she pulled her scarf tight around her face so that only her eyes were showing. Hannah did the same.

People traveled in both directions. Some stared at them, a boy and two girls traveling without an adult. He glared at them, fists clenched, daring them to say anything. Perhaps it worked, because nobody spoke. He gave it up, though, when he noticed Danna's eyes crinkling. She was laughing at him. Nine days, maybe more. That's how long he would have to put up with this. Maybe he could leave her at her grandfather's farm. They would be there in four days. That would show her. But what about Hannah? He did feel a tiny bit of relief at having someone else along to watch out for her. Too bad it was Danna. And now Hannah was holding her hand. She seemed to like this Danna person more than she liked him, her own brother.

He frowned at the girls. If only he didn't have them slowing him down. He could have been past Nippur by now. Maybe he could even cut a whole day off the journey. Who knew what Gimillu was cooking up? Would he return to Nar Kabara to find that his house had been burned down like his barley field?

"Slow down!" The voice from behind pulled him out of his thoughts. Danna. They were several paces back, stopped in fact, right on the road. The older girl's lips were pressed together in a tight line. Hannah was breathing hard next to her.

"Are you trying to catch Bavel before it runs away?" she asked. "Your sister's legs are short. It's hard for her to keep up when you're rushing ahead like that."

"You're the ones who demanded to come," he retorted. He stood waiting for them to catch up.

Instead, Danna pointed to a palm orchard just ahead. "We'll rest there," she said.

There she went again, as if she were in charge instead of him. In fact, though, it was getting very hot. He swallowed once and nodded.

But when they got to the orchard there was already a Chaldean man there, eyes closed, resting with his back against one of the trees.

Zakaryah signaled that they should move on, but Danna shook her head and walked to another tree, dragging Hannah with her. He motioned silently for them to come on.

"No," she said.

The man's eyes opened. He looked at the three of them, then did a double take. "A Kushite!" he declared in Akkadu, staring at Danna.

Her face froze and she went still. Zakaryah waited for the ferocious retort he knew was coming, but it never did. She just stood there staring down at nothing. He recalled how she had recoiled when Banayahu rubbed her arm to see if the darkness would come off on his fingers. True, she was a thorn in his side. Even so, it wasn't right. He opened his mouth to speak.

But Hannah was standing directly in front of the man, hands on her hips, fixing him with her strange grey eyes. "She's my sister," she told him. "You be nice to her."

"I'm sorry! I was surprised, that's all."

Hannah nodded once and walked over to where Zakaryah was standing with Danna.

Moved by an impulse he didn't understand, he put his arms around both girls. He felt Danna stiffen briefly, then she yielded and let him pull her closer. "We're going to rest here," he said, looking hard at the man.

"I'm sorry," the man repeated. "I didn't mean to be rude. I'm Nurea. Who're you?"

"Zakaryah." He paused for a moment, considering. But there didn't seem to be any reason not to introduce the girls. "This is my sister Hannah and my other sister—half-sister—Danna. We're going to Bab-ili to join our father."

"Bab-ili! Then you haven't heard. It's under siege."

"Siege?"

"By Kurush of Parsu," he responded. "Five days ago. Nobody can get in or out."

But Hannah shook her head.

"No siege," she told them. "Bab-ili fell. Yesterday."

CHAPTER 15

KING KURUSH AND HIS RETINUE of fifty men entered Bab-ili through the Marduk gate in the eastern wall of the city. The king rode a dark war horse. Gaubaruva rode beside him. Kurush's soldiers manned the walls alongside the gate and lined the small gate plaza and the street leading deeper into the city.

Gimillu walked just behind the king.

Once the king and his soldiers had passed through the gate they stopped. Ahead and around the column, people of the city were kneeling on the ground, foreheads touching the earth. Kurush's soldiers kept a wary eye on them, but they held their weapons casually, seeming to Gimillu not to be particularly tense.

Among the hundreds kneeling, he spotted his father and brother.

Kurush murmured something to Gaubaruva, who then called out, "Mushezib-nabu, stand forth."

Gimillu's father rose to his feet and bowed deeply toward the king. Kurush looked him over. He said, "Mushezib-nabu, I return your son to you." At his nod, Gimillu left the group.

As he stepped away from the rest of the retinue, Gimillu heard some in the crowd hissing "traitor." But he had saved them all, hadn't he? Wouldn't they have died if Kurush had attacked? Maybe he should have expected it. And he didn't really care, did he? What did they know of the dangers he had faced? What mattered was that he had done what had been required of him, had done it at great personal peril, and would now be standing next to his father in the presence of the new king.

"Don't just stand here," his father demanded in a whisper as he shuffled up to him. "Kneel down with your brother."

Kurush was speaking again. "I understand there's a dog in the household."

"Yes, my lord," Mushezib-nabu responded, frowning.

The king nodded at Gimillu's brother, still bent over on the ground, his face in the dirt. "This is your other son?"

"Yes, my lord."

"Send him to fetch the animal. He will bring it to us at the palace."

"Yes, my lord." He nudged Kudurru with his foot. "You heard the great king," he said. "Go!"

Gimillu snuck a peek at his brother and caught the venomous glance Kudurru directed at him as he rose and rushed off.

"Where is your former king?" Kurush demanded. "He was to be presented to me in irons."

"Great King," Mushezib-nabu answered, "the individual

you refer to managed to escape. We believe that he is hiding somewhere in the water tunnels. He has nowhere to go. We will certainly find him and bring him to you."

"And his former soldiers?"

"Most have joined the priests in honoring your victory here as Marduk's redemption of his city. They have sworn loyalty to you and are now under the command of your officers. Those who have not so sworn are in custody, awaiting your judgment."

The king nodded and spurred his horse forward, the crowd parting before him. "Come with me to the palace. Bring your Gimillu."

Mushezib-nabu pulled Gimillu to his feet and the two of them walked alongside the king's horse. The crowd immediately began flooding the street behind the king's party.

Gimillu was intensely aware of the anxious chatter of the people around him. He could make out very few of the individual conversations, but it was clear from those fragments he could discern that people were trying to make sense of their new ruler and what he would mean for them. Bab-ili had had many conquerors over the centuries. He had learned about them during his scribal training. Some had been brutal, some had been respectful. Which would this King Kurush be? He had been in the king's camp for more than a day and he had no idea.

When the slow procession reached the palace, his brother was waiting there with Shulmu. The dog caught sight of Gimillu, barked once, and ran straight toward him, tearing the rope Kudurru was holding right out of his hand. Gimillu caught him as he jumped up, and the two of them fell to the ground, Gimillu laughing and crying, the dog licking his face furiously.

The king said, "I return you to your Shulmu."

He rode forward through the palace gate with his retinue, beckoning Mushezib-nabu to follow.

CHAPTER 16

NEWS OF BAVEL'S FALL emerged in bits and pieces over the next two days. Travelers warned them to turn around. What could be so important, they demanded, that you would walk straight into the heart of the storm? Flee! Flee while you can!

So Hannah had been right. Bab-ili had been conquered by this Kurush.

"But how could she have known that?" Danna asked him while they were walking on the third day. "It would have taken almost five days for word to reach us back there."

Zakaryah shrugged. She had asked the same thing several times since they had left that date orchard. He had no better answer now than he did then. But maybe this time he could have some fun with her. He said, "With horse messengers it would be much faster—maybe just two days."

"Did you see horse messengers?" Danna demanded, taking his bait. "Did any gallop past us since we left the school that morning? Did one of them stop and talk with her when we weren't looking?"

"Then maybe she's a prophet, like that Yirmeyahu." He kept his expression serious, but when he couldn't hold it any longer, he broke out in a wide grin.

She sucked in her breath, letting it out slowly and audibly, glaring at him the whole time.

THEY FOUND THE OLD MAN in his field. Danna called out, "Grandfather!" and ran to him, throwing herself into his arms.

Danna! Tough, cynical Danna, running and shouting for joy when she saw her grandfather. He felt his sense of her changing as he watched, felt his cherished irritation with her slipping away. This was more disturbing even than being on the wrong end of her sarcasm and arrogance.

Her grandfather hugged her fiercely while she breathlessly introduced Zakaryah. When he released her, he took a long moment to look Zakaryah up and down.

"Ya'el's grandson," he said, shaking his head. "And this is your sister?"

"Hannah."

But then the old man scowled at Danna. "You came here alone? With a boy?"

"And Hannah," she replied. "We said I was his half-sister. Anyway, most of the people on the road were running away from Bab-ili. They didn't seem very interested in us."

"I tried to stop her from coming," Zakaryah told him. In fact, there was nothing he had wanted less than to have her along.

Abir-ilu just shook his head.

But this was all so strange. This old Chaldean man—grey haired and a little stooped, with his short grey beard—had been young once, had known his grandmother when she was also young. Zakaryah couldn't even imagine her as a girl. She had always just been his grandmother. He knew in his head—of course he did—that his parents and grandparents had had lives of their own. Still, he couldn't shake the feeling that they had sprung into existence the moment he was born, or maybe even later, at the time of his first memories.

"How did you meet my grandmother?" he asked. "She wrote about you in her scroll but just said that you were a guard."

"Her scroll? The scroll still exists?"

Danna said, "Yes, I've seen it. We left it with Michal for safekeeping. Your name is in it."

"Ah. I wish I could see it. That scroll caused her such trouble. They tried to kill her three times. But she was stronger than them, even when she didn't know it."

Someone had tried to kill her? Three times? Because of the scroll? This was so confusing, like trying to predict where a fish would jump out of the river next.

Best to start at the beginning. "How did you meet her?" he asked again.

The old man's eyes lost their focus. Before the silence could become uncomfortable, he looked at Zakaryah, then at Hannah. "She hated me at first. It was back in Al Yahudu. Not the one here, the real one. Yerushalayim in your language. It was in a ruined house. She was backed into a corner, terrified, no place to go. A soldier was about to kill her."

He shuddered, steadying himself finally with a deep breath. "Me. The soldier was me. I almost killed your grandmother."

IN HONOR OF THEIR VISIT, Abir-ilu had a servant slaughter one of his lambs. It was during the meal that Zakaryah got the story—some of it at least—of how Ya'el and the old man met. Danna's grandfather had been ordered by another soldier to kill her after the Chaldean forces had breached the walls of the city. When he realized that she could read, he captured her instead, because King Nevuchadnetsar wanted scribes. Really, he was glad to have the excuse. "I never was much of a killer," he told them.

"How did you know she could read and write?" Zakaryah asked.

"She had that scroll with her. She recited a blessing from it."

"What blessing?"

"Let's see. It started out with something about that god of hers protecting her."

"May Yahweh bless you and protect you," Danna said. "We learned that at the school."

"May Yahweh shine his face on you and be gracious to you. May Yahweh lift up his face to you and grant you peace." They all stared at Hannah as she completed the recitation of the blessing, the first time she had spoken since their arrival at the farm.

"You can't even read!" Danna exclaimed. "How do you know that?"

Hannah shrugged and gazed off into the distance.

"She'll have heard it at Shabbat gatherings in Nar Kabara," Zakaryah offered.

"Yes, that was the blessing," Abir-ilu acknowledged. "You know, I wanted to marry her."

"Marry her?" Zakaryah exclaimed. "Wasn't she only twelve? That would be like me wanting to marry Danna here." That drew a baleful glance from the girl herself and a speculative gaze from Hannah. He wished he hadn't said anything.

"Well, I would have waited. Anyway, that was later, after she stopped hating me. And that's enough for now." He addressed Danna. "Tell me why you're here."

"Zakaryah wants a judgment against a boy who burned his barley crop and conspired to steal his date orchard. He thinks he can find an honest judge in Bab-ili." She rolled her eyes. "Hannah insisted on coming too. She hasn't said why."

"And you," her grandfather said, "you're still hoping Immeru or his business connections might have heard something."

She nodded silently. Zakaryah saw the tears collecting at her lower eyelids and felt his sense of her shifting again. What was she hoping to hear about? Why was she crying?

But the grandfather was addressing him. "From what I've been hearing, this new King Kurush has left things in Bab-ili mostly as they were. You might be able to find a judge, but an honest one? I haven't run across many of those. And things there are still very unsettled. Nobody knows how long it will be before this Kurush starts hunting down supporters of the former king. It could be very dangerous."

Danna dried her eyes. "And this boy has family connections at court. Or anyway he did, before the new king took over."

"Oh?" her grandfather asked. "What family?"

"The former tax aggregator is the boy's father," she responded. "Mushezib-nabu." She looked at Zakaryah, who nodded his agreement.

"I haven't heard about him since Bab-ili fell," Abir-ilu mused. "But then, we don't get much news out here. Maybe the new king cast him out."

Zakaryah sighed. There was hope. Bab-ili would be in turmoil, he was sure of it. But somewhere there would be an honest judge, or at least a sympathetic one. Kurush wouldn't have been able to replace all the judges in the short time since his conquest of the city.

No, he would go on. One way or another he would get justice.

And if not justice, then revenge.

PART III

Late Spring, Year 1 of King Kurush

Their idols are silver and gold,
   the work of human hands.
They have a mouth, but do not speak,
   they have eyes, but do not see;
   they have ears, but do not hear,
   a nose, but do not smell;
   they have hands, but do not feel,
   they have feet, but do not walk;
   nor do they make a sound in their throat.
Those who make them,
   whoever trusts in them,
   will become like them.

PSALM 115:4-8

Ziggurat of Marduk
in Bab-ili (Babylon)

CHAPTER 17

A SLAVE WAS QUIETLY CLEARING the eating vessels from the morning meal when Gimillu walked into the room. He had slept late, unable to rouse himself after the terror and exhaustion of the past four days.

Nidintu and Kudurru were both there. There was no sign of his father.

"You shamed our father in front of the new king," Kudurru greeted him.

"What? What?" Gimillu shrank back from the accusation, rubbing his eyes to get the night grit out of them.

"He told us this morning before he left for the palace. You cried, the king said. The snot dripped down your face."

"I thought I would never see Shulmu again."

"That stupid dog," Kudurru answered. "I should have thrown it out the door the minute we pushed you into the canal."

"From what I hear," Nidintu commented, "King Kurush

would have been very angry. Didn't he make a promise?"

Was this Nidintu defending him? But she was baring her teeth at Kudurru in a smile that displayed no affection.

"Father made me fetch that animal like I was a slave." He glared at the servant holding the vessels. The man hunched his shoulders and hurried out of the room.

"You know," Nidintu remarked, getting back to the original topic, "Father didn't say that he felt ashamed. He said the king mentioned our young brother's courage. What courageous thing have you done lately, older brother?"

Kudurru didn't answer, just stormed out of the room, nostrils flaring.

Gimillu stared at her, eyes wide.

"Don't let it go to your head!" she snapped. "Still, what you did took courage, like the king said."

He reddened, thinking about his decision to run away and leave them all to face the new king's wrath. He opened his mouth to say something, but she cut him off.

"Be careful of Kudurru. He won't forget his humiliation."

"Aren't you worried too?"

"He's afraid of me. With good reason. But he's not scared of you," she declared. "Not at all."

GIMILLU STAYED IN THE HOUSE that day and the next, unwilling to face the reactions of the people in the city. The atmosphere in the house wasn't much better, though, and the following day he escaped as early as he could.

He wandered around the city, Shulmu at his heels.

People crowded the streets. They streamed to work. They hawked food, firewood and dung. Goats bleated as their owners led them along the streets and into and out of alleys. In the markets by the gates, vendors shouted from their stalls, offering delicacies and hard goods from the farthest corners of the kingdom, and even from places across the great sea in the northwest.

How could it look so normal, just three days after King Kurush conquered the city and two days after he rode in to take his place in the palace?

In the market by the Ishtar Gate, Gimillu exchanged a small piece of cut silver for a handful of tasty fried locusts. He nibbled them as he headed south along the broad processional way. He remembered the boulevard from when he had lived in the city—how could anyone forget?—but it had never gleamed like this. Paved with bricks and wide enough for five chariots abreast, it must have been cleaned up for the formal consecration of the new king that would take place the next day. The tiles that lined the walls on either side shone a rich and brilliant blue. Lions marched in relief along the walls in full color, reminding visitors and citizens alike of the power and prestige of the kingdom established three generations before by the glorious King Nabu-kuduri-utsur. What would that king think of how the city had fallen without a struggle to a new king from a distant land? What would he think of Gimillu himself and the role he had played in bringing about that downfall?

It wasn't hard to imagine what some people were thinking. As Shulmu tired in the heat he stopped running wildly around and kept pace at Gimillu's heel. Here and there people noticed and stood whispering in small clusters when the two of them passed. Had they seen him enter the city with Kurush? Or had the story simply spread of a boy with a dog who had betrayed the city?

He lowered his eyes and walked past them into a cross-street, pretending not to notice.

Had he ever really felt at home in this place? If so, he couldn't remember when. Maybe it was being sent off by his father to be educated among strangers, far from the city. Maybe it had been his lack of friends, scared away by his father's station and reputation for settling scores. Maybe it was neither of these. If only his mother had survived. She would have made a place for him in the family, would have forced his father, brother and sister to treat him well. He was sure of it.

He looked down at Shulmu, trotting quietly alongside him, tired from his earlier running around. Why couldn't people be more like that?

He headed back toward the intersection with the processional way. The boulevard there was teeming with people hurrying in both directions. Where were they all going in such a rush? Maybe they were hurrying so much that they wouldn't notice him and Shulmu.

While he was still twenty or so paces from the intersection, he could see that despite his initial impression, not everyone was rushing along. There was one old man in particular with a walking stick who was moving slowly enough that the crowd flowed around him the way the waters of the river parted around the piers of a bridge. He was towing some young people along in his wake. They were craning their heads in all directions as if they had never before been in Bab-ili. One of them, a boy, looked in Gimillu's direction, turning away without seeing him as something else caught his eye. Rust-colored hair, nose slightly bent, leading a young girl by the hand.

Gimillu sagged against the side of the nearest house and slid to the ground, his pulse pounding in his throat.

Zakar-yama.

CHAPTER 18

ZAKARYAH, HANNAH, ABIR-ILU and Danna entered Bab-ili at the Urash gate in the southern wall.

"Is this the only way to get in from the south?" Zakaryah asked Abir-ilu. They had had to take a ferry to cross the first of the two moats. It didn't seem very practical for a city that traded with virtually the whole world.

Danna was the one who answered. "There are ten gates in all, including the ones on the western side of the river."

He tried to suppress the flash of annoyance. Of course she answered. She had spent summers here, she said. She knew her way around. In fact, she seemed to know a lot about everything and was happy to let everyone know it. That's what rankled. She made him feel stupid. But he didn't try to make other people feel dumb, did he?

"It's huge," was all he said. And it was—larger and more populated than any place he had seen, or even imagined. "How many people live here?"

This time Danna remained silent and Abir-ilu answered. "I don't think anyone knows for certain, but there must be at least two hundred thousand."

Two hundred thousand people! He couldn't begin to imagine.

That changed the minute they walked through the gate. People rushed everywhere. Donkey carts plowed through the crowded streets. Drovers herded camels. Merchants carried baskets with geese, ducks, small furry animals, bats and more. Owners dragged goats along at the ends of ropes that frequently snagged walkers, bringing the unfortunate person face-to-face with the unhappy animal. There was shouting, cursing, bleating, quacking, loud conversation, all coming from everywhere.

He had never been in any place like this. He began biting his lips, darting his gaze all over. His breath came in short gasps, sweat breaking out on his face. He grasped Hannah's hand harder, only realizing it when she tapped his arm with her other hand.

He caught Danna looking at him. She quickly averted her gaze and said in a loud voice, "We're turning at that next intersection, aren't we, Grandfather?"

"Yes," he answered, his brow creasing as he looked at Zakaryah. "It's not far now."

Zakaryah took a deep breath and let it out slowly. He forced a smile to show Danna that he wasn't actually panicking. He asked Abir-ilu, "These are Danna's relatives we're visiting?"

"Yes, through my wife Elisheva."

As he led them there he explained that when he came back from the war he looked for a commercial connection to distribute the produce from his father's growing farm. The wealthy old families with ties to court and temple wanted too large a cut of the profits, so he sought out newcomers who were hungry to grow their business. He found a Yahudu family from the earlier deportation. They were open to the proposition, but he would have to marry the youngest daughter to tie the families together. His father had agreed, and so had he.

Danna asked, "Was that because you couldn't have Ya'el?"

"And you thought she only talked this way to you," he said to Zakaryah. But he didn't answer her.

They turned right at the first major intersection. There was a huge building just back from the corner on their left. Its outer walls were covered with beautiful yellow tiles, glazed to gleam in the light of the sun as it transited daily across the southern sky.

"What is it?" he asked.

"It's the Ishhara temple," Danna responded.

"Ishhara?"

"A sex goddess. Want to go in?" She looked at him out of the corner of her eye. He blushed and didn't answer.

They came presently to an enormous street, wider than any he had ever seen or imagined.

"The processional way," Abir-ilu announced. "We turn left here. If we walked all the way north we'd come to the Ishtar Gate. Danna!" he warned as she opened her mouth to speak. "No more about sex goddesses. You've embarrassed poor Zakaryah enough."

"He said it would be ridiculous for anyone to marry me."

"Hmm," her grandfather said. "Not quite the way I

remember it. Zakaryah, it's very crowded here. Keep holding onto your sister. We don't want to lose her."

They walked up the processional way, Zakaryah swiveling his head in every direction, his panic forgotten.

Ahead and to the left a huge building reached into the sky, looming above everything around it. It was higher than anything he had seen. How many men would have to stand one on top of the other to reach that high? Forty? Fifty? It was built in a succession of seven stages, each stage smaller than the one below it. A huge stairway ran halfway up the outside. The first six stages were a grayish-white in color. The topmost and smallest stage was a stunning blue as deep as that of the sky just before the setting of the sun. Every side of the building gleamed, catching the late light of the day.

Abir-ilu followed his gaze. "The ziqqurat of E-temen-anki," he said. "The foundation of heaven and earth. The building at the top is the temple of Marduk. There's a giant statue of the god inside, or so I've been told."

Danna sniffed. "What kind of god needs a statue?"

"Yes, yes," he answered. "No statue for your Yahweh. But don't you wish that just once you could see what he looks like?"

Hannah reached out and tugged on the sleeve of his robe. When he looked down at her she spoke for the first time that day. "What does the wind look like?" she asked him.

THAT EVENING they took their meal with Immeru, the cousin of Danna's mother. Zakaryah looked closely at the man. He was wearing a light linen robe. Prosperous, then. Medium height, dark hair, full beard, smile lines around his mouth.

Immeru pulled Danna into his shoulder so that they were both facing Zakaryah. "Checking to see if there's a family resemblance?" he asked, smiling. "Of course, she's a little darker than I am. Must be the sun, right, Danna?"

Danna laughed and Zakaryah turned bright red. How did the man know what he was thinking? It occurred to him that it had been a long while since he had thought of her as a Kushite. She was just Danna, annoying, bossy Danna. And this was the first time he had heard her laugh.

Immeru's wife, Zmira, gathered Danna and Hannah, and together they brought the food from the courtyard where she had prepared it to the shaded pavilion on the roof of the second story where they were now sitting. The three of them were accompanied by a swirl of small children. Zakaryah counted five, the oldest among them appearing to be a girl of about four years.

As he sat watching the children, Zakaryah stared around at the city that was spread out beyond the parapet of the house. From this vantage point he could see more of the true extent of Bab-ili. Buildings of varying heights stretched away in every direction. Here and there great edifices punctuated the skyline. Temples? Like that Ishhara temple they had passed? If so, this city had a huge number of gods. It was ridiculous. There was only one God, and he wasn't the one in that massive ziqqurat, or the Ishhara temple, or any of the others. Why did he allow these god-houses to stand when he had let his own house in Yerushalayim be destroyed?

There were some things Zakaryah would never understand. Temples aside, most of the buildings looked like private houses. Many people were out on the roofs, eating together under canopies like the one of his host. There didn't seem to be any sense of fear or panic, from what he could see.

"How did the city fall?" he asked Immeru.

Immeru didn't answer at once. Instead, he grabbed the four-year-old girl when she passed close to him and tickled her until she fell down, giggling and gasping for breath all at the same time. He laughed as she squirmed on the floor, then gave her a gentle swat on the rear end and she crawled off, tears streaming down her face.

"What do you know about how this city works?" Immeru responded when he was able to catch his breath.

"There seem to be a lot of temples."

"Yes, and the most powerful is Esagila, the temple of Marduk. It's as powerful as the king in some ways. It even has its own soldiers. The Esagila priests hated King Nabu-na'id because he neglected Marduk and diverted silver from them to Sin, the moon god. A high official in the palace struck a deal between the priests and King Kurush, and here we are."

Zakaryah shook his head at the stunning foolishness of these people. They had sold out their city for a statue that they themselves had made. "Everyone seems so calm," he observed.

"So far," Immeru said, "this King Kurush hasn't taken any action against the city. In fact, tomorrow he's going to be formally consecrated and blessed by Marduk's priests. Isn't that why you're all here? To see it?"

"No," his wife answered. "Danna told me while we were bringing up the meal. She's hoping you've heard something from your merchant connections."

At Danna's expectant look, he shook his head slowly. Her face lost all expression but her shoulders slumped. What was this about? Hannah had been with them. Maybe he could get her to tell him.

Whatever it was, something was wrong. Just in time, he stopped himself from reaching out to Danna. She would slap his hand away, she would scowl, she would make some cutting remark that would humiliate him in front of these others. So he said nothing and made no gestures, quashing the strange impulse to offer comfort.

After they'd finished eating, the children began chasing each other around the rooftop, screaming and giggling. The littlest child, a boy maybe two years old, started trying to climb up the parapet.

Zmira shouted, "Oryah! Shanitu! Grab your brother before he figures out how to climb that. Hannah," she said, "you can go play with them if you want."

Hannah looked at the children with a puzzled expression but didn't respond and didn't move. Zmira raised an eyebrow.

"Are all five yours?" Zakaryah asked her, shaking his head at the thought of Hannah playing and shouting like the other children.

"No, the two bigger ones belong to Immeru's sister. She and her husband live right in this next house." She pointed to an adjacent home that shared the same courtyard. "Now, why don't you tell us why you and your sister are here?"

He told them everything that had happened, the danger that he was in, and that he had come to obtain a judgment against the boy who caused it all.

"I see. And who did this to you?"

"His name is Gimillu."

Abir-ilu, resting with his eyes closed, said, "Gimillu. The son of Mushezib-nabu."

"Mushezib-nabu? The man who plotted to bring King Kurush into the city? His new chief scribe and adviser? *That* Mushezib-nabu?"

Abir-ilu opened his eyes. "I hadn't heard what happened to him when Kurush took over."

"You know," Immeru said, "there's a rumor that it was his son who carried the message out to Kurush's army. This Gimillu, is he about your age? With a dog?"

Zakaryah just stared as the implications sank in. He sagged in place. He had pinned his hopes on this trip to Babili, even in the face of Danna's and then Abir-ilu's skepticism about finding an honest judge. Where else was he going to go, anyway? The end of the month was just days away. Gimillu's uncle, Guzannu the tax aggregator, would be waiting to have him hauled off. Maybe there would be a few days' grace because of the new king, but if so it was sure to be a temporary reprieve.

"Husband," Zmira said, "you can't leave it there. Look at him. The boy's devastated. Surely there's something you can suggest?"

"I don't have any good ideas at the moment. But I'll be

going to the consecration tomorrow. Mushezib-nabu will certainly be there. Maybe something will occur to me. Does this Gimillu know you're here?"

"No."

"In that case you should be safe enough. Just stay here tomorrow. The consecration is early in the morning. The king has declared a feast day and the streets will be busier than normal. We'll be able to sneak you out of the city during the celebrations."

Zakaryah barely slept that night.

In the morning, Zmira and the girls prepared porridge and baked bread. After everyone had eaten, Immeru left to go to the consecration. The girls removed and scrubbed the eating vessels.

Zakaryah found a quiet corner on the first floor of the house and huddled there, eyes closed, his face buried between his knees, dizzy and numb at the same time.

Someone came into the room he was in, walked over. Danna. She sat down next to him and put an arm around his shoulder. He resisted for a moment, cringing inside at how he had held back from comforting her the night before. Then he sighed and let himself lean against her.

After a while he lifted his head and opened his eyes. She was regarding him, her face serious. "You know you can't sit here all day," she said. She stood and held out her hand.

Zakaryah stared at her hand, then at her face. No sign of mockery there, just concern. He extended his arm and she pulled him to his feet.

He frowned, looked around the room and the parts of the house that he could see. Then, still grasping Danna's hand, he pulled her out of the room and into the house proper.

"What?" she asked, dropping his hand and following him as he hurried out to the courtyard. Zmira was kneeling in the shade, kneading dough for bread. Her three children were in the far corner playing with some stones.

He swallowed hard, his breathing quick and shallow, hands clammy. "Where's Hannah?"

The two of them ran out of the house and looked down the street in both directions. The crowd on this side street was moving in the direction of the processional way. Zakaryah shaded his eyes, peering toward the end of the street. A small form was just visible close to the corner, alternately hidden and revealed as people shifted around.

It was her. It had to be.

The two of them raced down the street, bumping into people, shouting apologies, but never stopping to explain.

The next time they caught a glimpse of Hannah she had turned off the processional way and was passing through one of the side gates of the E-temen-anki enclosure. The ziqqurat stood high above everything, and the enclosure around it was rapidly filling with people. Once the plaza filled completely, he'd never find her.

They pushed their way through the crowd. There! Toward the front. It was Hannah—no doubt about it now. They dodged around clumps of people and finally caught up with her. She was standing calmly at the edge of a space that had been cordoned off with ropes. Stairs climbed up the side of the ziqqurat in front of her.

She smiled at him and Danna as they panted up to her. Grasping each by a hand, she said to Zakaryah, "Look, right over there."

He followed her gaze. Directly across the open space, not forty paces distant, in a group of well-dressed men, a boy in fine robes stood next to an elegantly dressed older man.

"It's him," Hannah told him cheerfully. "Your fire-starter." Gimillu.

The boy was listening to the man next to him, looking occasionally at the other men gathered around them.

Zakaryah stared and stared. He shivered in the morning heat, his heart pounding. Beads of sweat broke out on his forehead. His hands clenched, blood oozing out where his fingernails pierced his palms.

Trumpets sounded in the near distance, accompanied by the steady clomping of horses' hooves and the crunching of gravel under the wheels of many chariots.

Danna pulled his arm. When he didn't respond, she pulled again, urging him back into the crowd and out of sight.

Across the pavilion Gimillu swung his gaze idly in their direction.

The blaring of the trumpets became almost deafening. As King Kurush and his retinue filled the open space between them, Gimillu saw him.

They locked eyes.

CHAPTER 19

GIMILLU STOOD with his father by the steps of the ziqqurat, awaiting the arrival of King Kurush. In his wildest dreams he had never expected to be at such an event, but the king had demanded that his father bring him.

The previous evening, he had returned to the house thoroughly shaken from seeing the boy Zakar-yama walking along the processional way. He had determined on the way back to immediately tell his father. When he entered the house, though, Mushezib-nabu had demanded to know where he had been. The king, his father said, had insisted that Gimillu come to the consecration the next day. He needed to be measured for a decent robe. Nidintu would alter it from one of Kudurru's. Kudurru had glowered at him. Remembering their reaction when the matter of the barley field had first come up several days ago, he decided not to say anything about the Yahudu boy. And anyway, it was a huge city. He wouldn't see Zakar-yama again, he was sure of it, and at least the boy didn't know that Gimillu was here.

It all crashed down around him when his gaze crossed that of Zakar-yama as King Kurush was riding into the pavilion, his counselor Gaubaruva at his side.

But maybe he was mistaken. The two of them had looked at each other only for the blink of an eye, before the king's party filled the pavilion and blocked the view. That was it. Yes, Zakar-yama was somewhere in the city, he hadn't been mistaken yesterday. He had seen him then, no doubt about it. But this boy here was certainly just someone who looked like him. After all, how could a Yahudu boy have been invited to a place of honor right by the cordon? It was silly even to contemplate.

But then the horses shifted. Between them he caught a glimpse of the far side of the pavilion. It was indeed Zakar-yama. A small girl—his sister?—was holding his hand at the rope and an older girl was trying to pull him back into the crowd. There was something strange about that girl, but her head was turned away from him and he wasn't sure what it was.

"Father!" he said, leaning close so nobody else could hear.

"Quiet. The king is getting off his horse."

"But Father—"

Mushezib-nabu dragged his eyes from the pavilion and glared at him. "What is it? And be quick."

"That Yahudu boy," he gulped and continued, "the one with the barley field. He's here."

"Don't be ridiculous. You left him in that backwater town down the river."

"But he's here. He is. Just across there, past the king's horses. I saw him."

The horses moved again. Gimillu pointed through the gap between them. "There. There he is. With the little girl at the rope."

"You're sure that's him?"

Haven't you done enough damage? he heard Uqupu saying.

But he could shout something to the king!

Uqupu's voice answered him, implacable. *And what will happen to his sister when he's arrested?*

"Well?" his father demanded.

"I must have been mistaken, Father. It just looks like him, that's all."

His father shook his head in disgust and turned back to the ceremony.

The crowd fell silent as King Kurush stood at the foot of the stairway that went up the ziqqurat. Two men in the rich garments of priests were waiting for him there.

"Zeria and Rimut," his father told him without taking his eyes off them. "The two leaders of the temple."

One of the two handed Kurush a scepter. The other settled a mantle over his shoulders. All three men turned around and bowed deeply before the ziqqurat.

The three then climbed the stairs, the king in the middle and the two priests flanking him. Halfway up, where the stairway ended, they entered the structure through a gallery and disappeared from view. They reappeared, small figures at the very top, outside the exquisite blue temple of Marduk. They faced the entrance, got down on their knees and pressed their foreheads to the floor. The king then rose, and with scepter and mantle, entered the sanctuary, leaving the priests kneeling outside.

After a while he came back out, looked over the people gathered far below, and raised his scepter. A great shout went up from the crowd, and the king and the two priests then descended.

When they got to the bottom of the stairs, the priests left King Kurush and went to stand by the side.

"What happens now?" Gimillu asked.

"Be quiet."

The king raised his voice and began to speak. Scribes stood on makeshift pedestals throughout the crowd to repeat the king's words so that all could hear.

"To the great anger and grief of Marduk, a low and unworthy man installed himself as lord of this, Marduk's great country. He spoke insolence every day and was not afraid of Marduk's wrath. He halted the daily offerings and interfered with the rites. He did yet more evil to Marduk's holy city every day. But Marduk had mercy on the people of Bab-ili. He checked all the countries for a righteous king and took me, Kurush, king of Parsu and Anshan, and with his very hand he appointed me king of Bab-ili. Without fight or battle he had me enter Bab-ili and save his city from destruction. He delivered into my hands Nabu-na'id, the king who would not revere him.

"When I entered Bab-ili in peace, I took up my abode in the royal palace amidst jubilation and rejoicing. Marduk, the great lord, bestowed on me the wide heart of someone who loves Bab-ili, and so I do revere him every day.

"I am Kurush, the great king, the mighty king, the king of

Bab-ili, king of the land of Sumer and Akkad and the land of Beyond-the-River."

As the voices of the repeaters faded out to the far distance, Gimillu saw everyone in the crowd fall to their knees and press their foreheads to the ground. He hastily followed suit.

The king handed his scepter to an aide and mounted his horse, turning it around to ride out. But instead of immediately leaving the pavilion, he held up his hand and stopped, looking straight at Zakar-yama. A chill ran down Gimillu's spine. What was going on? Was the other boy going to denounce Gimillu to the king?

The king gestured to a nearby guard. He pointed not at the boy, but at the girl who had been trying to pull him back into the crowd. "Bring her to me," he said.

The guard grabbed hold of the girl's arm. She started, struggling, but the man's grip was solid. He lifted up the rope and stepped beneath it, dragging her with him. He bowed deeply before the king and pulled her down into a bow as well.

The girl was shaking uncontrollably in front of the king. And now Gimillu could see what was different about her. She was a Kushite! Her skin was a deep brown color, as dark as the ebony wood that came in the merchant caravans from the far south.

Behind her, the boy Zakar-yama was struggling in the grip of his little sister, seemingly wanting to dash after the girl. The sister couldn't be more than six years old. How could she be so strong? And yet she was holding him.

"Release her," King Kurush commanded the soldier. He did so, and at a nod from the king, stepped back.

"Relax," the king said, addressing the trembling girl. "No harm will come to you. I've never seen your kind before. Where are you from?"

"I . . . I'm from here, my lord, from the land of Sumer and Akkad."

"I didn't think there were Kushites here. Are there more like you?"

"No, my lord."

"And how did you come here?"

"My father was . . . is from the land of Kush."

"Was? Is?"

"He left with a trading caravan three years ago, my lord."

"And he hasn't returned?"

She shook her head. Behind her, Zakar-yama stopped struggling in his sister's grip, his eyes wide.

"Ah. I understand that the land of Kush produces excellent warriors. Are you a warrior?" the king asked with a smile.

"N-no, my lord."

"Well then. I'm afraid I can't use you in my service." He gestured to the guard to take the girl back to the place by the rope.

Before they could move, though, Gimillu saw the sister, the little girl, duck under the rope and run up to the Kushite girl. Now Zakar-yama lurched forward, eyes wild, trying to get under the rope, but the people nearby grabbed his arms and held him back. He thrashed around to get loose but was unable to escape the grip of the other bystanders.

Meanwhile, several soldiers had run forward, swords in hand.

The king held up his hand and they stopped.

While Zakar-yama continued to struggle, the sister took the hand of the Kushite girl and bowed to the king.

"And who are you?" the king asked.

She smiled up at him, and in a clear, high voice that Gimillu could hear perfectly, she said, "Yahweh, God of Yisra'el, God of Hosts, God of heaven and earth, says this. Before I put you in your mother's belly, I knew you. See, I am opening before you all the gates of the nations. None may stand before you. The time I appointed for the exile of my people is fulfilled. I charge you now to let them go up to Yehudah that they may rebuild my house in Yerushalayim. I am Yahweh."

The king frowned down at the two girls. He raised his voice to the crowd. "Who knows this Yahweh?"

Gimillu's father pushed him forward. "Go!" he said. "You live among them. Tell the king. And find out who that girl is. I want her. And the boy" Another forceful push had him stumbling in front of King Kurush. He tried to turn it into a deep bow.

"M-my lord," he stammered.

"The boy with the dog," the king said. "You're full of surprises. What about this Yahweh?"

"He's the god of the Yahudus, my lord. They were brought here by King Nabu-kuduri-utsur. They believe he's the only god, that he created the world and everything in it."

The king looked up at the magnificent ziqqurat from which he had recently descended, then down at the girl dressed in her plain robe. He smiled. "What poor god lets his people be uprooted from their country and then speaks to me through a small girl? But no god should feel slighted." He leaned over to Gaubaruva and said something Gimillu couldn't hear.

The king urged his horse forward, beckoning as he did so to Mushezib-nabu and other ministers to follow.

As he followed the king, his father snarled at him. "Get her," he said.

Gimillu found himself standing only a couple paces away from the two girls. The Kushite glared at him, fists clenched. He shrank back. If not for all the guards around she would have launched herself at him, he was sure of it. The sister, on the other hand, was studying him without expression. Her eyes, grey, solemn, locked with his, shaking him to his core. Then she smiled.

There was a commotion over by the rope. Zakar-yama had shaken off the hands of the people holding him and was coming straight for him. The Kushite girl broke away and ran to intercept him. Gimillu hissed to the sister, "Get out of the city before my father catches you both."

He turned and ran after the king.

"WHO WAS THAT GIRL?" his father demanded at the house that night. Gimillu's siblings watched curiously.

"Girl?" Gimillu asked, pretending not to understand. .

"You know who I mean."

"Oh. That girl. I thought her brother was Zakar-yama, but I was wrong. I don't know who they are." Why had he pretended that he didn't know them? And why had he told the sister to get out of the city? But he couldn't tell the truth now, could he? He shuddered at the thought of his father's reaction. "I want them. His sister said those things to the king. Very clever. Now Kurush is planning to issue a proclamation letting these people go back to whatever mud hole they came from. He could issue it in three to four days."

"Would that be so bad, Father?" Gimillu's voice shook with the thought of stirring his father's wrath. But if Zakaryama left, there would be nobody to accuse him, nobody to expose him to the unpredictable justice of this new king.

Mushezib-nabu didn't answer, but Kudurru did. "The king gave Father his tax quota today. He has plans for further conquests, big plans. He needs to fill the treasury fuller than it's been since the days of Nabu-kuduri-utsur."

"If they leave, how will I replace their taxes?" his father demanded, addressing all of them. "I'll lose my position. He could imprison me." A long pause. "He could imprison all of us. And he's thinking of including other groups in the proclamation so their gods will favor him like this Yahweh."

Mushezib-nabu looked Gimillu in the eye. "You know these Yahudus. Tomorrow you'll go out with a squad of soldiers. You can start with the merchants. They know everything. If you can't find them in the city we'll send horse soldiers out into the countryside. When we find them they'll be arrested."

"But how will it help to arrest them?"

"The boy will confess to the king that it was a lie. He put the words in the girl's mouth and she spoke them."

"But what if he doesn't confess?"

"He'll confess," his father said. "He'll confess."

And when he did, Mushezib-nabu would understand the extent of Gimillu's deceit.

CHAPTER 20

AFTER DARK, IMMERU LED ZAKARYAH
and the others out into the streets and toward the Enlil gate,
the nearest one to the house.

It seemed as though every person in the city was out. The
noise of the revelers was deafening. People wandered around,
carrying food of all descriptions in palm leaves. The palace
and temples provided meat in every plaza. Roasted lamb, ox,
rabbit, goat—all and more were available for anybody who
wanted them. From the noise, the tumult, and the pushing
and shoving around the food stands, it was clear that everyone
did want them.

Beer flowed in abundance. Zakaryah saw more than one
person vomiting up his drink at the side of the street before
lurching off for more.

He recoiled each time somebody in the crowd staggered
into him. His eyes darted all around as they neared the gate.

Gimillu would surely have told his father. Why had he insisted on coming here? There was no chance of getting justice. There never had been. He should have listened to Abir-ilu. Even Danna had known better. And now guards would be out hunting for him, celebration notwithstanding.

People were coming and going through the gate in great streams, some coming into the city from the local countryside, and some, having eaten and drunk their fill, leaving it for the fresher air outside the walls. There, in front of the gate! Soldiers. Were they scrutinizing everyone who passed through? They would be looking for a child with a Kushite girl and a boy. Danna would stand out. They couldn't miss her. When they caught her they would catch him too.

He pulled his hood tight around his face and fell back to the rear of the small group. He didn't feel any safer. And what if he got away but they caught Hannah and Danna? He would hate himself forever.

As it happened, though, the soldiers were drinking beer and eating, chatting with each other and not showing the least interest in the people passing through.

Even so, it was only after he and the others had put the gate far behind that the tightness in his neck and back finally loosened.

When they were well outside the city, Immeru hugged Danna, nodded seriously at Zakaryah and Abir-ilu. He let his gaze rest for a long moment on Hannah, opened his mouth to say something, then shook his head and turned back toward the Enlil gate.

Since it was the very end of the month there would be no moon during the night. Abir-ilu told them that even without the moon they would easily find their way to his farm. If they hurried they would arrive there well before dawn.

Zakaryah stumbled along in the near-perfect darkness, able to see the ribbon of the road in the starlight but not its surface. Between his stumbling, his exhaustion and his constant backward glances, he had neither the desire nor the strength for conversation. The others were equally quiet.

By the time they arrived he could barely lift his feet. He collapsed onto the pallet that Abir-ilu pointed out to him and lay awake for a while with his eyes closed, listening as the others took their places. Then he fell asleep.

He woke late in the morning. The pallets around him were empty.

He staggered out into the courtyard, rubbing his eyes and squinting against the intense morning sun. The others were sitting on straw mats, eating and talking.

Abir-ilu noticed him. "Good," he said. "You're here. We've been waiting for you. Danna, get him bread and beer."

To Zakaryah's amazement, she got up and served him without objecting. When she had reseated herself on a mat he began to eat, surprised at how hungry he was. He finished one of the small round loaves and was halfway through a second before he started to slow down.

Abir-ilu took a deep breath. "Hannah," he told her, "it was dangerous to run off the way you did. Look what happened to Danna."

Hannah raised her small shoulders up toward her ears and let them fall again.

"What could possibly be so important?"

When she didn't answer, Danna spoke. "She told him that Yahweh required him to let the Yahudus go back to Yerushalayim."

Hannah's words to the king hadn't sunk in at the time, terrified as Zakaryah had been for her, though he'd had plenty of time to think about them afterward. He shouted, "He could have killed you for that!"

Another shrug. She still didn't get it. Zakaryah opened his mouth to yell again.

Abir-ilu quelled him with a glance. "Hannah, what about that boy Gimillu? He definitely saw your brother. Zakaryah could have been arrested. You would never have seen him again."

"He said for me to get us out of the city."

"Did he say why?"

"He didn't want his father to catch us."

"Why didn't you tell us this?"

She looked around the courtyard and at the date palms rising from the orchard beyond the walls of the house. "We're out of the city."

What sense did this make? It was clear that Gimillu was after him, that he wouldn't be satisfied until Zakaryah was imprisoned or worse.

"You must have misunderstood," Zakaryah told her. "Gimillu would never help me escape. Have you forgotten what he's done?"

Hannah pushed some food around in her bowl but didn't answer.

"We were lucky," Abir-ilu observed. "He didn't know where you were staying and we got away quickly. Does he know where you live?"

Zakaryah shuddered and looked down at his hands, not really seeing them.

"I see," said Abir-ilu. "Where will you go?"

It was Danna who broke the long silence that followed. "He doesn't know about Michal's school. We can go there."

"You can hide there for a little while," her grandfather responded. "Al Yahudu isn't that big, though. He'll find you eventually."

"But it will give us some time," Zakaryah said, brightening. It would also mean more time with Danna. He could ditch her, though, as soon as he figured out the next step. He darted a glance at her. She was regarding him closely, a small frown bending down her lips. He had a funny feeling in his stomach, but it wasn't guilt. He didn't have any reason to feel guilty, did he? It wasn't as if he had asked her to come. She had just attached herself to him and Hannah. He didn't owe her anything. Anyway, she needed to continue her studies. He would be doing her a favor.

He took a deep breath and shook himself to banish his doubts. There. Much better.

WHEN IT WAS TIME TO LEAVE, Zakaryah went in search of Hannah. Maybe he could grab her and slip away without Danna knowing. That would be even better than leaving her behind at the school.

He looked first in the house. Nothing. He went to the outbuilding where the sheep and goats were housed at night. No Hannah. She wasn't in the barley field.

In the palm orchard he found Abir-ilu. "Try out there by the edge of the marsh," the old man told him, pointing beyond the farthest barley field.

His breath came fast and shallow. The marsh! She could fall in, or get sucked into the mud. "Why would she be there?" he asked, his voice squeaking.

"Don't worry. She'll be with Danna."

He rushed off in the direction Abir-ilu indicated, relief warring with aggravation. Danna wouldn't let anything bad happen to Hannah, but there'd be no chance now of escaping without the older girl.

He found them in a grassy area where his every step sank a finger's depth into the wet soil, leaving a trail of watery footprints behind.

The girls looked at him briefly as he came up to them.

"Get back!" Danna ordered him.

Why did she always have to be this rude? But he moved back. He noticed as he did so that a cord was hanging in a long loop from her right hand. At the bottom of the loop there was a small pouch, and in the pouch was a round stone. A sling! That must have been what she went back for when they left the school.

He stepped back farther.

Danna swung the stone backward a short distance, then forward very fast, accelerating it in a tight circle above her head. She let go of one end of the cord and the rock sped off faster than he could see. There was a loud thwack from a tree a hundred paces away, followed by angry squawking as several crows launched themselves from an upper branch.

"Can I try?" Hannah asked Danna breathlessly.

"This sling's too big for you." Danna turned to Zakaryah. "Do you want to?"

He shook his head. There was no way he was going to embarrass himself in front of this girl. "How did you learn?"

"I had to watch the sheep during harvest season when my grandfather had all the boys out cutting grain. Jackals would come looking for the lambs. It took a while, but they learned. The ones that survived, anyway."

She shaded her eyes with her hand and studied the position of the sun in the sky. "Let's get going," she said.

Still acting like she's in charge. But he took another look at the sling dangling from her hand, swallowed, and said, "All right."

ABIR-ILU STAYED BEHIND this time. He had servants make up packs of provisions for them, along with heavy skins of beer for mixing with the river water to make it safer to drink. He gave each of them a blanket so they wouldn't have to sleep directly on the ground as they had on the way up.

Before they left, he spoke to Danna.

"You know this still isn't right," he said, looking at Zakaryah.

"We came all the way here. And I'm not of marriageable age."

"Still, if anyone finds out it will be impossible for me to find you a husband from a good family."

"You can always make *him* marry me," she answered, looking at Zakaryah.

Zakaryah shuddered and she laughed. "It would serve you right," she told him.

As soon as they left the farm, Zakaryah asked why her grandfather hadn't simply forbidden her to go along.

"He's not my father. And anyway, he knows I'll do what I want."

The next day, the first full day of the return trip, when it was time to take a break from the crushing heat of midday, he insisted that they pull well off into the brush. That way, he told the girls, nobody would be able to see them from the road.

The band of vegetation was dense but not very wide. They couldn't be seen in their resting spot, but they could hear the occasional passersby who were willing to brave the heat and stillness of the road. During the middle of the rest, when the heat was most oppressive, Zakaryah heard the hammering of horses' hooves approaching at a fast pace. *Shh!* he hissed at them, gesturing to them to sit very still. As the sound faded into the distance, some of the tension left his shoulders.

"See," he said, "they're looking for us."

Danna responded that it could have been anybody, that he couldn't know for sure.

"They're looking for us," he murmured, closing his eyes as his fatigue overtook his anxiety. He stretched out on the ground and fell asleep despite the flies buzzing around his head.

That night Danna suggested that they travel on during the early evening. "You're so nervous," she told him. "You're making me nervous too."

He agreed and felt a bit better as the traffic on the road dropped off near sunset. But the light faded and he started worrying again. Would there be robbers on the road after dark? How could he avoid them if he couldn't see them? What if someone attacked the girls? He picked up a heavy stick he found at the edge of the road. When Danna asked him what he was doing with it he blurted out his worries. She rolled her eyes and asked him why robbers would be out at night if nobody else was. Who would they be robbing? He felt a flush creeping across his face, hoping she wouldn't notice in the gathering gloom. But he kept the stick.

As they walked on into the night, he was glad to have the weight of it in his hand. The night noises sounded completely different out here on the road than they did when he was safe inside the walls of his home. Bush crickets rasped deafeningly around them. There were constant rustlings in the vegetation along the road, wherever it passed close to the river. Something, a mouse maybe, jumped onto his foot before scurrying away. He felt its sharp, small claws on the naked skin next to his sandal straps. Frogs croaked and rumbled and chirped. Somewhere behind them he heard the grunting call of a lion. The second time he heard it, the sound was so close that he spun around with his stick raised, his hair on end.

Was it just him, or were the girls spooked too? It would be intolerable if he were the only one nervous. He couldn't see their faces in the dark, but he was gratified to find Danna walking much closer to him than she normally did. He could tell, even in the darkness, that she was constantly looking left, right, left again, behind, back to the front. Once, when a loud scuffling sounded right behind them, she practically jumped into his arms. And his sister? Hannah was walking with the same indifference she always exhibited. She had no sense of danger. She had shown that over and over again, like when she ran to confront King Kurush. How could he protect her if she kept putting herself in danger?

When the sun rose in the morning they hid in the bushes, ate from their provisions and drank water mixed with beer. Zakaryah slept as best he could, swatting at the insects that swarmed around his ears, mouth, and nose, moving when the shade moved with the shifting of the sun. Danna and Hannah wrapped their robes and scarves tightly around themselves, covering their faces and even their eyes, apparently more concerned with protecting themselves from the flies than with staying cool.

While he was sleeping during the day, tossing and turning in the heat, he had another dream. He was standing alongside one of the giant square kilns made of mud bricks. Inside the great cube a fire had been lit, baking the bricks from the inside out. As he watched, the mud bricks turned to stone. Stone was already hard, he found himself thinking. Why would it need to be baked? Then the whole structure fell apart, and stones scattered everywhere. A note sounded, like the string of a lyre being plucked. The stones stirred. Another note. Some of them settled into new positions, outlining the foundation of a building. More notes, more stones shifting into place. A long, last note reverberated in the stillness, and when it finally faded, a large building stood before him. Then it, too, faded.

As the sun sank into and below the horizon, he woke.

At dawn on the fourth day, they made it to Al Yahudu. Danna led them through the town to the school. She banged on the door, yawning as she did so. When there was no answer, she banged again.

Zakaryah heard footsteps approaching the door from the other side. The wooden bar grated as it was pulled aside. When the door opened, Michal stood in front of them, rubbing her eyes. She swept her gaze across the three of them and stepped aside, saying, "Inside, quickly!"

They crowded past her into the small courtyard. She closed the door behind them. She studied them for a long moment before remarking, "What a mess. Filthy, covered with insect welts, and my do you stink." Then she gathered all three of them into her arms and hugged them.

As she released them she said, "Zakaryah, someone was here looking for you."

He started trembling. Looking for him? Gimillu? Had Gimillu tracked him here after all? "Who was it?" he asked, voice shaking.

"He said he was your father's friend."

"Ovadyah? Was that his name?"

She nodded. "He brought you a bag. Your mother's things, he said. He told me to say he was sorry, that was all he could rescue when they came to confiscate your land."

"My land?" he gasped.

She nodded slowly, reaching out to place a hand on his shoulder. "For the taxes. The house and the barley field. The date orchard has been claimed by Banayahu."

He sank to the ground, numb.

"And there was one more thing," she continued, her voice gentle. "He says not to come back. They're hunting for you."

CHAPTER 21

SHULMU GREETED GIMILLU joyously just outside the door to the family house, leaping straight into the air and trying to lick his face. He dropped to a squat and hugged the dog. "I can't believe they threw you out of the house!" Shulmu didn't seem to mind, though. He jumped at Gimillu's chest, knocking him back onto the ground and barking.

His father, brother and sister stopped talking and stared at him as he entered the house with the dog.

The sky above the open courtyard was darkening. Night birds, evening hunters, were chirping and swooping in wild thrumming dives, sheering off as they approached the rooftops before soaring back up into the evening. Hunting for insects, probably. And finding plenty above the adjacent canal, Gimillu was certain, scratching at a recent bite.

"So," Mushezib-nabu said to Gimillu. "Two days of searching the city and you found nothing."

"No, Father. We talked to most of the Yahudu merchant families but nobody knew of this boy."

His father looked at him for a long, speculative moment that made him squirm inside. How much did Mushezib-nabu know?

As if in answer, his father looked at Nidintu. "Bring me the tablet." He didn't specify which one, but she evidently understood. She picked one from the stack at the end of the low table and brought it to her father.

"The tablet you brought from your uncle," he said, glancing briefly at Gimillu. He ran his finger along the lines of characters, stopping about halfway down the tablet. "Here," he announced. "Guzannu names this boy, this Zakar-yama. You should remember. You wrote this, mistakes and all. Read me the rest of the line." He held the tablet in front of Gimillu's face.

Gimillu stared at the line, fixated before it like a mouse in front of a snake.

In the silence that fell, he could feel the weight of the gazes of his brother and sister.

"Well?" his father demanded.

"It . . . it mentions that he has a sister."

"And how old is this sister?"

"Six years, about."

"And that boy you saw who you first thought was Zakar-yama. The little girl, the one who caused all the trouble. How old, do you think?"

"I'm not sure. Maybe eight? We don't know if she was even his sister." He was babbling, he knew. His mind raced from lie to desperate lie until it came to rest on a single fact that might save him. He snatched the tablet from his father's hand, heedless of the consequences of this show of disrespect. He ran a trembling finger along the line of text as his father had done. At the end of the line he looked up, brow creased as if in puzzlement.

"The boy at the investiture was with a Kushite girl. My uncle doesn't say anything about her. She would be the only Kushite in Nar Kabara. He would have mentioned that. It couldn't have been Zakar-yama!"

"She might have come from anywhere." His father sounded less sure, though.

The glimmer of hope Gimillu felt at this was quickly dashed when Mushezib-nabu continued. "Still, I can't help feeling that you've been lying to me. Kudurru!" Gimillu's brother jumped at his father's peremptory tone. "Kudurru, tomorrow you're going to go out to question the other merchant households, not the Yahudus. See if any of them know about a Kushite girl. Then you'll come back and report to me. Your brother will go with you. And," he added, staring at Gimillu, "I'll expect a full and truthful report."

KUDURRU SPOKE TO HIS FATHER the next day. "A girl in one of the merchant houses remembers this Kushite." Gimillu sat dejectedly in the corner, petting Shulmu and listening. He knew what his brother was going to say. It wasn't going to go well for him.

"Go on."

"This girl used to play with a Kushite named Danna."

"What else?"

"This Danna's father was a trader. Same as what you said she told the king."

His father nodded.

"Well," Kudurru continued, "he married a Yahudu woman from a farmstead with ties to the Yahudu merchant community."

"And this farm family?"

"The girl didn't know who they were. She just said the Kushite girl would come into the city during the summers. The two girls stopped playing together three years ago."

"Why?"

"The Danna girl was going to go away to a school in one of the Yahudu towns. Sort of like a tablet-house, she thought. She didn't know which town."

"A girl? Going to a tablet-house?" Mushezib-nabu addressed Gimillu in his dark corner. "The Yahudus teach their girls to write?"

"I don't think so, Father," Gimillu answered. Mushezib-nabu wouldn't be satisfied with that, he knew. He needed to obscure the trail further. "I never heard of a school for girls in Nar Kabara."

"What about that Al Yahudu? You were there. Spreading bribes around, as your uncle writes."

Gimillu flushed. "There's no school for girls there. I'm sure of it." At any rate, he was sure he had never heard of such a school. But he didn't say that.

"What you're sure of doesn't mean much to me. Tomorrow you and Kudurru will set off with four of my fast horse soldiers. You'll start by talking to your uncle Guzannu. If there's a school for girls anywhere in the Yahudu settlement area he should know. That Kushite will lead us to the girl and her brother. There isn't much time to stop the king before he issues his decree. The rumors have already started."

"What rumors, Father?"

"Many people at the consecration heard that little girl. The word has been spreading. The Yahudu merchants are asking about it, and other groups are starting to as well. The king's counselors are all against releasing these people, but nobody dares to tell him."

"Have you told him, Father?"

"Find her," Mushezib-nabu ordered with a chilling glare. "Find the Kushite."

GIMILLU HAD NEVER in his life been so miserable. His whole body ached. His inner thighs were rubbed raw. His tailbone sent waves of agony through his pelvis with every little jolt of the horse's stride. And his back! He had ridden almost the entire three days scrunched over, holding an anxious, writhing Shulmu while trying desperately to prevent the two of them from falling off the horse. At one point three soldiers in the king's robes rode past them at high speed. They galloped along so easily. He hated them. For that matter, he hated the four soldiers accompanying him and Kudurru. They never mocked him out loud, but it was clear from the murmured conversations and sly smiles that they found his agony endlessly amusing.

His only consolation was that Kudurru wasn't doing much better.

Finally, though, they reined in at the front of Guzannu's house.

He climbed slowly and painfully down from his horse, setting a very wobbly Shulmu down beside him. Kudurru also dismounted gingerly, glaring at Gimillu as if this were all his fault.

The soldiers swung down easily. One nodded at Kudurru, grabbing the leads of the horses and walking them off to water while Gimillu and Kudurru banged on the door of the house.

"That animal stays outside," Guzannu greeted them, pointing at Shulmu as he ushered them in. He kicked at the dog, slamming the door shut before Shulmu could enter.

"So your father got my message," Guzannu remarked to Kudurru. "But I didn't ask him to send anybody, especially not this one." He glanced at Gimillu.

"What message?" Kudurru demanded. "There was no message."

"Must have crossed you as you were coming down. It was about confiscating that Zakar-yama's land for non-payment of taxes. I've had soldiers looking for him. When they find him he'll be sold as a slave and so will that sister of his. He won't be any more trouble."

Gimillu shuddered. *It's all your fault*, the Uqupu voice told him. *Your fault.*

"We're not here about him," Kudurru responded. "Or maybe we are. I'm not sure."

Gimillu stared at the floor.

"What's this about, then?"

Kudurru explained about the events at the investiture ceremony, about the peril in which it put the entire family, including Guzannu; and about the Kushite girl who now seemed to be the key.

"This boy at the ceremony. What did he look like?"

"I wasn't there. Gimillu?"

There was no way to lie about this. His father had seen the boy too. What if he had told Kudurru?

"He had rust-colored hair, curly. His nose was a little bent. A thin face. Apart from that, ordinary-looking." There, truthful enough.

"Yes." His brother looked at Gimillu appraisingly. "That matches Father's description. Uncle, what about this Zakar-yama?"

But Guzannu had never seen the boy himself, and when his soldiers had questioned the townspeople in Nar Kabara, the descriptions they got had been very vague. "They could tell we were hunting for him. We never got a straight answer. But Gimillu here knows."

Both men looked at him.

What could he do now? If he gave the true description they'd know he'd been covering up. *You can't let them catch him*, Uqupu whispered. *What's one more lie?*

"He's about my height," he stammered. True enough.

A good start, anyway. "He has straight black hair, like everyone. His face is normal, maybe a little round." This was going more easily than he expected. One more detail would complete the misdirection. Not a lie, not really. After all, he had struck Zakar-yama once when the taunts had become more than he could bear. Maybe it had left a mark, though he didn't recall seeing one. "He has a scar over his right eye."

They nodded without challenging the description.

Kudurru changed the direction of his questioning.

"So we need to focus on this Kushite girl. Uncle, is there a scribal school somewhere in the Yahudu areas? The girl is apparently studying at some such school."

"I've heard there's a school in Al Yahudu. But what kind of scribal school would teach girls? It's ridiculous."

The hairs on the back of Gimillu's neck began standing up. Why?

"Still," his brother said, "we need to check it out. It's the only chance we have of finding the girl."

"Why does your father want this girl so badly? Surely the boy was telling her what to say?"

"Father said anyone who can convince the king that easily is too dangerous to have loose. She could tell him anything. She could say Father is stealing from the king's treasury."

"Isn't he?"

"No more than is proper for his station!"

"Well," Guzannu responded, "while you're there you can talk to the judge Bel-shunu and that wealthy Yahudu Bana-yama. They've both met this Zakar-yama."

He looked directly at Gimillu. "They'll give you a true description."

THEY MADE IT TO AL YAHUDU in the late morning of the next day. Strangely, there were very few people about. Gimillu sagged in relief. No people meant no Banayama, no Bel-shunu, and nobody to contradict his description of Zakar-yama.

"Maybe it's their day of rest," he offered. To Kudurru's blank look he said, "Their god orders them to rest one day in the week. Their Shabbat, they call it." That didn't seem right, though. He counted out the days. Tomorrow, tomorrow was Shabbat. So why were the streets empty?

Eventually they did find someone who could direct them to the school. They made their way there and banged on the door. There was no answer. Kudurru pushed it open.

Inside they found papyrus scrolls, some filled with Yahudu writing and others partially blank. Next to them were strewn pointed styluses and small black ink cakes. The ink in the center of the cakes was still wet.

There were no people.

Outside the school once again, Gimillu thought he could hear a sort of susurration in the distance. The streets nearby wandered randomly through the town, but with a turn here or there, the sound would get louder.

Eventually they found themselves on the edge of a large square where most of the population of Al Yahudu seemed to be gathered. As they watched, a few more people trickled in.

At the far side, a man in the robe of a king's scribe sat on a large horse, accompanied by two mounted soldiers. The scribe looked at the assembly and nodded to himself. He gestured and the crowd quieted.

"The order of Kurush," he declared in a voice that carried clearly, "great king, mighty king, king of the land of Sumer and Akkad, king of the land of Beyond-the-River. Yahweh, god of Yisra'el, has promised me all the kingdoms of the earth, charging me to rebuild his house in the land of the Yahudus. Any of his people among you may go up to his city, which is called in your language Yerushalayim, there to build his temple, and may your god be with you. The expenses of the journey shall be paid by the palace. Those who remain in the land of Sumer and Akkad will furnish them with silver and gold, with goods and livestock, for the temple of the god Yahweh."

He and the two soldiers wheeled their horses around, heading for one of the many streets that opened onto the square.

As the scribe and his soldiers disappeared from view, people started talking in small clusters, then in larger ones. One of the clusters drew Gimillu's scrutiny. At first he didn't understand why, but as he studied the group he realized that it was mostly children, both boys and girls. Then he noticed the woman who seemed to be the focus of their attention. It was the school. It had to be. And if that was the school . . .

He spotted her on the edge of the little group. A girl, about his age. Her scarf was bound at her neck but above that it had fallen open, revealing her face. As he watched she glanced

CHRISTOPHER FARRAR

abruptly left and right, then wrapped it tight again. She dropped
her hands quickly, but not before he saw them too.

And next to her? Zakar-yama, together with his sister.

His heart pounded. The reins suddenly felt slippery in his
hands. He looked at his palms, wiped them on his robe, then
wiped them again.

He couldn't let his brother see them.

But Kudurru was already staring there. He straightened,
his hand shading his eyes against the glare of the sun. He got
the soldiers' attention and pointed, jerking his head in the direction of the school group. His mouth was a tight line.

The soldiers kicked their mounts into movement.

Gimillu sat paralyzed on his. The last soldier in line
grabbed the reins out of his hands, tugging the animal along.

The crowd was dense enough to impede their progress,
parting only slowly in front of them.

Look over here, Gimillu willed the Kushite silently. Here!
Here!

But it was the sister who saw them. She tugged on the
older girl's arm and said something in her ear when she bent
down. The girl straightened abruptly and spied the riders making their slow way through the mass of people. And now the
whole school group was staring at them. Zakar-yama grabbed
the hands of his sister and the Kushite girl. The three of them
dashed to the edge of the square and into the mouth of one of
the streets.

Kudurru cursed and jumped off his mount, yelling at the
soldiers to follow and at Gimillu to stay with the horses. He

165

plowed ahead on foot. The woman with the children shouted something at the people around her. The crowd congealed in front of Kudurru and the soldiers, slowing them to a crawl.

Gimillu gathered the reins of the horses. He held his breath as his brother and the soldiers finally broke through, running into the street, down which Zakar-yama and the girls had disappeared.

Horses in tow, he worked his way closer to the woman with the children. When he saw that she was looking in his direction, he shouted to her. "They know where your school is. Don't go back there."

As the people around him dispersed, he led the horses back through the town to an irrigation ditch near the river where they could drink. His brother would find him here, close to the river road. He located a broad patch of shade in a palm orchard and settled down to wait.

CHAPTER 22

GIMILLU AGAIN! Wherever Zakaryah went, Gimillu was following him, hounding him. It wasn't enough that the boy had destroyed his livelihood, stolen his date orchard and set the tax-collector uncle after him. No, not nearly enough. Now he was chasing him with armed soldiers. If he and the girls had been caught in the open instead of being in the middle of the crowd, they would have been run down for sure.

One day, he promised himself, one day he would requite Gimillu for every wrong, for every hateful act.

First, though, he had to get away.

And where were they now? When he had seen the horse soldiers he had grabbed Hannah's and Danna's hands and rushed them toward the nearest street. As soon as the plaza was out of sight, Danna had dropped his hand and raced ahead. For once he didn't mind following her. She knew this town, could thread her way through the maze of the streets.

He ran after her. When Hannah had trouble keeping pace, he scooped her up and carried her. He wouldn't be able to do that for long.

And where were they?

"Danna," he gasped, "where are we heading?"

"Give me a scrap of cloth," she yelled.

"What?"

"Cloth! Any small piece. Hurry!"

He shifted Hannah's weight to his left arm and searched around in a pocket. There. A piece of the robe where the stitching was loose. He ripped at it as he ran, feeling it come free. He gave it to Hannah. "Here, hold onto this." She took it and he was able then to use both arms to carry her.

At the next intersection, Danna stopped and held out her hand. "The cloth. Quick."

Hannah passed it to her. Danna dropped it around the corner but clearly in view in the adjoining street, then ran farther down the street and dropped one she had found in her own pocket.

She ran quickly back. In answer to his unspoken question she panted, "It's . . . a major . . . cross street . . . Maybe they'll see . . . the two pieces of cloth . . . and think . . . we went that way."

She said nothing more, but as they ran the area began looking familiar. Michal's school, that's where she was taking them.

"They must know about the school," he shouted. "We shouldn't be here."

"They're lost somewhere in the town. We have time to grab our things and go."

At the school, Zakaryah set Hannah down. He leaned against the side of the building to catch his breath. Hannah pulled on the hem of her robe to straighten it but otherwise gave no indication that anything unusual had happened.

The door to the school was ajar. Danna approached it, slipping around the side of the door without touching it. She disappeared inside, reappearing a moment later.

"Nobody here," she told them quietly. "We need to be quick."

They split up to retrieve their traveling bags. Zakaryah also grabbed the small sack of his mother's things. He slipped back through the door and into the street to keep an eye out for their pursuers. Danna showed up a moment later with her bag. Hannah appeared after that, carrying both her bag and the sack containing Ya'el's scroll. He gave her a quick hug, glad that she had thought of it.

"Where now?" he asked Danna.

"Follow me. Hannah?" She held out her hand and Hannah took it.

Still the same Danna, he thought, annoyed that Hannah would rather walk with her than with him. *Can't answer a simple question, except when you don't want her to.*

But he followed her as she led them back into the warren of narrow streets.

ZAKARYAH REALIZED that the old lady looked familiar, even when she was well down the street. Who was she? The muscle in his upper arm twitched and he remembered. Ginat, the woman who had first taken him and Hannah to meet Michal. Danna had brought them to Ginat's house.

"Won't they be able to track us here?" he demanded.

This time Danna answered. "They won't think of it. She's not connected to the school. She's just a friend of Michal's."

Ginat studied them as she walked up to her house. "That was a nice little show you three put on in the plaza."

"They were chasing us!" Zakaryah retorted, offended.

"Well come inside before someone tells them where you are."

She opened the door. They went in and sank onto the mats on the floor.

"Let's see," Ginat said. "Danna, of course. And Zakaryah, if I remember rightly. Though my memory's not what it used to be. And Hannah. Yes?"

Hannah stood and bowed. Zakaryah stared at her.

"No need to be so formal, child," the old woman told her. Zakaryah thought she looked pleased, though.

"Are you going to be all right?" he asked her.

"You mean because you three are here? We're the only ones who know, right? I'm not telling. Are you?"

He shook his head vigorously.

"Well then. I should be fine. And anyway, that King Nevuchadnetsar ripped me from my home and my family and made me march more than three months to get here. Do you think a few Chaldean sheep-turds can scare me?"

"What about Michal?" Danna asked.

"They won't catch her. She'll be with friends. She sent the children home, the ones from here anyway. The children from along the river she put with local households. We talked about it after you lot ran off. Someone shouted at her not to go back to the school. I didn't see who it was."

Hannah leaned over and whispered something in Danna's ear, looking at him the whole time. Danna's eyes widened and she looked at him too.

"What? What are you talking about?" But neither girl answered him.

Ginat didn't seem to notice the byplay. "Tomorrow's Shabbat. The community will gather in the same square to talk about the king's decree. I think you should come."

"They'll catch us there!" he exclaimed.

"Not if you split up and hide in the crowd. And if you, Danna, keep yourself well covered."

Zakaryah said, "I can't be separated from Hannah." It was beyond argument and he stated it flatly. He wouldn't be where he couldn't protect her.

"Then we'll just have to make you look like someone else. You and Hannah will be with me. Danna?"

"I'll be fine."

"Good," Ginat declared. "It's settled. Now let's eat." She smiled at the girls. "Luckily I have two young women who can prepare the meal tonight. Zakaryah, you and I will play Twenty Squares while these two fix the food."

She pulled out a game board and began setting it up.

Danna glared at him. He felt a smile tugging at his own lips. He picked up his playing pieces and held them in his hand where she couldn't help seeing them.

For the first time that day, he felt just fine.

CHAPTER 23

THE PERSON WHO APPEARED first at Gimillu's resting spot wasn't Kudurru. No, to his great surprise, it was his uncle Guzannu who rode up.

"What are you doing here, Uncle?"

Guzannu favored him with a frown. "Where's your brother? Where are the soldiers?"

"They—we found the Kushite girl. They're somewhere in the town trying to capture her." *And I'm sitting here hoping they don't.*

Guzannu grunted. He grabbed a sack that was hanging from the saddle, tied his horse up with the others, and sat down in the shade of a neighboring palm. He took a beer skin out of the saddle bag and drank.

The sight reminded Gimillu that he was thirsty himself. "May I have some, Uncle?"

His uncle tossed the skin to him and he drank from it. He

tossed it back, stretched out on the ground and dozed off.

He woke to the sound of his brother talking quietly to Guzannu, relating the events of the day. Maybe they were keeping their voices down so they wouldn't disturb him. But his family was never that considerate. No, it had to be that they didn't trust him. *Fine. I don't trust you either.*

He kept his eyes closed and his breathing even.

"You were lucky you didn't catch them," his uncle was saying.

"Don't be ridiculous. Father wants them. Everything depends on it."

"You're not much brighter than our young sleeper there, you know."

Gimillu could almost see his brother's sullen expression. He opened his eyes to slits and quickly closed them again. Yes! Sullen would be an understatement.

He struggled to keep from smiling as Guzannu began upbraiding his brother. The situation had changed, his uncle said. The king had issued his decree. What did Kudurru think the king would do when he learned that Mushezib-nabu had ordered the arrest of the boy who had got his little sister to pass on that flattering message from the Yahudu god? What would he do to the one who actually made the arrest? Yes. You. Had Kudurru ever seen a man hanging from a wall with his entrails dangling to the ground? Why did he think Guzannu had ridden here as soon as the scribe reached Nar Kabara with the king's decree? Kudurru had listened to the whole proclamation and had still gone after those children like a jackal

CHRISTOPHER FARRAR

after a hare. Now everyone in Al Yahudu knew he was trying to catch them. How long would it take that news to get back to the palace?

Did he think his father had risen so high by being as stupid as Kudurru?

"What can we do?"

"You're a scribe," Guzannu told him. "You'll write a letter to your father. We've stumbled onto a plot. The Yahudus know that this boy got his little sister to pass the message of their god on to the king. Some among them are afraid of the power and prestige they'll lose if the people return according to the king's decree. They think they can stop it by assassinating the boy. We're trying to find him and bring him to safety."

"Do they really know it was the boy?"

"Who cares? Your father will know what to do with the message. We'll send it back with your four soldiers. For what comes next you won't need them."

What *would* come next? Gimillu waited to hear, but the whispering had stopped. Anyway, the beer was having its effect. He needed to get up.

He stretched and rubbed his eyes, doing his best to look as if he were just coming out of a deep sleep. In a way, maybe he was, because now he knew what he needed to do.

"Uncle, brother?"

When they were both looking at him, he continued. "You've found the children we've been looking for. You'll catch them, I know you will. I don't think I can help now."

Guzannu and Kudurru looked at each other.

His uncle was the one who spoke. "What are you suggesting?"

"I want to see my dog." They would sneer at that, but it would be believable. Anyway, it was true. "And I've missed weeks at the tablet-house. May I go back?"

There was another silent consultation between the two men. Guzannu nodded minutely at Kudurru.

"It was entirely your own stupidity that caused you to miss your lessons," Guzannu declared. "Still, your father is paying a lot for your education. Yes, go. Go now."

"Now? This late in the day? I'll never make it back before dark."

Guzannu yelled some instructions at the soldiers, who had taken the horses away to rest and water them. One soldier brought Gimillu's horse over.

"Here's your horse," his uncle told him. "Take it."

He climbed onto the horse and set off down the river road. Just before the first bend, he looked back. They were staring after him. Then he was around the bend and out of sight.

He turned off the road and headed back into Al Yahudu. When he arrived at the school, the door was ajar. He dismounted and knocked, not wanting to enter unannounced. Footsteps approached. A woman appeared, the same woman he had shouted to in the plaza. She regarded him and the horse, eyes narrowing.

"Please," he said, his voice hoarse. "I need to talk to you. Can I come in?"

CHAPTER 24

THE WOMAN looked Gimillu up and down, face tight. "You were with those soldiers in the plaza, weren't you?" She addressed him in Akkadu. "And now what? I suppose you've brought them here with you." She scanned up and down the empty street.

He jerked his eyes left and right. Nobody. They hadn't followed him. "No! No! They don't know I'm here. They'd beat me if they did. Or worse."

"What made you come here after you warned me not to return?"

"I thought you might have come anyway." He stumbled over the words. "I took a chance."

She stared at him again for a long moment. "Open your robe."

"What?"

"I want to be sure you're not carrying any weapons. Open your robe."

He flushed all the way down to his chest, but he complied, baring himself to his loin cloth.

She nodded. "Sorry to embarrass you," she said. "After the plaza, I needed to be sure. And if you don't want them to know you're here, you'd better do something with that horse."

He craned his neck to peer past her into the courtyard.

"No! No horses in my school. There's an abandoned house down the street. You can put him in the courtyard there. When you come back I'll give you a bowl and some water that you can take to him."

He followed her directions, leaving the horse tied to a pillar and out of sight. He left, returning shortly with the promised water.

When he came back she opened the door wider and he entered. He stood there, shifting his weight from foot to foot, sneaking glances around the place as he endured her continued scrutiny.

She sighed finally and said, "You don't seem all that dangerous. Sit down." She pointed to one of the raffia mats. "Do you need food or drink?"

He shook his head. He was too nervous to eat anything anyway. He imagined the Kushite girl sitting over across the room studying one of the open scrolls. Did she know how to read?

"Is this where you teach girls?" he blurted as he sat.

"You're that Gimillu, aren't you?"

He pulled his arms and legs closer to his body, dropping his chin to his chest. "Zakar-yama told you, didn't he?"

"His name is Zakaryah. Call him that while you're here."

"I've made a real mess of things." He blinked hard. Tears again, just like when he was taken to King Kurush. Why couldn't he be brave like his father?

"Why don't you tell me about it," she suggested. Her severe expression softened for the first time. "And I'm Michal."

He relaxed a bit. As he did he noticed that she was in fact quite pretty, in an ancient, two-decades-plus sort of way. He realized he was staring, then blushed again. She raised an eyebrow.

He stammered at first. He and Zakar-yama—Zakaryah, he corrected himself—had never got along. He was one of the slowest students at the tablet-house and Zakaryah was one of the best. Zakaryah used to make fun of him.

"I could see him doing that," she interjected.

When it got too much to take, he started trying to catch Zakaryah and beat him up.

"And did you?"

"Sometimes."

She nodded, not saying anything.

The rest of the story poured from him then. The snake. The barley field. His uncle. His father. The Kushite girl. The sister and the king.

"What?" she interjected. "Hannah told King Kurush to release us back to Yahudu?"

Yes, he told her, but of course it was really Zakaryah. But the sister had convinced the king. That's why they were chasing both of them.

He continued, telling her about his warning to the sister—Hannah, you said?—to get Zakaryah out of Bab-ili. And now it had gone too far, it was all his fault, he needed to stop his father from catching them, could she please, please, find the sister, Hannah, and let him talk to her? She had listened to him once, she would listen to him again. She had to.

"Why don't you talk to Zakaryah himself?"

"I can't. He hates me. He must. He won't believe anything I tell him. He'll think it's a trap."

"Well, I don't think he'll let me bring Hannah here by herself. And we can't exactly tell him what this is about, can we?"

He shook his head.

"And there's another reason," she told him. "I'm not sure I can trust you."

He hung his head, his hopes crashing. She was right. There wasn't any reason for her to trust him. She was the first person in a long, long time who had listened to him. She had even seemed sympathetic. But it wasn't that way after all, was it?

What could he do now? Maybe he should give up and go back to the tablet-house like he had told his uncle. They would catch them and that would be the end of it. The boy would disappear without a trace and so would Gimillu's problems. And it wasn't as though Zakar-yama was completely innocent. But what about the sister and the Kushite girl? They would disappear too.

He shuddered and raised his eyes. Michal was watching him closely. She had been the whole time, he realized.

"Have you made up your mind?"

"Wh-what do you mean?"

"Are you going to help them or just walk away?"

He shrank back from her gaze. How did she know what he was thinking?

He steadied himself with a deep breath. "I don't want them to be caught."

"So you're going to warn Hannah. But they already know your uncle is hunting them. What can you add to that?"

"I have an idea how he's planning to catch them."

She rose and stepped to the door.

"Where are you going?"

"Stay here. Don't touch anything." She disappeared through the door.

With her departure, the house became very quiet.

At first he sat where she had left him. As her absence dragged on, though, he started worrying. Where had she gone? Maybe she was out rounding up some Yahudu men to beat him. But her arms were muscular from grinding grain. She could probably have done that herself if she wanted to.

Or perhaps she had left in search of his uncle and brother to turn him over to them? But that was ridiculous.

To keep his mind off these kinds of ideas, he stood, stretched, and looked around the small courtyard. He walked over to the table he had spied earlier, the one with the open scrolls. *Don't touch anything*, she had told him. She hadn't said he couldn't look.

He leaned over one of the scrolls. The text was indecipherable but the letters were familiar. They were basically the same as the letters that the more advanced scribes wrote on the edges of tablets to label them so they could easily be picked out when standing with other tablets on a shelf. He was supposed to learn about that next year in the tablet-house. Not that there would be a next year for him, despite what he had told his uncle. He wouldn't be going back there, not after this. When his father found out about his deceit, about how he had thwarted him in capturing Zakar-yama and the sister, he wouldn't pay for an education any longer. Gimillu would be thrown out of the house and the family and be disinherited. That was the least that would happen.

Why hadn't he thought it through before he came here? He was always doing that, wasn't he? Just like he had burned down Zakar-yama's barley without thinking. *You never think,* the Uqupu voice told him. *You just plunge ahead and ruin everything.*

But maybe there was still time. He had the horse. He could ride to Guzannu's house, pick up Shulmu, then race off to Babili. He could be there in three days if he pushed it. He would tell Mushezib-nabu about his deception, that it really had been Zakar-yama the whole time. He had been weak, he could say. *I'm not strong like you, Father.* He had a change of heart when he realized Kudurru's stupidity in chasing the Yahudus. *He imperiled you, Father,* he would tell him. *He endangered the whole family.* He would grovel and throw himself on his father's mercy.

That was it. That's what he had to do.

He started for the door. As he reached out for the latch, the door opened of its own accord.

"Going somewhere?" Michal asked.

Behind her was the Kushite girl.

She was beautiful.

"I THINK they'll go to that Bana-yama," Gimillu said. He paused, half expecting Michal to tell him to use the man's Yahudu name.

She said nothing.

The Kushite girl—no, it was Danna, her name was Danna—she said, "He's the one you forged the loan contract for."

She regarded him. Her eyes bored into his, stark against the darkness of her skin.

"My uncle made me. And I was scared."

"You seem to be scared a lot."

"Give him some credit, Danna." That was Michal. "He's here and he's trying to warn you."

"Is he?" Danna demanded without taking her eyes off his face. "Maybe it's another one of his plots."

"I understand you don't trust me," he said.

"And he has a gift for the obvious," she told Michal. "You shouldn't have brought me here."

She rose as if to leave, but Michal pulled her down again.

"What harm will it do to listen to him, Danna? Hannah said that he warned her in Bab-ili. You told me that yourself. How could that have been a plot? And how could this be one?" Michal nodded to him to continue.

When had the woman turned into an ally?

"I don't know anything specific," he started.

Danna looked away shaking her head, lips thin.

"They wouldn't talk about it," he rushed on, "even though they thought I was asleep."

"Tell Danna who you mean by 'they,'" Michal ordered.

"My uncle Guzannu and my brother Kudurru. They know they can't act openly now that King Kurush has made his proclamation. They'll need to get someone in the Yahudu community to do it for them. They think it's still early enough to stop people from leaving if Zakar-yama—sorry, Zakaryah—disappears. They know he put the words to the king in his sister's mouth."

Danna and Michal exchanged a glance. "I'm not sure they're chasing the right sibling," Michal remarked.

What did that mean?

"They need someone to accuse," Danna observed. To Michal: "Would Banayahu do that?"

Before the woman could answer, Gimillu said to Danna, "It's not enough for Zakaryah to disappear. They'll need to make you and Hannah vanish too."

Danna bit her upper lip and looked toward the door.

"Don't worry," Michal reassured her. "They don't know where you are. But you need to go to the assembly tomorrow. It's the safest place for you, and for Zakaryah and Hannah. You'll all be invisible in the crowd if you cover up well. Don't say anything about Gimillu to Zakaryah."

She turned to him. "You'll go too. You'll stay with Danna. She doesn't know what your brother and uncle look like. You'll keep an eye out for them and get her to safety if they start closing in. I'll be watching Banayahu." Her stare made him feel like one of the frogs that soldiers speared for fun when they became bored.

"And I'll be watching you."

CHAPTER 25

PEOPLE BEGAN GATHERING for the assembly early on Shabbat morning.

Zakaryah ran his hand through his hair without thinking. It came away grey. He stared at it, just for a moment. Of course. Ashes from the cooking fire. If they were looking for a boy with rust-colored hair they wouldn't notice him. At least that's what Ginat had promised, and Danna had nodded in agreement. He had also turned his robe inside out to make it look even more ragged than usual.

They would also be looking for a six-year-old girl, and here was Hannah, standing just on the other side of Ginat, almost within reach of his arm. Would that be a giveaway? But there were a number of other small girls nearby, standing with parents or grandparents. It would be safe enough, he hoped.

Danna was somewhere in the growing crowd, well covered up. She had objected strongly the afternoon before when Ginat had suggested it. She changed her mind later, though, after Michal had come for her to help get the school ready for lessons. How had she known Danna was with Ginat? Anyway, it wasn't likely Gimillu and the soldiers would find her. Even he couldn't tell where she was, and he knew what to look for.

Ginat had brought them to the square early in the morning. She wanted to be near the front, she said, because her feeble old ears didn't hear as well as they used to. Not that he could tell. She had seemed to hear just fine the night before when he had told Danna in a whisper how much fun it was to play Twenty Squares. Ginat had looked straight at him. "Tomorrow you'll do the cooking, young man."

A makeshift platform of planks laid over palm trunks had been erected before the start of Shabbat the previous evening. It looked precarious. Wouldn't the trunks roll when someone stood on the planks? Then he noticed the stones that had been wedged in to prevent just this. Still, he wouldn't trust it.

It was within a short distance of this platform that Ginat had stationed them.

"Who's going to be on the platform?" he asked her.

"The head of the community here, probably," she told him. "Fellow named Zerubavel. Some sort of relation to the old king, I think."

"Which king? Zidkiyahu?"

"No, no. The first one brought here. Yehoyachin. Nobody survived from Zidkiyahu's family. Nevuchadnetsar killed them all."

An older man stepped up onto the platform. His father's age? Or rather, the age his father would be. Should be. Perhaps half a decade past thirty. Streaks of grey showed in the man's hair and beard, but there were no other signs of age and certainly no signs of feebleness.

"Zerubavel," she confirmed. "That's his wife Misha'el down in front. Their two sons are with her."

He nodded but kept his attention on the platform. "Who else will be there?"

She shrugged, but by then he knew the answer. He pulled back until he was partially obscured behind her. He grabbed Hannah's robe and pulled her back too.

Banayahu had climbed up and was standing next to Zerubavel.

Ginat took in Zakaryah's clenched fists and the tightness of his jaw. "Oh yes. You know that one, don't you."

By that time the square had mostly filled. The noise of the crowd was deafening enough to distract him from thoughts of Banayahu. There were so many people! The entire population of Nar Kabara would account for maybe one corner of this plaza. But then he thought of Bab-ili. How loud would it be if the entire population of that city was together in one place?

Zerubavel held his hands out. As people noticed they stopped talking. Soon the quiet had spread to the entire plaza. A few oblivious folks kept on, but they were shushed by their neighbors, and before long the silence was complete. The only remaining sounds were the distant chirping of birds, the shuffling of sandals on dirt and the sneezes and coughs that were always heard in any group.

"Listen, Yisra'el," Zerubavel began. A few near the front said it with him.

"Listen, Yisra'el," he repeated more loudly. The entire crowd was with him now, the voices filling the square and, thought Zakaryah, the world beyond. "Yahweh is our God. Yahweh is one!"

As the last echos of the word "one" faded, he spoke into the subsequent silence. "We all heard the words of the great King Koresh. Yahweh has breathed compassion into his heart and given us a chance we couldn't have imagined a few short months ago. We can leave this country of our captivity, in fulfillment of the words of the prophet Yirmeyahu. We can rebuild Yahweh's house in Yerushalayim. We can reestablish the people of Yahweh in the land of Yahweh. The land that has been silent and desolate for more than two generations will once again fill with the sound of our prayers, the voices of our children and the sweet smoke of our sacrifices rising to the nostrils of God.

"It is my great hope that we will do this."

A nice enough speech, Zakaryah thought. But there was only sporadic cheering and clapping.

Zerubavel nodded at this and said, "It's a frightening step. I anticipated that there would be concerns. The honorable Banayahu here has agreed to address those concerns."

He stepped back and Banayahu stepped forward. "As the honorable Zerubavel has said, we're confronted with the unprecedented opportunity to return to the land from which our parents and grandparents were uprooted over two generations ago. What other people has received a boon like this from the ruling powers?

"What does it matter that we would be leaving everything we know for a land our grandparents experienced only as children?"

At this point Zakaryah noticed some people near him leaning over to whisper to their neighbors.

"What does it matter that it's a journey of months and months to get there?

"Do we care that we'll be sleeping each night in makeshift camps by the side of the road? That robbers, snakes and scorpions will plague us in the dark?"

Is this what Zerubavel had asked Banayahu to talk about? Zakaryah thought it unlikely. A glance at the community leader showed him listening stone-faced to Banayahu. No, this wasn't at all what he had expected.

"Do we care that we'll be digging trenches every night for our own excrement? That women, men and children will need to share them?"

The whispering in the plaza had increased to a dull roar.

"But why should we care about such things? How can minor annoyances like these stop us from following our dreams back to the land we came from?

"Does it matter that we'll be leaving culture and learning stretching back thousands of years for a benighted backcountry where ignorance and superstition reign? Where the inhabitants will spit and hiss at us for usurping their land?

"Or that we'll be abandoning the abundant food we enjoy here for a primitive life of privation?

"No! None of this matters because we'll be doing it all for

the honor and praise of Yahweh. Of course, we know that we can honor and praise Yahweh right here, right in the land of Sumer and Akkad. We know from our great prophets Yirmeyahu and Yehezkel that Yahweh hears us here as he would everywhere in this great world of his creation. But what is that to us?"

And now the whole plaza was in an uproar. Zakaryah stood on his toes, shading his eyes from the morning sun. As far as he could see, people were shaking their heads, scowling, talking with great animation. Near him, he heard snatches.

"We'll never go."

"Who does this Koresh think he is?"

"Zerubavel—dreamer."

"We have food here."

"Here we have the king's law."

"But my business is growing!"

When he turned back from studying the crowd, Hannah was gone.

"Ginat." He pulled at her sleeve. "Hannah! Where is she?"

"She was here a moment ago."

"We have to find her!"

The two of them searched the immediate vicinity. No Hannah. Had she gone off in search of Danna? But she didn't know where the older girl was any more than he did.

He ran through the crowd, grabbing people by the arm. "A little girl, six years old. Have you seen her?"

No, people answered with a shake of the head or a puzzled look. Another no, and another, and another, until: "You mean that one?"

In his panic he almost failed to hear that last response. When it did register, he followed the hand pointing to the platform.

Hannah.

She was standing on the platform in front of the two men, holding a scroll. They were looking at her, Zerubavel rubbing his forehead, Banayahu blinking rapidly.

Soon a woman near the front noticed. She nudged her neighbor, who whispered to his neighbor. He jostled the shoulder of the woman next to him and pointed. Before long the entire community was staring at the platform.

The stillness became profound. Hannah regarded the crowd for a moment. She opened the scroll to the end. *What's she doing there? She doesn't know how to read.*

She began to sing in a child's voice, high and clear. The words of the song, though, weren't the words of a child.

By the waters of Bavel,
There we sat, sat and wept,
Remembering Yerushalayim.
There on the poplars we hung up our lyres
For our captors asked for songs,
Our tormentors for amusement.
Sing us a song of Yehudah.
How can we sing Yahweh's song on alien soil?
If I forget you, Yerushalayim
Let my right hand wither.
Let my tongue stick to my palate

If I cease to think of you,
If I do not keep you in memory
Even at my happiest hour.

Zerubavel stared at Hannah, his eyes wide. Banayahu looked as though a wagon full of straw had fallen on him.

Next to him, Ginat was weeping. "I remember it, I remember it. Ya'el's song."

Hannah rolled up the scroll and slipped off the front of the platform. She made her way back to them. Silence trailed her, the crowd parting for her like the sea before Moshe.

Zakaryah watched without really seeing her. In his thoughts, he was back on the day of his father's burial as his barley crackled and flamed in front of him. A single leaf swirled up on a column of smoke. His spirit went with it as the wind whipped it west.

West. Toward Yerushalayim.

He felt a yearning open up inside, a longing that he realized had been there since his earliest days.

I don't belong here, he realized. *I never have.*

CHAPTER 26

GIMILLU COULDN'T UNDERSTAND the words to the song the little girl was singing, but there was no mistaking the effect on the crowd. Every eye was directed at the platform. Even Danna, standing next to him, was focused on the girl. It was a relief, really. It was the first time this morning that she wasn't glaring at him.

The girl's voice was the only sound that could be heard in the plaza, other than the distant calling of crows near the river.

The young girl—Hannah, that was her name—finished singing. She rolled up the scroll she had read from and swept her eyes over the crowd. Her gaze seemed to settle on him. How could that be? She didn't even know he was here. And how could she pick him out of this crowd? He had to be wrong. But no, those silvery grey eyes locked on his in recognition but without surprise. She nodded.

His hair stood on end from his head to his knees. What had been Michal's murmured comment? *They're after the wrong sibling.* That's what she had said.

Well, they might be focused on the wrong sibling, but this Hannah was still a target, and she had put herself right where Bana-yama could grab her.

He risked a quick glance at the Kushite girl next to him. Had the same thought occurred to her? Danna was staring at Hannah as she came off the platform. Danna's body was rigid, her breathing fast and shallow. Her face was mostly covered, but her eyes looked strained and what he could see of her dark forehead was beaded with sweat.

"What are you staring at?" she hissed when she caught him looking. "He'll catch her for sure. This was your plan all along!"

He grabbed her sleeve to stop her lurching off in Hannah's direction. "Don't be stupid," he whispered at her, intensely aware of the Yahudus crowded around them. And it was so unfair. He had taken huge risks to come here, to warn them, to save them. And here she was accusing him of helping her pursuers. "Bana-yama can't do anything to her in front of this crowd. He'll have her followed when she leaves the plaza. Look, he's bending down to talk to someone at the side of the platform. One of his men, probably."

She shook her arm free of his grip but stopped trying to run off. "Yes, I see. But then they'll get Zakaryah too, and Ginat. And I'm not stupid!"

"Well then, think before you dash off." He choked as soon as the words were out of his mouth. *He* was telling *her* to think before acting.

Better change the subject before she noticed.

"Who's Ginat?"

She looked away as if she hadn't heard, but at least she didn't pounce on him. It wasn't much, but it was something.

Without looking at him, Danna began making her way through the plaza. It was a good thing he was paying attention, because after six paces she had practically been swallowed up in the crowd. He hurried after her, afraid of being left behind in this crush of Yahudus. Did her eyes dart in his direction as he caught up to her? If so, it was the only sign that she noticed. She was certainly making no secret of her feelings.

Where was she heading? There. Up ahead. Michal was searching the plaza, hand shading her eyes against the brightness of the morning.

"Your uncle and brother," Michal demanded as soon as they broke through to her. "Where are they?"

"I haven't seen them," he answered. "There are too many people here. But we should be more worried about Bana-yama."

"He'll have hired someone to grab them as soon as they leave the plaza," Danna told her with a glance at Gimillu. "We need to warn them."

"That's not enough," Michal replied. She tapped the shoulder of a stocky man next to her. When she had his attention she said something to him and pointed to where Hannah was visible from time to time as the throng headed to the streets leading from the square. He scowled and nodded, then gathered two of the men around him. The three men picked up three more on the way, and soon there was a phalanx of six strong Yahudu men surrounding Hannah.

"Zakaryah and Ginat are there too," Michal told them. "They'll all be safe now."

"But Banayahu will know where they are," Danna objected.

"It's the best we can do at the moment. Do you have any other ideas, Danna? Gimillu?" They both shook their heads. "In that case, let's go back to the school and think of some."

Michal and Danna were silent on the way back. Gimillu remained silent as well, trailing behind the other two. Michal looked like his sister Nidintu from behind, with a striking figure and long dark hair covered by a scarf. In personality, though, they were nothing alike. Where Nidintu was bitter and sharp, Michal was thoughtful and a careful listener. Even though she didn't trust him, he felt comfortable with her, as much as he could under the circumstances. His mother would have been like Michal if she had lived. He was sure of it.

Danna, on the other hand, still looked like a boy. Except for the scarf, of course, and the robe she wore. Even so, something drew him to her. If only she wasn't so terrifying.

When they reached the school, an old lady was sitting on the ground by the door. Her elbows were on her knees and her head was in her hands. At the sound of their footsteps she raised a gaunt and desolate face to them.

Michal squatted down, grasping both the woman's hands in her own. "What happened?" she asked.

"They got them," the old lady whispered. "They got Hannah and Zakaryah."

CHAPTER 27

"THERE WAS A BREACH in one of the major dams," the old lady explained when she had calmed down enough to talk clearly. "That's what they said."

They had moved inside. The women had removed their scarves. They were seated on mats just at the edge of the small courtyard.

"Ginat," Michal told her, "you'll need to speak in Chaldean for our guest."

"And who is this?" Ginat asked in that language.

"I'm Gimillu," he stammered.

"*The* Gimillu?"

He hung his head, unable to hold the old woman's gaze.

"It's all right, Ginat," Michal told her. "We can trust him. I'll tell you the story later."

She trusted him! His eyes welled with tears and a warmth he had never felt before flooded his whole body. At the same time, he cringed inside at the memory of what he had done that had led him to this moment. He snuck a glance at Danna. She was staring at him, lips tight and thin. Michal's declaration of trust didn't seem to apply to her.

"Who said the dam had collapsed?" Michal demanded, returning to Ginat's account. "Who said that?"

"The men protecting us had taken us as far as my house when somebody ran up shouting, 'The retention basin! The dam has collapsed! The fields are flooding!' Many of the people around us rushed off, and the men with us took off too. But three stayed behind. They pushed me down and grabbed Zakaryah and Hannah. When I got up they had already disappeared down some side street." Her voice broke and she began crying openly.

"Ginat," Michal said, "Gimillu has told us that he thinks Banayahu is behind this. The boy's uncle and brother will have persuaded him. Not that it would have taken much effort. How will you pay your taxes, they'll have said, when all your workers are gone? Who will tend your fields? How much will your profits go down when you have to pay more for workers? But if Zakaryah and Hannah just disappear, he'll be able to persuade everyone to stay, like he started to do before Hannah got up there. That's what he thinks."

Ginat said, "Then we just go to his house with a dozen strong men and demand them back."

"They won't be there," Michal responded. "His men will have hidden them somewhere. They caught them, now they'll wait for his orders."

"It's all *his* fault." Danna looked Gimillu up and down, nostrils flaring.

"Yes," Michal retorted. "And here he is trying to help. How are *you* helping?"

The girl opened her mouth to answer, then shut it again.

He felt a lump growing in his throat. She had spoken for him again. Nobody did that, not ever. He looked at her through a growing mist. *Think of something,* Uqupu's voice whispered. *Think fast or they'll be dead. You owe it to them. To her.*

"You said he thinks if they vanish he'll be able to convince everyone to stay," he told Michal. "Can we change that?"

Michal's eyes grew wide. "Give me a moment here," she told them. They sat and waited. Her gaze turned inward. She rested her chin on her palm, her finger slipping up to partially cover her mouth. She nodded to herself from time to time, sending waves of light rippling down the dark length of her hair.

A long silence ensued. It ended when she straightened and said, "All right." She looked at Ginat and at Danna. Her gaze came to rest on Gimillu, eyebrows raised in a mute question.

"Just tell me," he said. "I'll do it, whatever it is."

"Good. Danna, go to the children's houses and have their parents send them over immediately. Ginat, find Zerubavel and ask him to come back here. Gimillu, there's a bowl of clay over in the corner that we use for teaching the children to make pots. Shape two tablets from it, the kind you use for writing. You'll find some pieces of wood there that can serve as backing. Oh, and you'll need to make yourself a stylus. We have writing sticks here for our lessons. Pick one and whittle it down to the right shape. Then go get your horse ready to ride. It needs to be well fed and watered. There's grain in the side room. Stay with the horse until Danna comes to get you. Danna, have you ever been on a horse?"

Danna shook her head slowly.

"Well then, I don't envy you your next couple days. All of you move, now!"

They moved.

WHERE WAS MICHAL GOING to find a horse for Danna? Gimillu hadn't seen any horses here in Al Yahudu, except of course his own. It was clear that she was very resourceful, though. No doubt she would find one somewhere.

He had been so sore for the first several days he had been riding. Poor Danna. He felt a grin spread across his face.

He dug a handful of clay from the bowl that Michal had referred to, plopped it on a small wooden board and patted it into a tablet shape. He did the same with a second handful. What did she want him to do with this? She was going to have him write something in Akkadu, that was clear. But what? Well, she would tell him soon enough.

He took the wet tablets and set them down on the table. Then he rushed out to take care of the horse. He would make the stylus when he came back.

WHEN GIMILLU RETURNED, having been retrieved by a silent Danna, the man Zerubavel was standing next to the door. His arms were crossed and he blinked as he scanned the room. His eyes came to rest on Michal, brows furrowed.

He doesn't know why he's here.

The children stared at Gimillu, some with eyebrows raised, some tilting their heads to the side. A little of the tension left his shoulders when Michal didn't explain who he was or why he was in the house.

She shot a glance at Zerubavel, then spoke to the children in the Yahudu tongue. They grabbed their writing styluses and straightened the blank pieces of papyrus that had been set in front of them. At another word from her, they wetted their ink cakes and sat with styluses poised.

She turned to Ginat and said something in the same language. The old woman scratched her head a moment and began reciting. A poem, clearly. Zerubavel's eyes widened. And then Gimillu recognized it even though he couldn't understand the words. It was the poem that Hannah had sung in front of the Shabbat assembly earlier that day.

In Akkadu, Michal told Danna to walk around and make sure the song was copied correctly. "We don't want any mistakes with this," she said. Danna nodded and started moving around the table, looking over the shoulders of the children as they were writing.

While Ginat was reciting and the children were copying, Michal stood and talked at length to Zerubavel, speaking in the Yahudu language. Gimillu heard her say his name. He turned from watching the children to find himself the object of Zerubavel's cold gaze. Well, the man had no reason to trust him. But Michal spoke sharply and motioned Gimillu to her side, putting her arm around his shoulders. Gimillu raised his hand to the spot where his amulet used to sit.

The man took in her arm around his shoulder. He looked Gimillu hard in the eyes. After an interminable interval, the Yahudu nodded. Michal released him.

By this time the children had finished. In all, they had produced over twenty copies.

Michal switched to Akkadu. To Gimillu she said, "I'm going to dictate two messages. You'll write them in Akkadu, one message on each of the tablets. One will be for your brother the scribe."

"My brother? How will you get it to him? I don't know where he is."

"Don't worry. Zerubavel and I are going to pay a visit on Banayahu. We'll give him a letter in Yehudit. You're writing the same message in Akkadu. Banayahu will give that one to your brother."

As she dictated the message, he pressed the words into the damp clay with the stylus he had made, arranging the wedge impressions in the familiar shapes he had learned in the tablet-house. The letter indicated that copies of Hannah's song had been dispatched to every Yahudu community along the Kabara canal. Banayahu had seen the impact of the song on the crowd earlier. The matter was out of his hands. There was no reason to hold or harm Zakaryah and Hannah. They would be returned immediately or a message with the full story and the names of the conspirators would be sent to King Kurush. Did the consequences of that really need to be spelled out?

CHRISTOPHER FARRAR

He made an extra effort with this so that his brother wouldn't immediately recognize his careless hand. In the end, though, it certainly wouldn't make any difference. They would know there was only one person who could have supplied the details included in the letter. He was already hopelessly compromised with his family. There would be no coming back from this.

The other letter was for King Kurush. He tried to take the same level of care with it, but the shaking of his hand made that impossible. He had carried a message to the king once and had been lucky to have escaped with his life.

The stylus started slipping in his grip. He set it down, wiped his hand on his robe, picked it up, pressed another character into the clay, then wiped his hand again.

Michal stopped dictating as he faltered. She regarded him silently as he struggled with his fear. But he remembered the weight of her arm around his shoulders and knew he would do anything she asked of him. Eventually he was able to nod at her. She resumed as if there had been no interruption. At the end she told him that if things worked as she hoped, the message would never be sent. "But it's going to depend on you and Danna."

"WRAP YOUR ARMS around my chest," Gimillu ordered Danna at the start of the ride.

"I would rather die."

He shrugged and kicked the horse into a trot. She yelped and grasped the back of his robe. He urged the horse to greater speed. She made a grab for his chest and clung to him as the horse surged into a gallop.

His point made, he eased the animal back into a walk. There would be no trotting or galloping in this damp heat.

She hadn't spoken to him since.

The whole way he could feel her angry glower behind him as she hung on. No girl had ever put her arms around him. He pretended to himself that she didn't hate him, and it was wonderful.

Because it was still Shabbat and they were traveling through a mainly Yahudu area, there were few people on the road with them. Those they did pass did a double-take at the sight of a boy and a girl on horseback, a girl with the ebony face of a Kushite.

Some people scowled and shouted curses. Where was their chaperone? Was he training her to become a whore?

He yelled back at them. How dare they call his sister a whore? He reached inside his robe as if to draw out a dagger. They desisted, perhaps because of the feigned threat, perhaps because a lot of families were still on the move after the Parsu conquest. How would anyone know they weren't siblings? Half siblings, anyway.

At the first stop she refused his help dismounting and tried to climb down by herself. When her hands slipped from the edges of the seating blanket, she fell onto her rear, landing hard in the dirt. The horse snorted and Gimillu laughed out loud.

After he dismounted she gave him a painful kick in the shin.

"Lead the horse into the palm orchard," she ordered as he rubbed the growing lump.

"Won't someone see us?"

"It's still Shabbat, stupid. Nobody's working."

At least she was talking to him now.

He led the horse into the shade, glad himself to get out of the afternoon sun.

Danna reached into the bag that was looped around her waist and extracted a piece of papyrus, one of those onto which the children had copied Hannah's poem.

With the poem in hand, she headed into the town. As Michal had directed, she would seek out one of the local priests, hand him the papyrus, point out Zerubavel's name at the bottom, and explain the importance of reading it to the community. Then she would return and they would ride to the next Yahudu town. Only Danna could do this, Michal had said, because she spoke the language and could talk to the Yahudus in terms they would understand.

She returned a short time later.

He climbed onto the horse and sat there as she stood below him, her eyes darting around the area. The first time Michal had found a stool for her that she used to climb onto the horse. This time there was nothing.

What would she do to avoid asking him for help?

He felt the lump on his shin again and covered his mouth with a hand, biting his lip to avoid laughing.

She studied him for a moment as he struggled to keep his sides from shaking. Then she grabbed hold of his foot, shoved up and heaved him off the horse. He landed on his back in the soft soil of the palm orchard. As he lay wheezing on the ground, unable to catch his breath, she grabbed onto the blanket seat, jumping several times before she succeeded in pulling herself up. The horse swung its head around to stare at her.

When Gimillu recovered enough to breathe again, he climbed back onto the horse and took a position behind her. She handed him the reins without speaking. He tapped the horse in the ribs, and they headed for the next stop.

NAR KABARA.

This was as far as they would make it today.

Gimillu remained on the horse's back. Danna slid down from her position in front of him, not arguing this time as he held her hands to lower her to the ground. Her hands were sweaty but fit nicely into his. He swung down after her.

Michal had directed her to visit Ovadyah, a friend of Zakar-yama's father. She would spend the night in town. As far as she knew, Gimillu would be sleeping in the bushes.

He had other plans.

After Danna disappeared into the town, he turned the horse around toward the bridge that they had crossed on their approach to the village.

He crossed the canal, turned left, and made his way toward his uncle's home, passing Master Nabu-ushabshi's tablet-house on the way. Maybe he would stop there on his return. For now there was something more important he had to do.

He tied the horse in a patch of shade a good distance from his uncle's house. As far as he could tell, the servants weren't home. They were probably taking advantage of Guzannu's absence to have a holiday.

He dismounted and walked closer to the house.

"Shulmu!" he called. Knowing what was coming, he sat down in the dirt.

When the dog raced up he leapt on Gimillu and knocked him onto his back, barking and licking his face furiously.

"It's only been two days!" Gimillu exclaimed, laughing and hugging him. The hugs turned into a wrestling match, the dog lunging and leaping away, Gimillu catching him and rolling him on the ground, the two of them growling like wild animals.

When they had tired each other out, Gimillu plopped himself down and stretched full length on the ground, chest heaving, lighter at heart than he had been for longer than he could remember. Shulmu spun around in a tight circle and planted himself in the hollow of Gimillu's outstretched arm, tongue out, panting in the evening heat.

After the dog's panting and his own breathing had slowed to a more normal pace, Gimillu stood. "Come, Shulmu," he said. He led the dog slowly toward the horse to reintroduce the two animals to each other.

With his uncle's house empty, he decided to spend the night there instead of in the bush with its biting insects and small nasty animals.

In the morning he mounted the horse, and with Shulmu trotting alongside, made his way back to the palm orchard by Nar Kabara where he was to meet Danna.

He saw her before she saw him. She was standing at the

edge of the orchard, wringing her hands and tugging at her robe from time to time. She was probably worried that he wasn't there where she had expected him.

He wasn't actually relieved to see her. It was just that he wouldn't be able to complete the job without her. That's all it was.

He stopped the horse a few paces away. Shulmu came to his side and looked around, nose in the air, sniffing.

A man stepped out from behind a palm tree. He was holding a heavy stick.

CHAPTER 28

THE DOOR TO THE SCHOOL GROANED
on its wooden pins as Zakaryah pushed it open. He stood in the
doorway, not moving, the early sun streaming from behind into
the dimmer courtyard within.

Hannah slipped around him, grasping his hand as she did
so and tugging him inside. She had been like this during the
whole ordeal, calm and composed. How did she do it? She may
not have grasped how dire their peril had been, but he certainly
did. Their escape hadn't eased his sense of danger in the least.
He was still trembling with it.

Michal was sitting on a mat in the courtyard in front of
them, her head in her hands. At the creaking of the door, she
looked up, squinting in the bright light. Her face was lined and
she had dark pouches under her eyes. Hannah went to her, knelt
in front and hugged her.

Michal freed an arm from the girl's embrace and beckoned Zakaryah to her, her eyes glistening. She patted the mat

beside her. He sat down and she pulled him in tight. The three of them sat like that for a long moment, silent.

The door opened again and a man came in. It was that Zerubavel, the man on the platform from the day before.

"A servant came from Banayahu," he announced. "He said his master had managed to track down the criminals who were holding the boy and his sister, and when Banayahu showed up with three strong men to rescue the children, the perpetrators fled. Was that what happened?" he asked, looking at Zakaryah.

"They had us in a back room with a man guarding the door. Last night I heard some whispering from in front, then the house door slammed. I looked and they had all vanished. They must have been in a hurry because one of them left this behind." He retrieved a short-bladed dagger from a pocket inside his robe and held it out for them to see. "When I saw they were gone, we walked out. It was dark but there was some moonlight. We wandered until we found a deserted house where we spent the night. This morning when there was enough light to see, we came here. I didn't know where else to go."

Ginat shuffled in from one of the side rooms. "I didn't think I could sleep," she said, rubbing her eyes. She noticed who was in the courtyard. "I'm so sorry." Her voice faltered. "They knocked me down and by the time I got up you were gone."

Michal released Zakaryah and Hannah. She groaned, rising from the mat. "You'll be hungry, I'm sure. There's food left over from last night."

"I'll get it," Hannah told her, rising.

Michal sank down again.

Hannah showed up a short time later with bread and barley porridge, both cold. She placed them on the mat and sat down. Ginat and Zerubavel joined them, the five forming a tight circle around the food.

As they ate, Michal explained how they had freed them.

"We had the children make copies of Hannah's poem. Then we sent Danna out with the copies to distribute to our communities along the river."

Ginat opened her mouth to say something but closed it again at a small shake of the head from Michal.

"What good would that do?" Zakaryah asked. It didn't make much sense. And what was that head shake about?

"Banayahu needed you both out of the way to persuade people not to go back to Yehudah. He knows it will hurt his business interests if a lot of people leave. It would have worked, too, except for Hannah singing Ya'el's poem. He blames you and Hannah for threatening his wealth. Those Chaldeans encouraged him to think that."

"Gimillu!" he exploded.

The adults exchanged looks again. "Actually," Michal responded, "his brother and uncle. But once we told Banayahu the poem had gone out to our towns, he knew he had lost. Then the risk of harming you became too great. King Koresh would have found out and he would have been killed."

Zakaryah made an effort to calm himself. "How would the king have found out?"

"We wrote a letter. If you hadn't shown up here this morning it would have been sent."

Remembering the food in front of him, Zakaryah broke off a piece of bread and used it to scoop up some porridge, chewing without tasting it. He looked over at Hannah. She ate without visible agitation, as if this all involved someone else. *I'll never understand her.*

And then the other thing Michal said got through to him. "Danna delivered the poems?"

"She's still delivering them today."

Danna, alone on the road. "What if they catch her?" he demanded, gnawing the inside of his cheek. "What if something happens to her?"

"She'll be back tonight," Michal responded. "You and Hannah should rest now. We all should. Later we'll talk about what we do next."

She pointed the two of them to the room that Ginat had come out of. He stretched out on a pallet, his thoughts slowing. The last image that came to mind as he drifted off was Gimillu's startled face as their eyes met in Bavel. *Strange, strange . . .*

WHEN HE WOKE, Zakaryah didn't rise immediately. Instead, he lay on his pallet with his arms folded behind his head. Hannah was still sleeping on the next pallet. Even though she hadn't seemed as affected by the ordeal as he had been, it was just as long for her as it was for him. It was good for her to rest.

He raised his head a little and looked out into the courtyard. The shadows there suggested that the sun was well along in its descent. He was surprised that he hadn't slept longer. He had been up almost the whole of the previous night, afraid to doze off in case their captors had a change of heart and came looking for them. He would have felt safer if they'd been able to make it to the school as soon as the men left. He just didn't know the town well enough to find his way in the dark, even with the light of the quarter moon.

He rolled off the sleeping pallet, stood and stretched. He wanted to go outside to relieve himself—surely there was an open area somewhere nearby—but the fear of being seen kept him from leaving the house. He would just have to make it until dark. For the first time he felt envious of Danna's relations in Bavel. They had an indoor privy, a hole in the floor that dropped directly to an underground water channel. It carried the waste straight off to the moat. Imagine!

Neither Zerubavel nor Ginat was in the house. Michal must have had as bad a night as he did, because he could hear regular breathing coming from the other room, the one he hadn't been sleeping in.

He went over to the low table in the side room just off the courtyard. This was where the children had been studying the first time he had come here. It must have been where they sat to copy Ya'el's poem, the poem that had resulted in him and Hannah being set free, at least as Michal told it. Had it really been that simple? They just told Banayahu that the poem was being sent off to all the local communities, and he set them free? What would Ya'el have thought? Somehow, knowing her, it wasn't surprising that she'd had this effect.

His thoughts were interrupted by a shuffling sound from the street outside the door to the house. *Someone was there.* Sweat broke out on his forehead. His breaths came rapid and shallow. He started backing away from the door but there was nowhere to go, no other exit from the house. Hannah was sleeping in the room behind him. Could he scale the wall of the courtyard? But he would need to carry Hannah over too. What if they had the house surrounded? And what about Michal?

The door creaked. It wasn't barred! It moved outward a hand's breadth and stopped. There was a low sound of voices from the other side. He was paralyzed, not able to move now or wrench his eyes away.

The door opened all the way and Danna stepped through. She stopped dead as soon as she saw him, then fell back against the door jamb and pressed her palms to her eyes, her chest shaking with suppressed sobs.

The tension drained from his body, leaving him sagging against the writing table. Behind him he heard sounds of movement from the sleeping rooms. Hannah? Michal?

There was a snuffling sound from outside. Danna's hand flew to her mouth and she spun around to face the street, flinging an arm out as someone stepped through the doorway.

Gimillu.

Zakaryah launched himself at the other boy, pushing Danna out of harm's way. He knocked Gimillu onto the earthen floor and fell on top of him, swinging his fists.

When a dog rushed in from outside, barking furiously and lunging at him, the room erupted. Voices shouted, there was a sound of vessels breaking, a door banged. Hands grabbed him from behind. He gripped Gimillu's robe tightly with his left hand while continuing to pummel the boy with his right. When he pulled his fist back for a strike at the boy's face, he was seized by the back of the robe and flung away, spinning and skidding until his head connected with the heavy wood of the low writing table.

Through the sudden haze clouding his vision he watched Danna sit down on the dirt floor next to the other boy, gently lifting his head to cradle it in her lap.

Zakaryah sank to the ground as the interior of the house lurched around him. He groaned and closed his eyes.

"IT WAS MY FAULT. I should have warned him." Michal's voice was tired and strained.

Zakaryah lay still with his eyes shut, fearful of the nausea that had seized him a moment before when he had turned his head to the side.

"Why did you stop Ginat? She was about to tell him." A man. Zerubavel?

"I was afraid it would be too much on top of the ordeal he had just been through."

"Tell me what?" Zakaryah whispered, not moving.

There was no answer. He opened his eyes to a narrow slit so the light wouldn't make him vomit. Michal was kneeling next to him, eyes shut tight, her lips moving silently in a rhythm that he recognized: *barachi nafshi et Yahweh, bless*

Yahweh, my soul, all my being his holy name. A prayer of thanksgiving. For him?

She opened her eyes and grasped both sides of his face, holding it steady. "Look at me," she commanded.

"I'm afraid. The nausea."

"Open your eyes all the way."

He did so, surprised that the light didn't bother him after all. The sun was so low now that the whole courtyard was in shadow.

She peered into his eyes for a long time, then smiled. "Your pupils look normal. You'll feel well enough after that bump on your head goes down."

Bump? He touched the back of his head and winced. Yes, a bump, half the size of his hand.

"What happened?" he croaked. "Where's Danna? Gimillu! He was about to attack her. How did he find us? We have to leave now!" He propped himself up on an elbow only to fall back, overcome by nausea.

"Shh." Michal put a finger on his lips. "You're not in danger. Neither is Hannah."

"Danna. What about Danna?"

"Danna is safe. She took Gimillu back to the empty house where he's keeping his horse. She's looking after him. You're not the only one who got hurt, as you might recall."

"I don't understand."

"Gimillu has been helping us." Hannah's sleepy voice came from somewhere in the room behind him. "I told you at the farm. You didn't believe me."

"Yes," Michal said. "He saved your lives. He and Danna.

He's devastated over the events he set in motion. Don't you wonder why he didn't defend himself when you jumped him?"

And maybe that was true. He had been so angry, so fearful, that all he wanted was to beat the boy senseless, grab Hannah and Danna and run as far and as fast as he could.

Gimillu hadn't even tried to cover his face.

But what they were saying was impossible. He saw again the flames rising over his field. Gimillu did that. And the date orchard. Gimillu. The judge Bel-shunu. Banayahu. The terror of the previous day. All Gimillu. He had tricked Michal, had tricked Hannah, had tricked Danna. He had fooled them all, had got them all thinking he'd had a change of heart, was filled with regret.

"Right," Michal said after regarding him in silence for a moment. "It's a lot to take in. When you're ready to hear the story, tell me."

He closed his eyes and straightened his body where he lay. His head throbbed. He was exhausted. He had no place to go, could barely move even if he wanted to. He might as well listen to what she had to say. Maybe when he heard the lies Gimillu had told them all he'd be able to convince them.

"Go ahead," he whispered.

She explained how Gimillu had been furious at him and had come up with the idea of burning his barley to punish him.

"Our food! Our taxes!"

"Yes. It was stupid and very, very wrong. Tell me, is it true that you used to mock him at the tablet-house because he was slower than you? That you put a snake in his meal sack? One that looked like the deadly kind?"

"It was a harmless little snake!"

She looked at him a long moment before going on: The uncle, the father, the danger that Gimillu's actions had created for them, the scheming of the adults to protect their positions. How they had made him forge the contract for Banayahu, made him bribe the judge.

So this was what Gimillu had told them, that he had been forced into it all. Ridiculous. How could these people be so gullible? But there was a huge hole in the story.

He propped himself up on his elbows, surprised to discover that he could do this now with only a little dizziness. He scooted back a bit so he could rest against the table. "So then," he said, "that should have been the end of it. They won. We wouldn't have been a danger. But he still kept chasing us."

"Because of *me*," Hannah announced. She sounded proud.

"Yes," Michal agreed. "But by then he was trying to protect you." She told him the rest of the story, ending with the desperate ride of Danna and Gimillu to spread the words of the poem to the communities along the river.

At that point the door opened and Danna stepped into the doorway. He hadn't heard her approach, he realized. *She must have been outside the whole time.* Her gaze settled on him. Without taking her eyes off him, she reached back through the doorway and tugged at something that was just out of sight. When it didn't move she pulled harder. A hand came into view, then a sleeve, then the whole person. Gimillu, eyes downcast, shuffling as she pulled him into the house.

When he was fully inside she pulled the door shut behind

them and positioned herself in front of the other boy. She addressed Zakaryah. "Are you going to behave yourself now?"

Hannah giggled. "I don't think he can get up."

It was infuriating. Here was Gimillu, right in front of him, and he probably couldn't even stand up. Worse, they were all looking at Zakaryah as if he were the villain.

"Well?" Danna demanded, looking not at him this time but at Gimillu. When the boy didn't answer she shoved him hard in the shoulder, making him stagger. Gimillu's face reddened but he kept his gaze on his feet and still didn't say anything. Zakaryah noticed a dark bruise on the boy's right cheek and wondered at it. He hadn't actually hit him in the face had he? So where did the bruise come from?

No matter. One bruise wasn't nearly enough.

The room was silent, everyone watching but nobody speaking.

Danna stood there with her hands on her hips, looking from Gimillu to him and back again. What was she waiting for?

Then she spoke. "So, let's see if I understand. Two boys, both as dumb as clay jugs, start a stupid schoolboy fight that goes totally out of control and ends up endangering all of us. Do I have that right?"

"Don't forget me!" Hannah interjected.

"You stay out of this," Danna snapped.

She shoved Gimillu again. "Go on. Say it."

He muttered something under his breath.

"Louder! We all want to hear."

"I'm sorry, I'm sorry, I'm sorry! I didn't mean for it to

get this bad. I was so mad! I wasn't thinking." He turned to Hannah. "I'm so sorry. I didn't know he had a little sister. I didn't know."

Hannah's lips turned up in a strange little smile but she said nothing.

Danna turned to Zakaryah. "Now you."

"Me?" he squeaked. "He attacked me! He burned our food, our tax payment! I would have been imprisoned. Hannah would have been a slave!"

He looked around the inside of the house for support. Michal, Zerubavel, Hannah, Danna—they were all tense, all staring at him. Only Gimillu was looking away. What did they expect from him? To apologize? For being the victim?

The silence dragged on, became excruciating. For some reason he thought of what his father had said when he had proudly told him about the snake. Instead of praising him for his cleverness, Shillemyah had asked how he thought the other boy felt when he saw it slither out of the lunch sack.

"I shouldn't have mocked him," he grated out.

"To him!" Danna insisted.

"I shouldn't have mocked you!" he shouted.

Gimillu flinched but met his eyes for the first time. He nodded.

There was a collective sigh and everyone relaxed. But it didn't mean anything, did it? It wasn't a real apology. He had said the words but Gimillu was still the villain, and he, Zakaryah, was still the victim. That was right, wasn't it?

Danna swung her gaze between him and Gimillu. She

shook her head. "Dumb as jugs," she muttered. To Michal she said, "I'll start fixing the evening meal. Hannah, come with me."

The two of them went off.

Michal and Zerubavel began talking in low voices. Zakaryah was too preoccupied with his own thoughts to pay much attention. He ignored Gimillu, who was leaning awkwardly against a wall, scanning the room nervously. The boy's gaze kept coming back to him, as if he expected Zakaryah to jump up at any moment and hit him again.

After the evening meal he went back to the pallet he had slept on during the day, exhausted both physically and emotionally.

As he lay on the edge of sleep, one image from earlier in the day came back to him. He had been lying stunned against the table and Danna—Danna was cradling Gimillu's head in her lap.

CHAPTER 29

WHEN HE WOKE in the morning, Gimillu lay on his makeshift pallet on the roof and did an inventory of his bruises. There was the one on his right cheek. How did he get that? Oh yes. The man with the stick at Nar Kabara. When he stepped out from behind the tree, Shulmu began barking. The horse spooked and dashed off, smashing his face into a low branch.

The man behind the tree was Ovadyah, a friend of Zakaryah's father. Danna had explained it as they were riding to their next stop. "He just wanted to make sure I was safe." Had she told the man about him, he wanted to know. No response, but the stick had been its own answer.

She had been nicer to him after that. It probably helped that the dog liked her. She had sat behind him, carrying Shulmu for the rest of the ride, holding Gimillu's robe with one hand and the dog with the other, laughing as Shulmu nuzzled her and licked her face.

His other bruises had been inflicted by Zakaryah, except for the one on his shin where Danna had kicked him two days before. They were all hidden under his robe, for which he was grateful. He was pretty sure there were no broken bones, but it hurt to take a deep breath. He squeezed several places on his legs and arms, wincing each time. Walking would be painful, that was clear.

But she had held him! He marveled at that, at the feeling of his head in her lap after Zerubavel had flung Zakaryah off him.

So much nicer than being shoved off the back of a horse.

WHEN GIMILLU STEPPED OFF the roof ladder and limped into the courtyard, still groggy from sleep, Michal, Danna and Zerubavel were already sitting there, cross-legged on their mats. Eating bowls sat empty in front of them, showing traces of barley porridge and date pits.

Michal held a bowl out to him. He took it and scooped some porridge from the serving krater that was there on the floor. He grabbed a round loaf from the stack of bread next to it.

"There's also beer next to the cooking pit," Danna told him. "And you'll need to wash your hands." She pointed to a bowl of water that was sitting close by the beer.

By now he had taken enough meals with these people that he wasn't surprised by the reminder to wash his hands. Still, he didn't see the reason for it. It wasn't as though he had been handling wet dung. He did as she told him just the same, fetching some beer and spilling the water over his hands to clean them.

Michal leaned toward him as he ate, her eyebrows drawn together.

"What do you want us to do for you?" she asked.

"I don't understand."

"Will you be able to go back to your family?"

Danna jerked her fist to her mouth at this, eyes wide, chewing on a finger as she looked at him. Was she thinking of her own family? But maybe she actually cared about him.

He felt a brief moment of elation before Michal's question sank in. Then it was like a cartload of dates had been dumped on him, burying him so deep he couldn't breathe. His brother and uncle would know by now that he had lied to them, that he had helped the Yahudus to escape. They would tell his father. He had known this before, had known it when he wrote out the tablet that Michal used with Bana-yama to free Zakaryah and Hannah. He had pushed it to the back of his mind but there was no running away from it.

He slumped as he met Michal's eyes, cursing himself for the moisture that was gathering in his own. She reached over and squeezed his hand.

The funny thing was that he had been ready to leave his family, his dog even, just before he had been captured by Kurush's soldiers. Why was this hitting him so hard now? They didn't care about him, his family. His brother blamed him for their mother's death. His father held him in such low regard that he had sent him off to the countryside to be instructed by a disgraced scribe while the older brother went to expensive and prestigious tablet-houses in Bab-ili. And Nidintu? What had made her so hard and bitter?

Michal brought him out of the whirlpool of thoughts that

was sucking him down. "They'll come after you, won't they?" Her voice was gentle.

And she was right. They would track him down wherever he went. What would they do when they caught him?

"What if I become one of you?"

"I'm sorry, Gimillu." She dropped her eyes, dabbing at them with the sleeve of her robe. "It's not possible. You don't speak our language. You worship idols and false gods. You know none of the prayers and incantations. When you washed your hands just now, Danna had to say the prayer for you. No one would believe you were my child."

That drew a sudden sharp glance from Zerubavel. She didn't seem to notice.

"And the worst thing," she concluded, almost whispering, "is that it won't stop them from capturing you."

Zerubavel addressed Michal, speaking for the first time. "Some outsiders have joined our community. They have to live like we live. It's hard, but if they do that, Yahweh accepts them. That's not the real problem."

She regarded him, eyebrows raised.

"The real problem," he told her, responding to the unvoiced question, "is that his family will eventually track him back here. He's a danger to all of us."

Gimillu's bowels loosened, his chin and lips trembled. This terrible man was going to cast him out. His father would order him arrested. He would be imprisoned, probably even killed.

"I won't throw him to them," Michal said.

But how long could she resist? It was true, what the man

said. There wasn't any alternative. He should have seen it before. He never did, though. He never thought things through. The man was right. If he stayed they would all be imprisoned, maybe enslaved. His father wouldn't hesitate, he was sure of it.

Gimillu looked at Michal. She was still, regarding him. He raised his hand to the absent Pazuzu amulet. He turned to Danna. She dropped her eyes. How could he endanger them? And Hannah? Even Zakar-yama. At least that was one person who would be happy to see him go.

He would manage somehow. He had thought once before about escaping south to the Sea Land, about taking passage on a boat to some distant country. He would miss them, especially Michal. Danna too, even though she still frightened him.

"I'll leave," he announced finally, the words catching in his throat. He rose. He had a bag somewhere, didn't he? He would grab that. He would collect Shulmu and the horse and that would be that. He would be gone.

Zerubavel stood too, shaking his head. He caught Michal's eye. "When they catch him, they'll retrace his steps to us. There's only one way," he told her. "The boy has to die."

THE ROBE WAS STAINED DEEP RED, the blood spread in random splotches around long gashes. Zerubavel folded it carefully, slipping it into a sack that he set down by his feet.

"I'll take the horse out into the marshes at dusk when people will be inside their houses eating. I'll lead it through the shallows to pick up some mud. After that I'll take it to Banayahu's house. He'll let the brother know."

Michal nodded. "That should work," she said. "There've been reports of a lion in the area so it will be easy to believe. And," she continued, "did I mention that there've been reports of a lion?"

He laughed. "Misha'el will worry. Send someone to tell her that I'll be back after dark."

She nodded and he left, pushing the door closed behind him.

Gimillu squatted in the farthest corner he could find, stripped down to his loin cloth, arms wrapped as tightly as he could manage around his naked torso. His bruises stood out clearly, dark and ugly where Zakaryah had pounded him. Over by the cooking pit, Hannah and Danna were plucking and gutting two headless chickens. They whispered to each other as they worked, breaking into helpless giggles each time they glanced at him.

He couldn't see his own face, but he was sure it had never been as red as it was now.

Zakaryah sat cross-legged on a mat, finishing his meal. Shulmu lay near him in the shade of a pillar, head on his paws. Zakaryah didn't look at the dog or Gimillu. Instead he scowled at the girls as they worked and laughed.

"You know, Zakaryah," Michal said, "you're going to have to talk to him eventually."

No answer.

Gimillu spoke from his corner. "I said I was sorry."

Still nothing.

Michal gestured to him behind Zakaryah's back. Come here, the gesture said. She pointed to a spot next to the other boy. He shook his head and stayed where he was.

She got up, crossed the courtyard and entered her sleeping room. She emerged carrying a light linen cover, strode over to Gimillu and dropped it at his feet. She went back to her place at the edge of the courtyard.

He wetted his lips, took a deep breath and stood, gasping with the pain. He draped the cloth over his head and wrapped it in front of his body, trying to figure out how to fasten it so it wouldn't gap open in front. There was laughter from the girls, stifled almost as soon as it started. He glared at them and they turned away, unable to conceal broad grins. Of course. With the cloth over his head and the front held closed, he looked like a woman. It was so unfair!

In the end he wrapped the cloth around him and tucked in the top so that it clung tight just under his armpits. It was the best he could do.

Michal gestured again. No choice this time. He shuffled over to the spot she had indicated. He winced as he lowered himself to sit cross-legged on the mat. He was a little over two arm's lengths from Zakaryah. Not as close as she wanted, but as close as he was willing to get. Shulmu left his spot to plop himself down next to Gimillu, between him and Zakaryah.

The two of them sat there like that, staring straight ahead, not talking.

In front of them, the girls' eyes met. They dropped their

birds onto the stone work surface and rose.

"Ow!" Gimillu and Zakaryah shouted in unison as each was kicked hard in the thigh, Gimillu by Hannah and Zakaryah by Danna.

The girls returned to their chickens.

Michal laughed and said, "Now that you have something in common, maybe you can talk to each other."

"You should control your sister better," Gimillu told Zakaryah. Hannah smiled without raising her eyes from the bird she was gutting.

"You should control your *friend*." Zakaryah spat the word out, his mouth tight, his face tense.

"Oh," Danna replied with a quick glance at Zakaryah, "I've kicked Gimillu lots. It was your turn this time."

Friend! Zakaryah had called her his *friend*. Only he hadn't meant just *friend*, had he? And she hadn't argued!

Shulmu peered up at Zakaryah, then rolled over onto his back, exposing his neck and the underside of his chin.

"He wants you to scratch his neck," Danna told Zakaryah. "Go ahead. He doesn't bite."

Gimillu leaned forward, blinking, as Zakaryah reached out with one tentative hand. Had this boy never petted a dog? "Like this," he said, running his fingers over the soft skin under Shulmu's neck. The dog drummed his tail against the dirt floor in a flurry of ecstatic thumping.

Zakaryah touched the dog's neck before jerking his hand back.

Shulmu rolled back onto his stomach, regarding Gimillu

with sad eyes and drooping ears. "Don't stare at me like that," he said. "It's Zakaryah's fault, not mine." But he ruffled Shulmu's fur just the same. The dog rolled onto his back again and rewarded him with a big sigh.

Gimillu went to work on Shulmu's chest and stomach. After a moment, Zakaryah stretched out a hand and scratched the dog's neck.

"When do we get to stop?" Zakaryah asked.

"Don't worry," Danna told him as she finished with her chicken. "He has to eat sometime."

"I heard you say you wanted to become a Yahudu like us."

It took Gimillu a moment to realize that Zakaryah was talking to him.

"Yes. I can't go back to my family. Zerubavel said it's possible. I have to worship only your Yahweh. I have to learn the blessings and incantations. I have to learn your language. I have to live like you do. Then your God will accept me. That's what he said."

By now Danna and Michal were paying close attention.

Hannah had washed her hands after cleaning her bird. She was sitting next to Zakaryah. "We'll be going back to Yehudah," he continued, putting his arm around his sister. "Hannah and I will be walking for more than three months. You'll never see your family again. You'll never see the land of Sumer and Akkad."

Gimillu swallowed hard. He and Zakaryah could barely stand to be in the same house. How could they tolerate being together for three months?

He turned to Michal. "Couldn't I stay here with you? I

could join the school and learn how to be a Yahudu. I could learn the language and the writing." And that way he would still be around Danna.

Michal lowered her eyes. "If you stay here, they'll eventually see through our trick with the bloody robe. Sooner or later they'll find you. I'm so sorry."

There was no choice, then. Gimillu blinked back tears. He would need to leave with Zakaryah and Hannah. He couldn't stay here with Michal. He reached for the missing Pazuzu amulet.

Zakaryah saw the gesture and said, "Yahudus don't wear graven images."

Gimillu dropped his hand. He would be leaving even that behind, the last remembrance of his mother.

"You'll need a teacher while you're on the road." That was Danna, speaking for the first time in a while. "Luckily for you, I'm going too."

Michal's mouth fell open. "What?"

"I'll be going with Zakaryah and Hannah," Danna told her.

"Why? I need you here to help with the teaching."

Danna looked down and said nothing.

But she would be going! Suddenly the journey didn't seem so terrible.

Danna turned to Gimillu. "You'll need a Yahudu name. I think we should call you Gemalyahu. That's like your Akkadu name. It means 'Yahweh redeems.' It fits you, I think."

"Gamal-yahu," he repeated.

They all laughed.

"You just said that Yahweh is a camel," she told him. "I

assure you, Yahweh is not a camel."

He tried saying the name again several times, until they nodded and agreed that it was passable, even if his nasty Akkadu accent might make people think of caravans crossing a desert.

"There's just one more thing you'll need to do to become a Yahudu," Zakaryah told him.

The laughing stopped.

"What? I'll do anything."

Zakaryah reached inside his robe and pulled out a small dagger. He smiled, leaned over and placed it in Gimillu's lap, close to his groin where the cloth wrap gapped.

"You'll need to be circumcised."

CHAPTER 30

IT WAS A WHILE before anyone in the house would talk to him. Really, why were they mad? Gimillu wanted to be Yehudi. They had all sat around and listened to him talk about it, had given him that Yehudi name, but hadn't mentioned the most important thing. Someone had to tell him. He was just helping, wasn't he?

But as he would drift off to sleep at night, he imagined his father looking at him reproachfully.

Hannah was the only one who hadn't been angry. Instead, she had smiled at him. That didn't make much sense either. After Zerubavel performed the circumcision, she spent a lot of time taking care of Gimillu, feeding him, bringing him clean cloths for bandages, emptying his chamber pot while he recovered. She sat and talked with him while he was lying on his pallet, asked him to recite the creation epic Enuma Elish and the story of Gilgamesh.

Why had she gone to Gimillu for this? He knew the stories too. He and Gimillu had both learned them at the tablet-house as part of their scribal lessons. In the end, though, he had let it pass. It wouldn't do any good to confront Hannah. She would just go about her business, whatever it was at the time, paying no attention.

No, the only person who really bothered him was Danna. Whenever she had a break in her work, she would squat at the foot of Gimillu's pallet, listening to him spin these tales to Hannah. And while it was Hannah who had demanded the stories, Gimillu would rarely take his eyes off Danna whenever she was there.

As Gimillu recovered, Danna and Michal began talking to Zakaryah again. Gimillu, though, made his feelings quite clear. For a time he would even refuse to enter a room where Zakaryah was present. That was fine with Zakaryah. There weren't that many rooms in the house, though, and it was hard for the two of them to avoid each other.

The standoff ended one evening as Zakaryah and Danna were waiting on the roof for a meeting on the progress of the preparations for the journey. As the sun neared the western horizon, a cooling breeze from the river stirred their hair and robes.

The branches making up the rungs of the ladder creaked against their bindings. Michal appeared, followed by Zerubavel.

When they had settled, Zakaryah asked Zerubavel how many people would be on the journey.

"There could be several thousand," the man answered, going on to cite the hardships that many people were experiencing now as inherited farm fields were sliced into smaller parcels with each succeeding generation of sons. "The king promised support from the palace. We need to write to him and ask for it. Danna, can you tell Gimillu to join us?"

She nodded and made her way down the ladder, disappearing into a room below. After a moment, Gimillu appeared, climbing carefully, carrying a large cloth. This he folded into a cushion before sitting down on it. Danna came up behind him.

"You look like you're recovering well," Zerubavel observed.

Gimillu glared at Zakaryah. "Yes, better now."

Zerubavel said, "It had to be done, Gimillu. Of course Zakaryah did choose a very unfriendly way to tell you."

Zakaryah opened his mouth to defend himself, but Michal shook her head at him and he closed it again. *I suppose I could have been nicer about it.*

Zerubavel addressed Gimillu. "I need you to write a letter to the king requesting the funds for the journey back to Yehudah."

Gimillu stammered, "Is that a good idea? They think I'm dead. My father might see it. He'd recognize my writing. Why can't *he* do it?" He jerked his chin in Zakaryah's direction.

They all turned toward Zakaryah.

Zerubavel said to Zakaryah, "I keep forgetting that you also read and write Chaldean."

"I can write it," he said. "But a letter to the king will have to be very formal." He turned to Gimillu. "Can you help me with the formalities?"

Gimillu's mouth fell open. He snapped it shut and nodded.

See, Zakaryah thought, *I'm not a monster after all.*

Zerubavel told Zakaryah and Gimillu what he wanted the letter to say. Zakaryah wrote it in Chaldean, pressing it sign by sign into the wet clay of the letter tablet, biting his lip in concentration as he did so:

> To King Kurush, great king, mighty king, king of Anshan, king of the land of Sumer and Akkad, king of Beyond the River;
>
> Greetings. We pray to Yahweh daily for the health of the king. May the king live forever.
>
> Be it known to the king that as the king has decreed in his wisdom and beneficence, we, of the people of Yahudu whom Nabu-kuduri-utsur brought to Babylon, are preparing to journey back to Yahudu to build again the house of Yahweh as our God has commanded us.
>
> Now, if it please the king, let us have letters to the governors of the province of Beyond the River, directing them to grant us passage until we reach Yahudu. If it further please the king, let us draw on the resources of the palace as the king has decreed, and let the king provide an armed escort to protect the many treasures that the king in his generosity has directed us to return to the sanctuary of our God Yahweh.
>
> May the king convey to us his pleasure in this matter.
>
> -Zerubavel son of She'alti'el

Zakaryah added a note at the bottom, as formality required, indicating that he was the scribe and that the letter was composed on the second day of the month of Dumuzu, in the first year of Kurush.

An image of Shillemyah came to mind, smiling at Zakaryah's successes in the tablet-house, frowning when he thought his son wasn't taking his studies seriously enough. *I miss you so much, Father.*

When they finished, Zakaryah and Gimillu read the letter to Zerubavel. At the man's nod, it was fired, cooled and dispatched by courier to the palace.

The response from King Kurush came back ten days later. The funds would be provided as requested. When they were ready to depart they were to assemble the returnees on the plain north of Bab-ili during the second week of Ululu. One hundred soldiers in two companies-of-fifty would meet them there to lead and protect them on their journey back to Yehudah.

Zakaryah read the letter aloud to Zerubavel, Danna and Gimillu. "But there are some characters I don't recognize," he said with a frown. "The scribe's name." He handed the tablet to Gimillu. "Here. You try."

As Gimillu studied the characters, the color drained from his face. He raised his eyes to meet Zakaryah's. "He signed it himself. To let you know."

Zakaryah's stomach was suddenly tight. "Who? Who signed it?"

"Mushezib-nabu. My father. He's coming after you," Gimillu told him. "He wants revenge."

.

CHAPTER 31

ZAKARYAH FELT LITTLE as he said goodbye to Michal and Ginat in the courtyard of her home. Oh, he would miss them, but Al Yahudu had been for him the place where he had first been honest with himself about wanting to leave. He had also spent the most terrifying time of his life there, a time when he had been chased and captured by ruthless enemies, when he was certain from moment to moment that he and Hannah would be killed. No, he was not sorry to go.

He did feel bad for Danna. She cried when Michal hugged her. It was strange to see this girl, so tough and clever, so quick with a sharp word, sobbing like a young child as she was held against the other woman's chest. Michal cried too, until she and Danna stepped back from each other, grasped hands one last time and let them drop.

Hannah also received a long, lingering embrace from Michal. His sister seemed more pleased than upset, eliciting a look of surprise from Michal by patting her on the cheek. Was Hannah trying to comfort her? How strange.

Strangest of all, though, was Gimillu. When Michal reached out to hold him, he began trembling, first his lips, then his hands. His eyes reddened. He slumped forward. He reached toward his chest, letting his hand drop before he completed the gesture. Then he collapsed limply against her, his whole body trembling. This was the fearsome enemy of his nightmares, the boy who had destroyed his life and Hannah's, who had set them on this course now that they had no choice but to follow. This terror, this Gimillu, was crying in Michal's arms. When Michal gently separated from him, he stood slumped over until Hannah tugged on his hand. She led him shuffling blindly after her as she stepped out of the courtyard, through the door, and into the street.

"SOMEONE'S FOLLOWING US," Danna announced.

Zakaryah's breath caught. He turned quickly and looked. It was early morning, but the road was already crowded both ahead and behind. There were people on foot. There were farm carts headed to market. There were shepherds with flocks of sheep. Dogs ran alongside them, keeping them together and moving forward.

"There are so many people. Maybe you're just nervous." He hoped so, anyway. He certainly was, after Gimillu's warning.

"He's the one walking the horse, way back," Danna answered. "Why would he be leading the horse instead of riding it? He wants to keep us in sight."

Zakaryah looked again. "He's riding now."

Gimillu shattered the moment. "He needs to get a good look so he can report to my father that it's really you. See? He's coming closer." He was biting his lip and mopping his forehead. "When he sees Shulmu he'll realize I'm here too."

"Here's what we'll do. . ." Danna said.

The rider passed them a short time later, scrutinizing them surreptitiously. By all appearances, they were two brothers with their young sister. They stared down at their feet, at the small clouds of dust raised with each step.

"He'll be riding ahead now," Danna said as she hurried up from behind with Shulmu. "He'll be checking everyone he passes."

"My father won't be pleased," Gimillu told them. "He didn't recognize you?"

"I turned away as he passed so he wouldn't see my face. I don't think even that was necessary, though. He saw the dog and the herd of sheep I was with. He didn't look any closer."

AS THEY STEPPED OFF the river road, Zakaryah scanned everywhere to see if they were being watched. Nothing.

Danna's grandfather was in the palm orchard. She ran there, throwing herself into his arms, pressing her face against his chest, laughing and crying at the same time.

Abir-ilu held her tightly and peered over her head at the others. His face contrasted strongly with the darkness of her cheek. "Zakaryah, Hannah," he nodded, unable to extricate himself to do more. He regarded Gimillu, his brows creasing. "But who's this?"

"Oh," Danna said without looking. "That's just Gimillu. The dog is Shulmu. He's very nice."

She must mean the dog. But Zakaryah caught himself. Gimillu wasn't the enemy anymore. If he just told himself enough times maybe he would remember.

Abir-ilu carefully untangled himself to hold his granddaughter at arm's length. "I should be surprised," he said, peering at Gimillu, "but somehow with you I'm not. You know, he doesn't look nearly as dead as he's supposed to be." He shook his head. "I can't wait to hear the story. In the meantime, Gimillu, welcome."

During the evening meal Danna explained how Gimillu had turned against his family. Now it would be unsafe for him to stay in the land of Sumer and Akkad. "And his father is hunting for us," she said, relating the incident on the road.

"But how did you hear I was dead?" It was the first time Gimillu had spoken since they arrived on the farm.

"Our relatives in Bab-ili told me that your father put on a big ceremony."

"Big?" Gimillu held his breath, his eyes wide, leaning forward.

"Yes. He invited high-level people from the court and the temples. It enhanced his position at the palace. So they told me."

Gimillu's face collapsed. "Oh."

"So what now?" Abir-ilu asked them.

Zakaryah and Hannah would be journeying on to Yehudah,

Danna explained, and Gimillu would be going with them.

"What about you?" Gimillu blurted.

Danna lowered her eyes.

"I have to leave you," she whispered to Abir-ilu. "I'm going to Mitzrayim to find my father."

ZAKARYAH LOOKED OUT over the plain from the top of a small hillock near where Zerubavel had pitched his tent. Four thousand people, maybe five! He shivered. Any of them could be an assassin for Mushezib-nabu.

Zerubavel had told him they would be safe with his household. "King Kurush knows I'm leading the return. Nobody will dare interfere."

But Zakaryah felt no such confidence.

And now a rider was threading an erratic path through the campsites, coming closer with the horse's every step. The spy from the road! It had to be. A sword glinted at his side.

Zakaryah ran to Zerubavel's tent. "A rider," he gasped. "Armed. Coming this way."

"Quick. Get the others and hide in my wife's partition," Zerubavel ordered. "She's out with the boys. You'll hear everything. If he's dangerous you can slip under the tent's edge and escape."

By the time Zerubavel had stepped out of the tent to greet the rider, Zakaryah, Danna, Gimillu, and Hannah were safely hidden behind the curtain that screened off the other room. They hadn't been able to find Shulmu. The dog was out somewhere exploring all the exciting new smells of the camp.

"I'm looking for a Zerubavel," a man's voice announced in accented Akkadu.

"That's me."

"I'm Manu, commander over the two companies-of-fifty that the king has provided for your protection. We need to discuss the organization of the march so that I can position my soldiers."

Beside Zakaryah, Gimillu stiffened.

"Excellent. Come into my tent and I'll tell you what we've planned."

The two men worked out their plans. When they were done, Zerubavel raised his voice. "Come out now."

Zakaryah pushed the curtain aside enough to slip around it. He was followed by Hannah and Danna.

The commander raised an eyebrow.

"My apologies," Zerubavel said. "Orphans attached to my household. There have been—incidents—that have given me concern for their safety. When you approached I told them to hide until we could judge whether there was any danger." He introduced them. "But we seem to be missing one. Hannah?"

She nodded and ducked behind the curtain, dragging Gimillu back like an obstinate donkey.

"The shy one is Gemalyahu. Gamal-yama in Akkadu. Also an orphan."

"Strange. He looks surprisingly like a youngster I captured during the siege. The son of a high official. Dead, though, some months back. Torn to pieces by wild animals, they say. Very sad." Another long look at Gimillu, a small smile shaping his lips. He swung onto his horse, turned its head, and rode away.

THE NEXT MORNING, the group moved out. Zerubavel placed his household in the middle of the pack. He said he wanted to be able to move up and down the line to deal with problems and keep the peoples' spirits up when they flagged.

The marchers, bunched up now on the assembly ground, would soon stretch along the road. Donkey carts would accompany them, spread out along the line of march to provide provisions at the end of each day, and respite for those too tired or sick to walk. Each household would bring along its sheep and goats, and there would be others given by the king for sacrifices when they reached their final destination.

Zakaryah walked with Hannah beside him, Danna and Gimillu a few steps behind, Shulmu dashing around sniffing everything.

Where the plain met the river road, Zakaryah turned for a last glimpse of the city and the land.

To the south he could see the famous gate of the goddess Ishtar, reaching above the city wall in which it was set. The gate was a stunning blue in the afternoon sun, even from this far away. A huge building sat to the right in front of the gate. The king's northern palace, Gimillu had told him. Was the king there now, looking out at them as they left? In the city itself the tops of several temples stood out. They were all dwarfed by the towering ziqqurat of the god Marduk. In its shadow he imagined he could see his field, his farmhouse, his grandmother's house. Had they ever really been his?

This land was an immense trap, one that had been tightening around him and Hannah since the death of their father, maybe since his own birth. Now they were left with a single way out, if that's what it was.

He was a stranger in a strange land, leaving now for another strange land, one he had never seen. And what about all the people who were staying behind, Danna's cousin Immeru, Ovadyah, Ginat, Michal, and the thousands and thousands of others? What would become of them?

How can we sing Yahweh's song on alien soil? That was how his grandmother had put it in her poem, the one that Hannah had sung in front of the crowd that day.

He turned for one last look. There should have been a figure, tiny with distance, watching, satisfied, as he and his sister marched unawares into the final snare of a vastly larger trap.

The plain was empty.

He took Hannah's hand in his. She squeezed it and they stepped out together onto the long road to Yerushalayim. Trap or no, his heart was lighter than it had been at any time since the burial. *Grandmother, Father, I wish you could see us now.*

PART IV

Late Fall, Year 1 of King Kurush

The Lord is the builder of Jerusalem;
    He gathers in the dispersed of Israel.
He is the healer of the broken-hearted,
    The one who binds up their sorrows.
The Lord heartens the lowly,
He casts the wicked down to the earth.

PSALM 147:2-3; 6

CHAPTER 32

THE LAND IN FRONT OF GIMILLU fell away in steep wadis and rocky hills toward the lake, the faded blue waters of which were just visible in the distance.

Before this journey, he had never seen a landscape like this, of jumbled stones, towering hills and deep, jagged crevasses.

He sat on a low boulder to watch the sun as it set beyond the lake, absently scratching Shulmu behind the ears.

Before long even the lake would disappear in the gathering darkness. The remaining light came from glowing red clouds that layered the far horizon, lit from below by the last gleaming of the sun.

Now, with day slipping inexorably into night, every rock, every leaf, every hill seemed etched from crystal. If not for the hills blocking his view, Gimillu would see to the farthest ends of the earth. He was sure of it.

And it was green, even now before the winter had properly

begun. Where the lands of Sumer and Akkad were dominated by desiccated browns and tans, the hillsides here were luminous with the green of new growth. At least during the day. Now they were darkening into invisibility.

Three endless months. That was how long he had been walking to get here, and there were still at least two weeks of walking ahead. How many times along the way had he gone over the events that had forced him onto this journey? At least the other four or five thousand people on the march had reasons for coming, for leaving behind everything they knew. Not him. For him, it was just a series of mistakes, one after the other, that had left him with no alternatives.

At least there had been no signs of pursuit and no attacks against Zakaryah and Hannah. That was something.

Shulmu closed his eyes and rolled onto his back, a clear demand to have his belly scratched.

Gimillu groaned and stood up. Behind him the wide plain was dotted with cooking fires as people boiled the allotments of grain obtained earlier from the wagons spaced out along the line of march.

With Shulmu at his heels, Gimillu wound his way between the cooking fires to Zerubavel's camp, located now at the head of the line of march.

Just in time, too. The others were preparing to eat.

"There's a big lake in the distance," he announced. "I saw it before the sun set."

"That would have to be Kinneret," Zakaryah told him. He pulled out Ya'el's scroll and began looking through it. Again.

Gimillu ignored him.

After the evening meal, Zerubavel made his way over to where the four of them were laying out their sleeping rolls. "Manu tells me that a courier came to him from the governor of Shomron. A delegation will be meeting us the day after tomorrow as we approach Beit She'an.

Manu. Gimillu shivered.

THE LINE OF MARCHERS stretched out of sight behind Gimillu. Ahead of him, Zerubavel rode side by side with the commander Manu. Gimillu had done his best to remain inconspicuous when the soldier was around, but after that first encounter back at the assembly ground, the man had said nothing further that Gimillu had heard of.

The road they were on descended from the high plateau of the camp, first through a steep canyon, then through broad green valleys, and finally in a succession of sharp switchbacks that dropped rapidly down to run along a small river.

As they descended, the air grew hotter and damper. Gimillu's robe and loincloth were heavy with sweat. Shulmu trotted at his heels, tongue out, panting rapidly. Fortunately, water was plentiful here. He opened the water skin he was carrying and poured some water over the dog's head to cool him.

Next to him, Danna wiped her forehead with the sleeve of her robe, then did it again. He wondered if he smelled as bad as she did.

"What are you staring at?"

He didn't bother answering her. Her temper had grown shorter as the journey had grown longer. Better to say nothing, he had learned, than to try to explain himself.

Two nights later they camped in a valley wide enough to accommodate the entire group of over four thousand returnees. The valley stretched west to a range of high hills. To the north, and well behind them now, lay Kinneret, the large lake that Gimillu had seen in the distance before they started their descent.

Zerubavel had his household, including his wife, his sons, Gimillu, and the others, set up camp on the east side of the river Yarden. "We'll wait here for the delegation from the governor. Manu says they'll come tomorrow around daybreak."

Gimillu walked over to a break in the band of vegetation along the river to stare at the slowly flowing water. This was the Yarden? This was the mighty river that Danna's Yahweh had split for Yehoshua so his army could capture Yericho? It was barely thirty-five paces from side to side. From the lessons she had been giving him along the way, it should have been as deep and wide as the great sea in the west.

As the sun descended behind the high hills just beyond the river, mosquitos rose whining out of the nearby vegetation. Between the heat, the dampness and the insects there would be precious little sleep tonight. He couldn't do anything about the heat and the dampness, but the mosquitos? He squatted down and scooped some smelly dark mud from the riverbank. He smeared it on his face, his hands and the lower parts of his legs where the robe left them exposed. There! He raised his arms and studied the backs of his hands. Dark, just like Danna's. He couldn't see his own face, of course, but that would be dark too. She'd think he was making fun of her. Something else for her to complain about.

As he stood up he spied movement in the distance across the river. A man on horseback had emerged from a bend that rounded the spur of a wadi. The governor's delegation? But where were the others? No matter, who else could it be? He would inform Zerubavel.

As he turned to leave, the man rode up almost to the far bank of the river. It was hard to make out details in the darkening air, but there was something about the man, something about the way he sat the horse. The man stared across at him but didn't call out and made no move to cross.

And then he had it. His knees started shaking. Sweat broke out on his forehead. He backed away from the riverbank, spun on his heels, stumbled once, and ran.

Kudurru.

THE FOUR OF THEM were cross-legged on the ground, sitting in a tight circle. Shulmu lay in the center, within easy reach of hands that could scratch and stroke him.

"Did he recognize you?" Danna's voice was pitched low.

"I don't know. I don't think so. I had already covered myself with mud. He probably thinks I'm a Kushite."

"Maybe he mistook you for me."

"I'm not a girl!"

She smirked at him.

"Anyway, he thinks you're dead," Zakaryah said. He looked down at the dog. "But he'll change his mind if he sees Shulmu."

The dog raised his head and looked at Zakaryah. When no more scratches were forthcoming, he sighed and laid his head down again.

Hannah stood, went to Gimillu's carrying sack, and extracted his eating bowl. She held it out to him.

"What?" he demanded. "What's this for?"

She pushed it into his hand and curled his thumb around the rim. "Go get mud."

"She's right," Danna told him. "Your mud will rub off overnight. Go get more while it's dark. Zakaryah can take a double portion of food in the morning. You can share that."

"Why me?" Zakaryah asked. "It's your idea."

"Hannah's, actually. But I certainly don't want his muddy fingers in *my* food."

IN THE MORNING, the delegation from the governor was on horseback on the far side of the river. There were ten men. No, eleven. Gimillu made out one who was keeping well back from the others. He couldn't discern the man's features, but there was no doubt in his mind that it was his brother.

Gimillu began slipping farther back, Shulmu at his heel. Before he could move very far, though, there was a splashing sound from the river. The horsemen were crossing to this side! What about Kudurru? But his brother had stayed put while the others forded the stream.

He let his breath out and remained where he was, close enough to see what would happen next, but not close enough to hear.

Zerubavel and Manu rode to meet the others as their horses emerged on the riverbank. They conferred with the man leading the group. Zerubavel reached into a pouch at the side of his horse and withdrew a clay tablet and a scroll. He presented these to the other, who scrutinized them carefully, then nodded and handed them back.

The leader then took out a document of his own and passed it to Manu. Manu read it and leaned close to say something to Zerubavel. Both of them turned around to look behind. Gimillu craned his neck to see, but his view was blocked by the people around him.

The leader gestured to his men. Two of them swept past Zerubavel and dismounted. Zerubavel jumped from his horse to go after them, but Manu, still mounted, restrained him with a grip on his shoulder.

There was a flurry of activity and muted shouting, then the men remounted, turned their horses and splashed swiftly back across the river. One rider held Zakaryah pinned in front, the other Hannah.

When they reached the far bank, Kudurru wheeled his horse and the three of them galloped off. As they disappeared around a bend, Gimillu sat down hard, burying his head in his hands. Shulmu licked him under the chin.

It was his imagination, it had to be, at this distance. Some part of him was sure, though. As the horsemen vanished from view, Zakaryah had turned to glare at him, face dark with accusation.

CHAPTER 33

ZERUBAVEL SPOKE to Gimillu and Danna.

"They've taken them to the governor's palace at Shomron. There was an order from the king's counselor for their arrest."

"My father," Gimillu said. He petted Shulmu without looking.

Zerubavel nodded. He fixed his gaze on Gimillu. "You should have told me when you recognized your brother."

Gimillu dropped his eyes, not able to meet those of the leader of the Yahudus. *Yehudim*, he corrected himself.

"It wasn't Gimillu's fault. We all knew," Danna told him. "We thought he had come to scare people into turning back. The most important thing was to prevent his brother finding out that Gimillu is still alive."

"And now you want to go after them, I assume."

"We can't just let them be dragged into slavery," Danna said.

"It's my fault. I did this." Gimillu's voice dropped to a

whisper. "I'll trade myself for them."

Danna placed a hand on his arm.

"And what makes you think that would even work?" Zerubavel demanded. "All three of you could end up as slaves." He stared at Danna. "All four of you. Slaves. Or worse." He fell silent.

After a long moment he shook himself and looked at Gimillu. "How much power does your father have? I don't understand how palace politics work with this new king."

He went to the entrance to the tent and stuck his head outside. Gimillu couldn't make out what he said. There was the sound of running feet as he pulled back in.

Not long after, the tent flap was pushed open. A man stepped through, looked around.

Manu.

Gimillu shrank back as far as he could, but in the tent there was no place to hide.

"We have a problem," Zerubavel told him. "Please sit." He indicated a vacant mat next to him on the floor of the tent.

The man raised his eyebrows and took his place as offered. "This is about the two who were arrested?"

Zerubavel nodded. "You've met Danna, I believe. Also her friend Gemalyahu?"

Manu addressed Gimillu directly. "You know that if I had wanted to denounce you to your father I would have done it by now."

Gimillu nodded slowly, and slowly relaxed.

"Someday I hope I can introduce you to my own son," the

man said. To Zerubavel: "In the meantime, what do you need from me?"

"I don't understand the workings of this new king's court. We have a counselor to the old king, now in high position with the new king, who has ordered the arrest of two members of my household. Is this the will of the king?"

"The man who presented the arrest order—his name was Shtar-boznai. He told me the new governor, a certain Tattnai, recently arrived to take up his post in Shomron. The arrest order was issued by Mushezib-nabu. But you're here as the leader of this group, under the king's decree, as are all the members of your household. It's reasonable to put the matter of the arrest before this Tattnai."

Gimillu shuddered. All this talking wasn't getting them anywhere. Hannah would surely be sold as a slave, and Zakaryah—who knew?

"I'm going to Shomron," he declared, levering himself off the mat. Shulmu scrambled to his feet, eyes on Gimillu.

Danna remained seated. "Where's Shomron?" she asked him, reaching out to pull the dog down beside her.

He pointed down the road that the party with Zakaryah and Hannah had taken.

"Is that the only road?" she asked. "How far is it? How many days will it take? How much food will you need? What will you do when you get there? What will Kudurru do when he realizes you're still alive?"

He sank back down on the mat, chagrined. "But I have to do something. I can't just sit here!"

Zerubavel said, "I agree with Gimillu. Gemalyahu. We need to get to Shomron quickly. Our route goes by there, but with these thousands of people it will take four days, maybe more."

"You and I can't leave the march," Manu said to Zerubavel, "but I can send a fast horseman ahead with a message that the new governor should hold back from taking action until the complexities of the case can be put before him. These two," he glanced at Danna and Gimillu, "need to stay with the main body. That will give them some cover."

He stood. "I have my duties." He left.

"As do I," Zerubavel said. He too left.

Gimillu's breath left in a rush. Four days! Four days of waiting, of walking along as if nothing was wrong. In four days anything could happen.

Danna squeezed his hand.

He didn't notice.

CHAPTER 34

"HE DIDN'T DO THIS."

Zakaryah didn't look at his sister. He knew where she was, just two arm's lengths away in the small cell where they had been put after two days of brutal jolting on horseback.

"I know," he answered, "but everything that's happened, all of this, has been because of Gimillu."

"It's your fault too."

He glowered at her. Was it Zakaryah's fault that Gimillu's father had sent that Kudurru ahead with an order to arrest them on the excuse of the missed taxes? Was it his fault that powerful people had conspired to make paying his taxes impossible? Was it his fault that King Koresh had decreed that the people were to be returned to Yehudah? No, it wasn't. None of it was. But his father's words echoed in his memory. *How do you think the other boy felt when he saw the snake?* How could that ever compare to the terrible things Gimillu had done?

Zakaryah sighed. It was past time to let go of his resentment. Gimillu was as much a victim as he and Hannah were.

He shifted his weight on the stone bench that jutted out from the blocks of the cell wall. It was no use. No position was comfortable, not with the bruises the horse's back had left on his tailbone. And then there were the oozing scrapes where his robe had rubbed the skin raw inside his thighs.

He pulled the robe tighter. How could it have been so hot in the river valley and so cold here on the mountain? In Bavel, if it was hot in one place it was hot every place.

Of course, the cold stones of the cell didn't help.

He looked at the stones more closely. They were irregular in shape, as if they had simply been gathered from the rocky hillsides and stacked on top of each other. In the gaps between the larger stones, smaller ones had been cunningly inserted, giving the wall a fairly even appearance overall. He tried pulling out one of the small rocks. It was wedged in tight, held in place by the weight of the stones around it. He remembered the strange daytime dream he had had after the escape from Bavel, where stones had floated into the air to settle into the perfect shape of a building. What would it take to construct a building like that out of stones like these?

He glanced again at Hannah. She was hugging herself to keep warm. Apart from that, she looked as serene as ever.

"Aren't you scared?"

Instead of answering, she said, "Read me the part about Halabu."

What? Oh, the scroll. Strange that she was thinking about

that now. But strange was the right word for Hannah. Sometimes, when she acted like a normal child of six, he forgot just how strange she really was. Not that it changed anything. She was his sister. It was his job to protect her. He hung his head. He hadn't been doing a very good job of that lately, had he? But what harm would it do to humor her? Perhaps it would distract him for a time from this dread that was chewing away at his insides.

He slid the scroll from its pocket inside his robe and unrolled it about halfway. Now where was the passage she meant?

He found it about a third of the way from the end. He placed his finger on the spot where Ya'el's account began. Hannah shook her head and plucked a slender twig from her robe. It must have stuck there when the horses brushed against some bush or other on the ride to this place. He took the twig and used it as he read aloud to track his grandmother's uneven scrawl.

The captives had been camped outside of Halabu when Ya'el decided to escape. She had fooled the guards, slipped outside the camp and entered the city, following a young soldier. Abir-ilu, Danna's grandfather. She got lost in the foreign city, panicked, and realized she had to return to camp. He had panicked that same way in Bab-ili. But she managed to find her way back to Abir-ilu. She was so clever! She persuaded him to arrest her so that they both could escape punishment when they returned.

Her terror and her desperation came through so clearly in her writing. But she hadn't given up then; in fact, had never given up. And here he was, and here Hannah was.

Ya'el hadn't given in to her fear. He wouldn't give in to his.

ON THEIR THIRD DAY in the small room, Hannah said, "Are you going to ask Abir-ilu?"

"What?" Her question had come out of nowhere, after one of the long silences that dominated their imprisonment. He had given up talking to her, lost in his nail-biting, and when the nails started bleeding, in the knotting of his gut. And the boredom! How could he be strangled with anxiety and bored at the same time?

His only relief from the boredom had been when the guard would come to bring their food and take away the chamber pot. From the twisting in his intestines, there was no relief.

"Well," she demanded when he didn't respond. "Are you?"

"What are you talking about? Ask him what? We're imprisoned here and he's back in Bavel, in case you haven't noticed."

"Oh, they'll let us out today. And then you can write to him. Will you?"

He drew in a deep breath, let it out slowly. There was no point getting upset with her. She lived in a world of her own imagination. Wasn't that a little like madness? He studied her carefully for the first time in days. Small. But then she was six. Straight black hair, well tangled now that she didn't have her comb. She was relaxed in the corner, wrapped in the blanket they had been given when he complained to the guard. She looked at him calmly, her silver-grey eyes as startling as ever, brows creased slightly as she waited for him to answer her incomprehensible question.

Maddening, maybe, but not mad.

But why couldn't she just explain herself? It would make things so much easier.

He took another deep breath. He would humor her. It was the only thing that ever worked. "What am I supposed to be asking Abir-ilu?"

"About marrying Danna, of course." Her tone clearly said, *are you really that dense?*

He froze, a strange prickling starting in his groin and spreading up his chest and neck. She *was* mad, after all. It was ridiculous. Danna didn't like him. She was heading to Mitzrayim to look for her father. He'd never see her again. She liked Gimillu. She was too young. So was he.

Hannah was looking at him, waiting for him to say something. He stammered, "That's . . that's—"

Before he could get out the word *crazy*, there was a grating sound as the bar was withdrawn from the cell door. A guard stuck his head into the gloom, wrinkled his nose and beckoned to them. "Come," he ordered them. "The governor wants to see you."

Hannah hopped off the stone bench, grabbed Zakaryah's sleeve, and pulled him out into fresh air and sunlight.

GOVERNOR TATTNAI was a slim man. That much was clear in the dim light of the small audience hall. He was seated, though, and Zakaryah couldn't see how tall he was. His beard was full and dark, suggesting that he was still fairly young.

"I understand there's a petitioner here to discuss these prisoners?"

The guard who brought them nodded. "Two, my lord." He stepped into a small adjoining room.

The first man through the door was Kudurru.

The tension hit Zakaryah like a battering ram. It was all he could do to stay on his feet. This was the man who was responsible for his arrest, his and Hannah's, and that was only the latest of the terrors he had inflicted on them. Zakaryah glanced at his sister, trying to contain his fear for her sake. She was silent, showing no emotion as she measured this Kudurru, the person behind their current misery and captivity. The man scowled at her. She looked at him without expression, then turned her face toward the governor, eyes down, as appropriate.

The second man was Zerubavel. Zakaryah felt the tension drain from his body like water draining from the wadis after a desert storm. He started to offer a greeting but stopped at the warning in the man's eyes.

"I'll hear first from the complainant."

Kudurru stepped forward and bowed. "My lord, I was sent here—"

"Your station and name."

"My pardon, my lord. Kudurru, apprentice scribe at court, son of Mushezib-nabu, High Counselor to Kurush, great king, mighty king, king of Sumer and Akkad, king of Beyond the River."

The governor rolled his eyes and Kudurru rushed on. "I was sent here by my father, the High Counselor Mushezib-nabu—"

"Yes. You mentioned that he's the high counselor. The same that betrayed the former king, if I remember?"

"No, my lord, that was my younger brother. Such a shock to my poor father." The sweat was beading on Kudurru's forehead.

"And yet your father acceded to his current high position."

"The king's mercy is legendary, as is his skill at recognizing talent." Kudurru opened the top of his robe, though the room was cool.

"So you were sent here by your father. With what objective?"

"To present a warrant for the arrest of these two, my lord, for failure to pay taxes rightfully due the king."

"A rather long distance to travel for a tax evader, isn't it?" The governor pointed at Hannah. "You, girl, how old are you?"

"Six, my lord," Hannah answered, bowing deeply and keeping her eyes lowered.

"Did you refuse to pay the king's taxes?"

"No, my lord."

Blushing and visibly flustered, Kudurru interjected, "The boy, my lord, the boy, he refused. The sister is not accused."

"And yet your warrant names her as well. Enough of this, though." He turned to Zerubavel. "You're here to present a counter-petition?"

"Yes, my lord governor. I am Zerubavel ben She'alti'el, appointed by King Kurush to bring the people of Yehudah back to the land to rebuild the House of Yahweh."

"And your relationship to these two children?"

"They are orphans, my lord, attached to my household."

"And your petition?"

"To be allowed to take them back into my household."

"Do you deny the validity of the warrant?"

"I have no basis for either affirming or denying its validity. I can say only that I have been commanded by the king himself to bring my people, including these two, to Yerushalayim to rebuild the house of Yahweh and offer sacrifices to Him there for the well-being of the king and the success of his endeavors. And I will say further that it was this young girl"—he bent his head in Hannah's direction—"who acquainted the king with Yahweh's will in this matter."

"My lord," Kudurru burst out. "She's dangerous. So is the boy. He put her up to it."

The governor glanced at Hannah, then back at Kudurru. "Dangerous," he murmured.

Kudurru's ears turned bright red.

The governor looked back at Hannah. "What did you say to the king..."

Zerubavel supplied her name. "Hannah bat Shillemyah, my lord governor."

"What did you say to the king, Hannah bat Shillemyah?"

"Nothing, my lord. Yahweh told the king, 'Before I put you in your mother's belly, I knew you. See, I am opening before you all the gates of the nations. None may stand before you. The time I appointed for the exile of my people is fulfilled. I charge you now to let them go up to Yehudah that they may rebuild my house in Yerushalayim. I am Yahweh.'" There was a resonance in her voice that Zakaryah had never before heard, a richness that seemed to seep into the very stones of the room. She raised her eyes to meet those of the governor and he recoiled in his chair.

Zakaryah shivered as the echo of her words died away.

Outside the audience hall sparrows chirped as they flitted to and from the nests they had built in the chinks of the walls. Crickets were starting their rhythmic evening songs. In the distance, hoopoe birds called *hwoo-hwoo-hwoo*.

Inside, the silence was profound. It was broken finally when the governor said, his voice small, "I will write to the king and ask his will in this matter." More forcefully: "In the meantime, the orphans will return to the household of Zerubavel ben She'alti'el. You"—and here he looked directly at Kudurru—"will make no further attempt to arrest these two and will not hinder or harass them, pending the response of King Kurush."

He grabbed for a cloth and blotted the sweat from his forehead.

CHAPTER 35

"I KNOW YOU BLAME ME," Gimillu said, trembling a little. "I saw you turn and stare as they were riding off with you."

They were walking near the front of the long line, following close behind Zerubavel. Every step brought Yerushalayim that little bit closer and left Bavel that little bit farther back.

"You couldn't have seen that," Zakaryah told him. "We were too far away."

"But you blamed me." *And I blamed myself.*

"Yes." He took in the glares he was getting from both Danna and Hannah and quickly added, "But I know it wasn't your fault. It was your brother."

"He's trying to win our father's respect. And . . . and . . ." Why was this so hard to say? "And his love."

"Like you," Hannah said.

Her words hit him hard and he sat down on the nearest

rock. Why hadn't he seen that before? It was so clear. All those terrible things he had done. He was no better than Kudurru.

Danna squatted in front of him and grasped his face in both of her hands so he was forced to look her in the eyes. "Don't pay any attention to Hannah. You aren't like him."

"She didn't mean it that way." His spirit lightened as he realized that was true.

The four of them formed a small stationary island, with the rest of the returnees streaming past them.

"Come on," Zakaryah said. "We're falling behind. Let's get moving." He extended his hand. Gimillu hesitated, then grasped it and let Zakaryah pull him up.

They began walking again. He looked around for Shulmu. The dog was well back in the pack, sniffing around a donkey cart. One of the wagons with meat, probably. He clapped his hands as loudly as he could, still not quite trusting his voice. It must have been loud enough because Shulmu came racing back to take his accustomed place at Gimillu's heel. Or was it at Danna's? Hannah's? Zakaryah's? It was hard to say anymore.

Gimillu asked the question then that had been on his mind as soon as Zakaryah and Hannah had rejoined them. "What about Kudurru?"

"He looked furious," Zakaryah told him. "He couldn't show it, though, not to the governor. When we left the audience hall, he stomped away without looking at us. But I was glad he wasn't carrying a sword."

"He won't give up. He would have to go back and tell our father that he failed. Again."

The road they were on cut west around the base of the hill of Shomron before turning south into a narrow valley between two hills. The air was clean, light with the spiciness of wild herbs, at least here at the head of the line where the dust of the marchers was not as thick. Gimillu still marveled at the wadis that cut through these hills, at the green fur they seemed to wear now that the season had turned cooler, and especially at the stone terraces that turned every hillside into stairways for giants. On these terraces he could see trees—almonds and olives—that simply didn't grow in the land of Sumer and Akkad. Grape vines were everywhere, some sprawling over terrace walls, some trailing up and over wooden or stone structures. Some of the terraces seemed to be used for pasturage, because he saw sheep and goats scattered through the higher reaches.

The train of marchers stretched back from here to beyond Shomron. In the time it took the line to pass this spot, Gimillu figured that the sun would have soared four or five handbreadths across the sky—a significant portion of the day at this season.

The road turned sharply west around another hill, then around a jutting spur. A tall round hill blocked the way south. His eyes followed the slope of the hill all the way to the top. Something seemed out of place, though it was hard to tell for sure because of the distance. A horseman, that had to be it, silhouetted broadside against the sky. The horse wheeled around so that the rider was facing them. One of the governor's men, checking on their progress?

But somehow he knew that wasn't it.

Six days later, as the head of the line passed the city of Mitzpah, just half a day's march from Yerushalayim, a stone flew from behind a wall and hit Hannah. She fell to the ground.

As Gimillu crouched to scoop her into his arms, the sky rained rocks.

"IS SHE ALL RIGHT?"

Gimillu had never before heard the note of concern that he heard now in Zerubavel's voice.

"I think so. It hit her on the side of the head."

Zakaryah was sitting, holding Hannah in his lap, cradling her in his arms. He hugged her tight for a moment, his eyes filling with moisture.

Gimillu squatted next to them, holding one of her hands. "Most of them got away, but Manu's men caught one, a youth of about sixteen years. 'We won't let you take our land,' he said over and over."

"I wonder who could have given them that idea."

Ah! The old cynical Danna. Gimillu realized that he had missed that side of her on this long trek.

He asked Zerubavel, "How many were injured?"

"Thirty or so with bruises. Two with head wounds like Hannah's. One with a broken arm when he fell running away from the stones."

"What will happen to the one they caught?"

"I'm not sure. He'll be brought before Governor Tattnai. He could be executed, I suppose."

Gimillu shifted his position so that he was kneeling next to Hannah rather than squatting. "Manu should let him go. He just listened to my brother. If stupidity was a crime, I'd have been executed a long time ago."

Hannah's hand tightened on his.

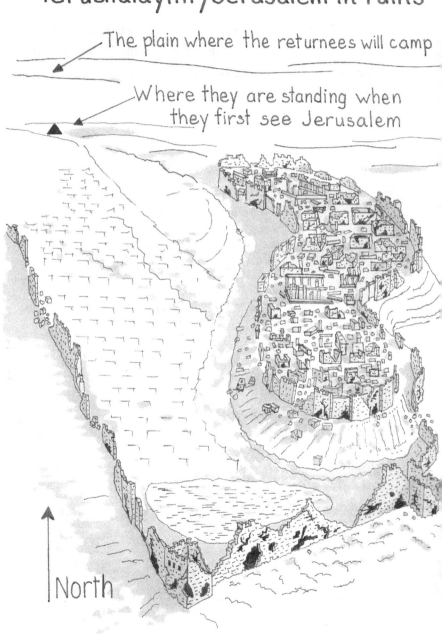

Yerushalayim / Jerusalem in ruins

The plain where the returnees will camp

Where they are standing when they first see Jerusalem

North

CHAPTER 36

ZAKARYAH STOOD shoulder to shoulder with Gimillu and Danna. Hannah was pressed close to his side, unable to see much over the heads of the others. Shulmu leaned panting against Gimillu's legs.

Four thousand people crowded behind them, silent except for muffled sobbing and the shuffling of feet.

In front of them were the walls of Yerushalayim.

Rather, what had been the walls.

Ten paces from him, a lizard twice the length of his hand lounged on a pile of tumbled stones, warming itself in the thin sun of early winter. From somewhere inside the city he could hear the mournful cry of a jackal, faint with distance. The only other sound was that of the afternoon wind as it moaned through the emptiness of the dead city.

He began to sway. He pressed his hand to his chest as pressure grew there, until he realized he wasn't breathing. A sob rose in his throat and he looked for a place to sit. Danna slipped to his side, supporting him with her shoulder. She steered him to a large stone and he sank onto it, burying his face in his hands.

After more than three months of a grueling march, months of high anticipation in which he had slept out of doors, carried much of his food and personal belongings, helped dig pits every evening and fill them in every morning, he was here at the sacred city, looking on a field of rubble forty paces across.

The rubble of the wall stretched right and left, higher than a man's head, meandering along the edge of Yerushalayim, becoming in the distance a blurred parody of a wall.

What had he expected? He had known the city was destroyed, that everyone who lived here had either died in the siege, been killed by the soldiers or been carried off to Bavel. What had he thought would be left?

They were near what had been the northern gate, now just a low spot in the rubble. The massive wooden doors that had kept Nevuchadnetsar's army outside for eighteen disastrous months were visible, charred and slowly rotting beneath the stones. Any army could simply walk over them, had there been anything within worth conquering.

Verses from a poem came to him. Ya'el had read it to him a long time ago.

My eyes are spent with tears,
My heart is in tumult,
My liver is poured out upon the ground,
Over the ruin of my poor people.

Was this how his grandmother felt when she was captured? He had never understood, not until now.

He raised his head and looked around, blinking to clear the dampness from his eyes. Where was Hannah? Oh, there with Gimillu. And Danna? He spotted her through the gate—through what had been the gate—in an open area with less debris. She was sitting on a large rock, her face toward him, eyes hooded, lips pressed tight together.

He pushed himself up from the rock and walked through the gate area, stepping carefully to avoid tripping. He glanced behind. Gimillu and Hannah were trailing after him, Shulmu following along. He walked over to Danna. She moved aside, making room for him. He sat and rested his head on her shoulder.

Hannah drifted over. "This was it," she whispered to them.

"This was what?"

"The place."

She addressed Danna. "Your grandfather. He captured her and brought her here. Ya'el. She sat on this stone. She cried."

ZAKARYAH CAME BACK ALONE after the evening meal, while there was still some light.

The terrible shock had faded, replaced by resignation. This was where he would have to make his home. He couldn't go back to Bavel. It would be hard, but he would manage somehow. He would rebuild one of these houses. Among the four thousand returnees there had to be a man who would agree to a bride match for his daughter. Of course, that wouldn't be for several years.

In his mind he saw an image of Danna sitting on the stone earlier in the day, her brows drawn together with concern for him. Then he grimaced. Hannah! She had put that thought into his head. It made no more sense today than it had back in the cell in Shomron. Still, it was too bad Danna would be leaving for Mitzrayim. He had become used to her, something he couldn't have imagined even a few months ago.

He walked over to the stone she'd been sitting on, ran his hand over its rough surface. He had re-read the beginning of Ya'el's scroll as he was waiting for the girls to finish preparing the meal. It took some imagination, but this did look like the market square she described, where she had been brought to await the start of the long march to Bavel. But this specific stone? He supposed Ya'el could have sat on it. Then again, she could just as well have sat on any of twenty or thirty others. But Hannah was probably right.

Hannah. He shook his head and sighed. In Shomron, Hannah had said the two of them would be freed from the cell and they were. And that first trip to Al Yahudu. He didn't want her to come, but she had said he would need her, and he had. She spoke to the king and he believed her, believed that Yahweh was talking to him. So did Governor Tattnai. He had seen it in the man's eyes. And even Gimillu's father—this terrible man he had seen but never met. Oh, he had set Kudurru on him and Hannah both, there was no doubt. Still, he was sure somehow that it was Hannah the man was afraid of, afraid enough to risk his position and perhaps his life to subvert the king's orders.

Zakaryah had laughed when he had baited Danna, when he had suggested that Hannah might be a prophet.

It didn't seem funny now.

How many times had he discounted Hannah's pronouncements, argued with her, tried to persuade her that she was wrong? It was all a show he put on for himself. The truth was, he had long ago stopped questioning the things she said, stopped wondering how she knew them.

Then she had been hit by a rock at Mitzpah, a rock she hadn't seen coming.

And what did it mean now that she as much as told him he would marry Danna?

He shook himself out of this train of thought and looked more closely at the tumbled stones of the wall. It must have taken Nevuchadnetsar's soldiers almost as much work to tear the walls down as it had for King Hizkiyahu's men to build them a century and a half before. How else to explain the extent of the destruction? On the long march from Bavel they had passed many ruined towns and hamlets, some of which had been abandoned for hundreds of years. They hadn't looked as ruined as this, deserted a mere two generations.

He walked over to the nearest pile and knelt, running his hand over a stone. It was squared off, maybe twice the size of a mud-brick. He spotted others like it, scattered around. But most of the rocks were irregular, with no discernible shape or pattern to them. He recalled the stones of the cell in Shomron, individually much more irregular than the bricks he was familiar with, but together presenting a surface that was almost flush. What kind of cunning had these people had, to build a wall with such crude materials, a wall that was able to stand for a year and a half against the army of Bavel?

He climbed to the top of the pile, careful to test each stone before he set his weight on it. To the outside, he could see the encampment of the returnees. Cooking fires dotted the plain, dying down now after the evening meal but still visible in the gathering shadows.

In the opposite direction, he could see far down into the city.

Many of the buildings had been destroyed, but to his surprise, many of what must have been private homes seemed intact. At least, their walls were standing. Some even had roofs. The larger buildings, though, were burned-out ruins. Those would have been centers for official functions, he surmised, or the mansions of the wealthy. Most of these clustered on the narrow ridge to the south and east. There they caught the last rays of the vanishing sun in a travesty of golden beauty.

Well to the south, but within the ruin of the walls, he was able to make out a dark gleam of water. That at least was something promising to hold onto. He would mention it to Zerubavel, and perhaps tomorrow he would venture to explore it further.

He turned, clambered down the rocks, and walked back to camp.

IN THE MORNING Hannah announced that she was going to the house of Yahweh.

"It will be like this," Zakaryah told her, gesturing at the fallen stones.

"I want to see."

"We don't even know where it is."

"It's right over there," Hannah told him, looking to the east to a hill separated from them by a narrow valley.

In the direction she indicated there was rubble that didn't look much different from what was in front of them. There beyond the wall, the collapsed stones gave way to open ground. An empty knoll rose to the north. It should give a good view down into the temple area.

Danna followed his gaze. "Zakaryah." She thrust her chin toward a low hill a bit farther to the north, where eight or nine locals were watching the returnees as they readied themselves for the day.

Trust Danna to have her eyes open.

"Gimillu, can you take her there?" He pointed to the hill he had been studying. "But don't go unless you can find a soldier to go with you. Leave your bag with me. I'll pack up your things."

Gimillu nodded, took Hannah's hand, and started off. "Come, Shulmu." The dog trotted behind, his tail batting the air, as the two of them went in search of a soldier.

Danna stayed behind. "I'm surprised you let her go."

"Have you ever tried stopping her? At least this way she'll have Gimillu and a soldier, and I won't worry about her running off in the middle of the night."

Shortly after, Zakaryah spied Hannah and Gimillu crossing the small valley to the east. Gimillu was carrying a large bundle of sticks, Shulmu trotting after him. There were two men with them, one a soldier and one wearing the robe of a priest. The priest had a goat on a short rope. Hannah was in front. She was leading them up the hill toward the house of Yahweh.

ZAKARYAH'S MOUTH FELL OPEN. "A sacrifice? You sacrificed on the altar?" He stared at Hannah's hands. No blood.

When Hannah didn't respond, Gimillu cleared his throat. "The priest did the sacrifice. First though he said several blessings to cleanse the altar. In case it had been desecrated during the destruction, or afterward."

"How did she get him to follow her? Nobody listens to a six-year-old girl."

"Or to a girl of any age," Danna said.

Gimillu just shook his head. "Would you like to say something, Hannah?"

She didn't look at him or acknowledge the question.

Zakaryah and Danna exchanged a glance. Danna nodded. "I'll tell Zerubavel."

She headed for his tent.

"Anyway, there wasn't much left of the altar. There was one stone at the corner with a sort of horn sticking up from it, and several stones of the original platform. We cleared branches and weeds from around it and moved a few stones into place as best we could, just enough for the sacrifice. It will need to be rebuilt, and so will the grates to burn the offerings."

Zakaryah asked, "What happened with the locals who were watching?"

"I don't know," Gimillu answered. "They were gone by the time we reached the top of that small knoll."

"Well, at least they didn't bother you. But I'm glad the soldier was there."

Danna returned after a short time. "He just stared at me and shook his head." She answered Zakaryah before he could ask. "He's very worried, but not about this. I think we'll hear more tomorrow."

Deep in the night, Zakaryah sat up. His blanket slipped down to his waist and he began to shiver. The moon was almost in its last quarter, too low on the eastern horizon to be casting much light. What had wakened him? Then he heard it—shouts coming faintly from the far edge of the encampment. The noise soon died down, though. He sank back into the warmth of his blanket and was quickly asleep.

ZERUBAVEL GATHERED THEM in his tent in the morning and told them about it.

"They threw rocks. Several people were hit, some seriously. After Mitzpah, Manu was ready for something like this. The soldiers drove them off before more were hurt." He frowned. "But it's disturbing. I thought the people here would welcome us. We're all Yehudim."

Zakaryah unclenched his jaw with an effort. "Was it the same group as Mitzpah?" He inspected the bruise on Hannah's temple and hugged her, pulling her into his shoulder. She removed his arm and pushed it gently back to his lap.

"I doubt it." Zerubavel ran his hand through his hair, greyer now than when he had been planning the journey that had brought them here. "Who would march half a night to pelt us with rocks and then have to march back? But that makes it worse, doesn't it?"

"Kudurru's here." Gimillu said it flatly, as if he were talking about someone he didn't know. "He probably sent those people we saw on the hill yesterday. To spy on us."

"Your brother doesn't speak Yehudit. How does he talk to them?"

"Someone must have taught him. We were preparing for this trip for a long time, and then it took us over three months to get here. Plenty of time to learn."

"I think it's time you told me more about this brother of yours."

"He won't give up. He's failed too many times already. He's afraid of my father. The only person who scares him more is Nidintu. My sister."

"Your sister?"

"My *father* wouldn't actually kill him."

Gimillu continued after a moment. "He wants to drive us—all of us—to return to Bavel. Except me. He doesn't know I'm alive. But the rest of us, all four thousand or so. My father has to collect the taxes that the king needs for his military campaigns. Every person who stays here is another person whose tax payments he needs to replace. And then there's revenge, like Danna said the other day. But that's personal, both for Kudurru and for Mushezib-Nabu."

"Fine, so maybe I understand your brother a little better. And I guess there's no way he can scare us off all by himself, so it makes sense that he's trying to put the locals up to it. What doesn't make sense is why they're listening to him."

Manu pushed the tent flap aside and stepped partway in. "For that you'll need to talk to them." He dragged a man in and pushed him down to kneel just inside the tent. "Fortunately, I have one right here."

"YOU LEFT FIFTY YEARS AGO. We've been doing fine without you."

The man was in the middle twenties of his life. His beard was short and already showing signs of grey.

"He only speaks Yahudu. You'll need to translate for me."

Zerubavel repeated the conversation in Akkadu for Manu's benefit. "His name is Adoniqam. He lives in the village of Anatot, half a morning's walk from here. He says they've been doing fine without us for fifty years."

Zerubavel introduced each of them to Adoniqam. When he got to Danna, the man said, "A Kushite. What's she doing here?"

Danna became very still.

Zakaryah said, "When we left fifty years ago I guess we took good manners with us."

The man just stared at him.

Zerubavel changed the topic. "Has a man from Bavel been talking to you?"

Adoniqam shrugged. "We know why you're here. You want to move into your old houses outside the city. We're living in them. You want to come back to your old estates. They're ours now. You want to bring back the priests, those leeches. They'll suck the food out of our stomachs and the silver out of our purses. You want to take over the country again and ruin it like you did before. Nevuchadnetsar was the best thing that happened to us. He got rid of *you*."

Zerubavel translated for Manu and said, "I can understand them being worried about this, but I don't understand the hatred."

"Gimillu's brother has been busy," Manu answered. "What do you want me to do with him?"

"Get him out of here. Take him to the small valley just east of here and let him go. I'll tell him that if he comes back he'll be taken to the governor for trial."

When Manu and the prisoner had left, he said to the others, "We need to find a more secure place for everyone. Zakaryah, you said something about exploring the city today?"

Zakaryah told him about what he had seen from the top of the stones. "It was hard to be sure, but there may be enough houses for everybody. Most of them will need new roofs, but there are many with walls standing. Also, I saw a pool of water off to the south."

"Good. We'll need that."

Hannah spoke. "We can't use the water yet."

They all stared at her. "Because of the bones," she said, not looking up. "Nevuchadnetsar. He killed them. He threw the bodies in."

That night, after they were asleep in their blanket rolls, one of the returnees was stabbed to death.

CHAPTER 37

ZAKARYAH SQUATTED just outside the tent. Zerubavel's voice rose loud enough to come clearly through the thin walls. "How did they do it? You're supposed to be guarding us."

"They snuck through our line." Manu's voice was pitched low and level. "I have one hundred men to protect your four thousand. And they need to sleep. They're on three watches during the night, so about sixty-five are on guard at any time."

"Can you catch them?"

"There were six or seven, based on the tracks. I sent a patrol out. The trail was clear enough until they got up into some rocks. The men will follow as long as they can, but they don't know the area."

Zerubavel said something that Zakaryah couldn't make out.

Manu's answer came through clearly enough. "My orders were to deliver you here and return to Halabu to await the king.

I can stay for five days, six at the most."

"We weren't expecting this when we planned the trip. We brought light weapons, swords and some spears, not enough for every man. Can you leave us any?"

"I can let you have a few but I can't deplete our spares too much. How many men do you have with fighting experience?"

"We've already started checking."

"After that's done we'll go into the city together. I'll help you plan which houses to put people in and where to station your armed men for the best protection."

"Zakaryah!" Zerubavel shouted. "I know you're listening. Go get Danna and Gimillu."

Zakaryah backed away from the tent, tiptoeing softly, then spun around and ran off to find them.

"THEY'RE PLANNING something." Zerubavel shook his head.

Zakaryah shivered. Cold! And after a miserable night sleeping in the open. He had even put on the second robe he had brought with him. It helped, but it didn't do anything for his feet. He uncrossed his legs and switched to kneeling with his feet beneath his thighs. Better. Soon, though, his knees and ankles would be sore and he would need to switch back.

Danna and Gimillu were on one side of him, Hannah on the other. Zerubavel hadn't told Zakaryah to bring her, but she was there anyway. No surprise. She was holding Shulmu in her lap, petting him and scratching behind his ears.

There were another ten people seated on the tent floor. They kept shifting their attention from Zerubavel to Hannah, no doubt imagining, as Zakaryah was, how much warmer they would feel with the dog in their own laps.

"Manu's soldiers found footprints just outside the encampment this morning. We need to get everyone and their animals into the city today. We have just over nine hundred households. You need to find houses for them."

"That's a lot of houses."

Who had said that? Oh, a man on the other side of the tent. Zakaryah didn't know his name.

"Yes. Each of you will pick four or five others to go with you. Families will need to share houses for a while, along with their livestock." He shot a glance at Shulmu, sprawled in Hannah's lap. "At least the animals can help to keep everyone warm. We'll organize groups out here so we can quickly get people into the places you find.

"Danna, the three of you will go together." Zerubavel reached behind him to the low table on the floor of the tent. He grabbed a water skin and a square piece of papyrus, each side about the length of Zakaryah's forearm. He handed them to her, along with an ink cake. "Manu will assign a couple soldiers to patrol the area where you and the other teams will be working. He doesn't have enough to accompany every group and also protect the rest of us. Stay within sight of each other. Shout if you need help.

"You'll concentrate on the area between the gate near us and the valley to the east. You," he scowled at Hannah, "will stay here. No more running off to the temple mount. Misha'el will look after you."

Hannah said nothing, but Zakaryah met Gimillu's and Danna's eyes. The man would surely learn eventually.

ZAKARYAH PULLED HIS ROBE tighter as they entered the city, but there was nothing he could do to warm his feet in the sandals. The mornings had been getting colder, true, but the sun had always brought enough warmth when it had climbed over the high eastern hills.

Not today. Today heavy grey clouds slid across the sky, driven by the same wind that was even now probing at every opening of his robe.

As Zakaryah had expected, Hannah was with them. How had she slipped away from Misha'el? Best not to know. It would be bad enough later, when Zerubavel found out. He would scowl, his eyes would narrow, he would blame his wife, he would blame the three of them; but really, the man should know better by now. The only way to keep her where you wanted was with ropes.

Danna headed down the main street leading into the city from the ruined gate. Zakaryah followed her, with Gimillu and Hannah following him. Shulmu danced around them, interested as always in all the new things to sniff.

The clouds above darkened and the air grew colder. Fortunately, the wind died down. As it did, though, small white flecks of *something* began falling from the sky. Manna, like during the escape from Mitzrayim? He tilted his head back, opened his mouth, and managed to catch some. It didn't taste like much and certainly didn't seem very nourishing. Cold, though!

The flecks became larger and started covering the ground with a thin layer of white. What was it?

"Shalgu!" Gimillu exclaimed. He turned to Zakaryah. "Don't you remember? We read about it in the tablet-house, in the military reports the master made us read. The army went into the mountains to the north and east, and had to turn around because of something called *shalgu.*" He used the Chaldean word. "This is shalgu. It must be."

And Zakaryah did remember. Shalgu. *Sheleg* in Yehudit. Snow. He had never seen it and hadn't made the connection. He shivered, and not just from the cold.

Danna led them deeper into the city.

Zakaryah hadn't thought this place could feel any more desolate, but he was wrong. The snow muffled all sound, even the sound of his footsteps. Shadows swirled on every side.

Danna looked the way he had felt when they had entered Bab-ili. Her jaws were clamped together, her face set. Her eyes darted from side to side. Her breathing was shallow and rapid.

He stepped forward a pace to walk beside her. "It's just empty stones," he told her in a voice too low for the other two to hear. "And the snow is like rain, only cold."

She turned toward him. As she did, the panic drained from her eyes. *Thank you,* she mouthed, squeezing his hand and releasing it. "It's not just that, though," she said softly. "I spent summers in Bab-ili. Smoke from cooking fires stung peoples' eyes. The air reeked from animal and human dung, from urine used in fulling wool. Streets were crowded. People yelled, they talked quietly, they argued, they complained, they bargained in the market places. Children ran around, shrieking and bumping into each other, bouncing off slower-moving adults. That's what it was like there. It was the same here, you can be sure. Now it's empty as a corpse."

When had she ever talked to him like this? He held his breath, afraid to say anything, afraid not to.

But she offered nothing more, and they walked on in silence.

Danna stopped when she found a large stone to sit on in one of the deserted houses. She drew the papyrus from its pocket and wetted the ink cake from her water skin.

Zakaryah grabbed her arm and jerked her toward him, clasping her tight and spilling both of them to the ground. She just had time to shout when the wall above her collapsed, crashing heavy building stones over the place she had been sitting. Dust billowed up around them.

Danna pushed herself off Zakaryah and the two of them stood up, not looking at each other.

Hannah retrieved the map from where it had fallen and held it out for Danna's trembling hand.

"These old buildings can fall any time," Zakaryah said. "We'll need to be careful."

"Didn't you hear?" Gimillu asked.

"Hear what?" Zakaryah and Danna demanded simultaneously.

"Footsteps. Running away. The wall didn't fall over. It was pushed."

ZAKARYAH WENT IN FRONT because Danna was still shaken. He led the group silently, eyes scanning in all directions, alert to any and all sounds. He looked for a building with sturdy walls in a place where they could see the approaches.

He found one not too far off. They would be able to continue their mapping mission after a pause to rest and eat.

Zakaryah turned his gaze to a wall that had caught his eye. Where he was standing it was intact up to about his waist. It rose an arm's length higher to the left. On the right it continued at waist height for a couple paces before turning into a pile of the debris that would have formed the missing parts of the wall.

Hannah's stomach growled, easily audible in the stillness. She reached into a sack she was carrying and retrieved chunks of dried goat meat. She handed one to each of them and put another on the ground in front of Shulmu. The dog gulped once and it vanished. He nosed the bag and looked up at her, eyes round, tail wagging with hope. She pushed his muzzle away. How did the dog manage to look reproachful and happy at the same time? Shulmu moved off a pace, spun around a few times and plopped himself down on the snow-covered ground.

Zakaryah bit into the meat and ripped a piece off, a little saliva spilling from the corner of his mouth. He must have been hungrier than he realized.

He chewed as he examined the wall, then handed the rest of the chunk to Gimillu to hold. He ran his hands over the stones. The ones on the ground had been part of the structure before. Rebuilding should be easy. He stooped and grabbed a stone lying near the base of the wall. He grunted and brought his feet closer to the stone, then lifted and pushed with his stomach to shift it into position. It wobbled. He found a smaller stone to wedge underneath.

"How is this helping us?" Danna demanded around a mouthful of dried goat. "We're supposed to be mapping this place."

"We'll be living in one of these. Who do you think will be rebuilding the walls?"

She sniffed and tore another hunk off the meat.

When they finished eating, they continued the mapping until Danna judged it was time to meet the group they were to escort in. At that point, she rolled the map back up and shoved it inside her robe. "Let's go." She began retracing her steps. Zakaryah followed, Gimillu coming after him.

After a few paces Zakaryah realized that Hannah wasn't with them. He looked back. She was spinning in a circle, her arms wide, her palms up, her face turned to the sky. Her mouth was wide open as she danced around, laughing as she tried to catch the snow on her tongue. Shulmu was dancing with her, snapping at the flakes as they fell. Every time one landed on his nose he shook his head and sneezed.

Zakaryah smiled despite himself. He couldn't remember ever seeing her so joyous. He looked at Danna and Gimillu. They had stopped and were waiting for him. They did need to leave.

Still, a little bit longer wouldn't hurt.

"SOMEONE FOLLOWED US."

The others stopped and looked at the tracks Zakaryah was pointing to. They were clear and crisp, whereas their own footprints from earlier in the day were blurred and softened with the snow that had fallen after.

"One of the members of another team, maybe," Gimillu offered, "finding his way back to camp?"

"Maybe. But walk next to the footprints. Try to match the stride."

Gimillu looked puzzled but did as Zakaryah asked, stretching a little farther than he normally would to be able to match the spacing.

After five paces Zakaryah said, "That's good. Now come here and look at them."

The two of them bent over the first footprint. Danna joined them and they studied it together. They went to the next, and then the one after.

Hannah played with Shulmu, packing snow between her hands and throwing it for the dog to chase. Shulmu dashed off, each time skidding to a stop and looking baffled when it hit and disintegrated.

"I'm not sure what it is," Zakaryah told the other two. "Something bothers me about these tracks."

"He's not wearing sandals," Hannah told them without turning. She packed another handful of snow and threw it.

Was she saying he was barefoot? "Gimillu, take off your sandals and do it again."

"No, silly." Hannah packed the next wad of snow and

flung it. "It was Kudurru. He was wearing boots. Like the king's soldiers."

There was the sound of a foot slipping on stone a couple houses away. A large rock flew toward Hannah, hitting her in the leg and dropping her to the ground. Shulmu yelped and scrabbled back.

A boy dashed out of a ruined house and began running.

"There he is!" Gimillu shouted, taking off after him, Zakaryah right behind.

At the shout, the boy looked behind him, eyes wide. He didn't see the stone in his path and tripped, sprawling forward. He hit his chin and lay there stunned, blood from his face and hands staining the snow a deep crimson.

Gimillu skidded to a stop. He shot a glance back at where Hannah was moaning on the ground, Danna kneeling beside her. Nostrils flaring, he picked up a stone larger than his fist. The boy curled into a tight ball, raising his arms to cover his head, whimpering and shaking all over as Gimillu raised the stone high.

Zakaryah caught up to him as he was preparing to bring the stone down. He seized Gimillu's arm, grabbed the stone and flung it away. He pointed at a half-ruined wall. "Sit there," he ordered.

Gimillu's shoulders drooped and he began trembling. He shuffled over to the wall and crumpled onto it.

Zakaryah bared his teeth at the boy on the ground. "Don't move!"

He yelled back to Danna. "How is she?"

Danna picked Hannah up. "We're coming." She carried her over, stumbling with the girl's weight and leaving deep scuff marks in the snow.

Shulmu trotted after.

Danna asked, "Can you stand?"

Hannah felt her lower leg and cried out softly. There were trails of tears on her cheeks, but she nodded and Danna set her down next to Zakaryah. She retained a hold on Hannah's arm so she wouldn't need to put her weight on the injured leg.

The boy looked to be perhaps eight or nine. He was staring wide-eyed at Danna and hugging himself, leaving red prints over the front of his robe. Zakaryah nudged him with his toe. "Sit up. Don't stand and don't try to get away. And stop staring at my friend."

Was everyone here this rude?

"You threw a heavy stone at a six-year-old girl," he said to the boy through clenched teeth. "No. Don't look at me. Look at her."

The boy wrenched his eyes from Zakaryah's face and stared at Hannah. She was looking down at her injured leg, holding it just off the ground. As he watched she put some weight on it, cried out, and immediately jerked it back. When she raised her eyes to him, her face taut with pain, the boy flinched, ears reddening as he dropped his gaze.

Zakaryah took a deep breath. "Why did you throw the rock at Hannah?"

"He said she's bad. She tells lies to bring you here. You'll steal our farms and our homes. We won't have any place to live.

We'll starve. You need to go back."

"Who's this *we* you're talking about?"

The boy thrust his chin out at Zakaryah. "All of us. The villages around here. Thousands and thousands!"

Thousands! The boy probably couldn't even count to twenty. Zakaryah shook his head. Thousands or just hundreds, they were angry and dangerous. *What have we walked into here?*

"Who's telling you this?" Really, it could only be one person. *But let's hear what he says.*

The boy pressed his lips together and shook his head.

Time to try something different. "What's your name?"

"N-Neryah."

"Well, Neryah, is he about this tall?" Zakaryah held his hand a little above his own head. "Has an accent?"

The boy slowly nodded, keeping his eyes on Zakaryah.

Gimillu was following the conversation. He met Zakaryah's eyes, then dropped his own.

"Neryah," Zakaryah said, "get out of here. If you come back I'll let *him* have you." He pointed to Gimillu.

The boy scrambled to his feet and ran off. He didn't look back.

"I'VE NEVER BEEN THAT ANGRY. I saw Hannah on the ground and I wanted to hurt him."

Zakaryah had seated himself on the wall next to Gimillu. "That's how I felt when you came into Michal's house. It's why I stopped you. You'd have hated yourself afterward. I know."

"Michal." Gimillu dropped his head, hands covering his eyes. "I can see her sucking in her breath. She'd be so disappointed."

"I don't think so," Zakaryah told him. "She forgave *me*."

He noticed then that Danna was standing near him. She was looking at him, regarding him with a strange smile he had never seen before. "What?" he demanded.

She shook herself. "Nothing. We have to go meet the group that's coming to our area. Hannah needs help walking."

"Gimillu can carry me," Hannah said.

Gimillu groaned, but he stood and let Danna place Hannah low on his back. "Now I'm a horse," he muttered.

CHAPTER 38

KUDURRU, WHAT HAVE YOU DONE TO ME?

Gimillu wasn't able to get the thought out of his mind as he carried Hannah just behind Zakaryah and Danna. They were walking in a tight cluster, eyes moving constantly. The sounds of their footsteps and his own heavy breathing were the only things he could hear, and even those noises were muted in the snow-filled city.

What would he have done if Zakaryah hadn't stopped him from smashing that rock down on the boy? He had never wanted to hurt anyone before. Well, Zakaryah maybe, when he had set fire to the barley field. And before that, when he tried to catch him after lessons at the tablet-house.

But those didn't count, did they?

Anyway, he didn't want to be that person anymore, and he had thought he wasn't. Until just now.

He trudged on, Hannah's weight slowing him and making

him cautious. Her arms were around his chest. He was carrying her on his hips, his arms looped under her legs on either side. If he tripped he wouldn't be able to save either of them.

Kudurru. His brother had told the boy to target Hannah, to hurt her, had told lies about her to get him angry and violent. This was more than trying to scare the returnees into going back to Bab-ili, wasn't it?

His arms and back were getting tired. Would he be carrying Hannah all day? But then he stumbled over a shallow ditch and she whimpered. He drew a deep breath and tightened his grip.

He heard a scrabbling sound from inside the ruin of a building up ahead. Kudurru? He cringed, half expecting a stone to come flying at them. His skin crawled as they drew even with it, but all he saw was a large hare that bounded off as soon as they came into view.

After that, though, as they walked toward the main city gate where they would be meeting their group, he did hear noises. Some were definitely animals—hares, jackals, rats, he imagined—scurrying out of the way. But once in a while he would hear what sounded like a quiet footfall, now parallel with them behind the buildings lining this street, now ahead, now at their rear.

"Zakaryah!" he called softly.

Zakaryah glanced back at him and nodded. He tapped Danna on the shoulder. They stopped and had a whispered conversation that Gimillu couldn't make out. Zakaryah stooped and picked up several fist-sized stones. He put some of them in a pocket inside his robe, gave two more to Danna, and held on to two others.

Danna withdrew a coil of cord from inside her robe. There was a loop on one end that she slipped over a finger. She grasped the other end in the same hand, letting the middle drop. There was a pouch there into which she placed one of the stones Zakaryah had handed her. A sling! She swung it back a short ways, then spun it up into a fast circle above her head. She let the stone fly and it cracked loud against the wall of a house forty paces away.

Gimillu's jaw dropped. "Where did you learn *that*?" he gasped.

She gave him a tight smile but said nothing.

He shuddered, thinking about all the times she could have slung a stone at him before she decided she could trust him.

They resumed walking. He continued hearing the footfalls from time to time, but they made it back to the gate plaza without being subjected to any more attacks.

A large crowd was waiting there for them.

Gimillu asked over his shoulder, "Can I set you down?"

He felt Hannah nodding against his back. He shifted his grip to her waist and lowered her behind him, letting her ribs slide gently through his hands. He turned around only when he felt her weight completely off him. He let out a long sigh and arched his back, arms stretched above and behind him as far as he could reach. "Phew!"

He rubbed his lower back without taking his eyes off her. "Show me your leg."

She pulled her robe up to knee height. There was a large purple bump in the middle of her shin. It looked ugly and painful, but she was supporting her own weight. No bones broken, then, thankfully.

Meanwhile, the group they would be escorting was filling the plaza. How many people were there? Based on what Zerubavel had said in the tent that morning, there could be four hundred or more.

He looked the crowd over but there were far too many to count, and that didn't include the sheep and goats. It would be very slow work to get four thousand people and their animals settled if only one group of four hundred could fit into the plaza at a time. More than the amount of daylight that was left, that was for sure. Well, that was Zerubavel's problem. He had enough to worry about.

Where were the soldiers? He spotted three of them talking with Zakaryah and Danna. They carried swords and spears and wore bows slung over their shoulders. Next to them was a man with a long stick, from the top of which a piece of linen hung.

Gimillu stuck his elbow out to Hannah. She hung onto it, supporting her weight on the side of the injured leg. He slapped his thigh twice for Shulmu to join them.

They proceeded toward the other two, Gimillu walking slowly, Hannah limping. Shulmu kept pace, running off from time to time to anoint a stone or just sniff around.

Danna spoke to them as they came up. "It's just these three soldiers."

"Three? For all these people?" His insides tightened. How much protection could three soldiers offer? Manu must not know what they were dealing with. For that matter, he didn't know either. But the four of them had already had several nasty surprises. It would be foolish to assume there wouldn't be more coming, and maybe worse.

"Three is what we get," Danna said, shaking her head. She looked over the crowd. "But at least some of the men have spears." And indeed, he could see eight—no, nine—nine spears, their sharp iron points floating above the crowd.

Danna bent to pick up a rock. She slipped it into her sling and draped the sling over her shoulder.

She touched Zakaryah's arm. He nodded and said something to the man with the standard, who began shouting and waving the staff above his head.

Danna and Zakaryah led the staff-bearer down to where the main street exited the plaza.

Gimillu followed them. Hannah limped at his side. Shulmu trotted with them, dodging between their legs in his normal excitement, until Gimillu yelled at him.

The group followed, a cacophony of voices giving way to quieter talking as they were squeezed into a narrower formation by the lesser width of the street. One soldier walked in the lead next to Zakaryah, another was roughly in the middle of the line and the third brought up the end. The men with the spears were spaced in between.

Gimillu estimated the line at about two hundred paces long, far too long to be guarded effectively by three soldiers, even with the spear-bearers. Progress was slow as people picked their way through the rubble that still littered the street. The snow churned into muddy slush with the passage of hundreds of sandaled feet.

It didn't look good.

And now the talking died down further in the deadness of the ruined city. People swiveled their heads right and left. Men grabbed fist-sized throwing rocks from the ground, filling the pockets inside their robes with as many as they could.

The wind picked up, hollow and frigid in the stone canyon they filed through.

Gimillu shuddered. It wasn't just the cold. It was the low, racing clouds. It was the collapsed buildings pressing in from all sides, the impossibility of seeing beyond the ruins facing the street. With every dark alleyway they approached, his breath grew shorter, his stomach tighter.

And it was too quiet. The people in the line behind had stopped talking altogether. The shuffling of feet, the creaking of cart wheels, the occasional curse of someone tripping or stumbling on the uneven surface, sneezes, coughs, cries of live-stock—all were muffled and dull.

Neither were there the soft scurryings of the small ani-mals that lived among the stones. They had been so startling at first. Now their absence was ominous. Of course he was at the head of a line of four hundred people. Naturally the creatures would disappear, would get as far away as possible. That at least was one silence he shouldn't worry about, wasn't it? He didn't need to be concerned with that one.

A shout from back in the line jerked him out of his thoughts. Shulmu was dashing around, barking furiously. Men appeared in the alleyways up and down the line on both sides, yelling and flinging stones. Two men materialized from an alley fifteen paces ahead, letting fly a barrage of rocks. One more stepped from behind them with a drawn bow, pointing it in his direction. There was a muted twang. A sheep standing between him and the bowman gave a piteous cry and collapsed, the arrow standing out of its side. The man fitted another arrow to the string, but the bow clattered to the ground, releasing the arrow harmlessly into a nearby wall. The archer fell to his knees, grabbing at his throat and dropping his clutch of arrows.

Two steps ahead of Gimillu, Danna placed another stone in her sling and swung it in a tight circle above her head. The stone cracked into a wall, shattering and flinging fragments in every direction. The other two attackers jerked as the shards hit them in the face and chest, then grabbed the bowman where he was lying motionless on the ground and dragged him off by the arms. They vanished into the alleyway as suddenly as they had appeared. The other attackers also withdrew, leaving weeping and wailing in their wake.

Just ahead of him, Danna was shaking, tears running down her cheeks. Zakaryah pried open her clenched fist and pulled the sling from her hand. He uncurled her fingers and pressed them flat between both of his hands, then drew her into his shoulder while she sobbed.

When the sobbing diminished, he released her. He opened the loop of the sling into a small circle and slid it onto her finger, holding her hand a moment longer than necessary. "In case there's another attack," he stammered, reddening when she turned her attention suddenly to his face.

She nodded, straightened, and fitted a stone into the pouch.

Hannah tugged at Gimillu's arm. He dragged his eyes away from Danna and Zakaryah. "The bow," Hannah said.

He nodded and ran to the alley mouth, scooping up the bow and the dropped arrows. They felt strange in his hand, heavy in a way that had nothing to do with their weight.

The line began moving again under the urging of the soldiers. Had they even had time to draw their weapons? He didn't know, but the bow of the soldier in front was out now and nocked. The men with spears repositioned themselves on either side of the line, close to the mouths of the alleys. They carried their weapons pointing to the side, level, ready for a new attack.

Back in the line, Gimillu saw people limping. Some of the stronger men were carrying others the way he had carried Hannah. From what he could see, it didn't appear that there had been any fatalities, though if they were far enough back he wouldn't be able to tell.

Hannah and Shulmu moved forward with the flow of people. When they drew even with him, he pulled Hannah out of the line. He knelt to bring his face even with hers, grasping her upper arms. She let him hold her, regarding him silently with silver eyes that looked much older than her six years.

He released a long-held breath and stood, letting go of her arms.

The two of them merged back into the river of returnees, Shulmu at their heels.

He tightened his fist around the bow. The arrow that it

launched had been pointed in his direction, but the bowman hadn't been aiming at him and hadn't been aiming at a sheep. He had seen it in the man's eyes.

He had been aiming at Hannah.

GIMILLU HAD EXPECTED that it would be Danna who would organize the assignment of houses. In fact it was Zakaryah who, map in hand, was directing people to the houses that the four of them had mapped out.

Danna was silent, sitting out of the way and staring into some empty distance.

Gimillu went to sit next to her, Shulmu following. He lifted the dog up and placed him in her lap. She stroked his fur without losing the distant look in her eyes.

"You should have answered yes," he told her.

"What?"

Ah! That had dragged her out of it. "When King Koresh asked you if you were a warrior. You should have answered yes."

A tiny smile flashed on her lips, to be replaced in an instant by the same dead and distant look.

"You didn't have a choice," he went on. "He was trying to hit Hannah." He thought of the sheep that had fallen over dead, the blood running from its side to stain the snow crimson. He didn't mention that to her.

"I've never killed anyone," she whispered, cradling her head in her hands. "I just shot at jackals and wild dogs. To protect our sheep."

"You don't know that you killed him. I think I saw his chest moving."

She raised her head and looked him straight in the eyes. "I crushed his throat."

To that he had no answer.

AS THE SUN WAS SINKING beyond the western hills, Gimillu found two small houses next to each other, separated by a mostly ruined wall. One still had a roof supported by wooden beams that had somehow survived the general destruction of fifty years before. Zerubavel had said that households should double up. Would he object if they took both of them, the roofed one for his family and the other for the four of them and Shulmu?

"With his household and us, we're eight," Zakaryah answered when Gimillu asked. "That's a lot to crowd into one little house. That's what I'll tell him. Anyway, the broken wall makes it like a single house."

Gimillu found Danna back where he had left her, still sitting, still silent, still staring. Hannah was next to her, Shulmu at her feet.

He picked up the bow and arrows from the side of the stone where he had left them. "Come with me," he ordered the two of them. They followed, Danna shuffling along, Hannah limping and Shulmu bouncing around as usual.

He led them to the house and ushered them into the interior. He pointed at the old fire circle in the floor of what had been the open courtyard. Now the whole building was open to the sky.

"They've built a communal fire in one of the ruined buildings in the next alley," he told them. "You can go there and get a burning brand and some wood. There's a cart of provisions too. I'll be back with Zakaryah."

There. Give them some work to do. That would get Danna out of her dark mood.

He went off to look for Zakaryah.

ATTACKS CONTINUED in the days after the returnees settled into their houses. Villagers would show up suddenly from empty streets or buildings, launch volleys of stones and then disappear into the maze of ruins. Occasionally there were bowmen with the raiders, and then the casualties would become serious.

Even before the returnees had fully settled themselves, Zerubavel sent a caravan of carts and armed men to the cities at the edge of the great sea in the west. Their instructions were to purchase spears, swords, bows and arrows. While he waited for the caravan to return, he sent patrols into the city to flush out villagers and prevent attacks.

During this period Manu and his soldiers departed for the far north, but not before they had refreshed the weapons-handling skills of the men in the group who had had fighting experience earlier in their lives. These men in turn trained the other men and the older boys.

Gimillu was haunted by an image of Hannah with an arrow through her chest, bleeding into the snow like the sheep. He launched himself into the training with seriousness and focus. He became proficient with the bow he had collected after the attack, sinking his arrows into targets farther and farther away as the training progressed. When he wasn't training, the weapon was never far from his hand.

Zakaryah was more interested in mastering construction than sword fighting. He would have avoided the training entirely, but Danna insisted that he go. "Gimillu and I can't be the only ones who know how to use a weapon," she told him, shuddering. He never became very good, and Danna wasn't reticent about sharing her disgust.

There was no further trace of Kudurru.

"WHAT'S THE POINT?" Zakaryah told Danna when she yelled at him once again about not taking his weapons training seriously. "It's been six weeks, the last three with no attacks at all. The villagers know we're here to stay. They can't chase us back now. And it's spring. It's beautiful, the days are longer and the soil is ready for farming. They'll be planting their barley. They don't have time for Kudurru's plots."

Gimillu didn't share his confidence. He could feel his brother's brooding presence, his fear of returning to their father to report another devastating failure. The villagers might be done with Kudurru, but Kudurru surely wasn't done with them. He wouldn't have given up, wouldn't have gone back to Bab-ili.

During the night of their seventh Shabbat, Gimillu woke feeling uneasy. He sat up on his pallet, pulling his wool blanket up with him. It was the middle of the month so the moon was full. Light streamed into the open courtyard, but the shadows were deep here in the back room. He heard Zakaryah's steady breathing next to him. On the other side of Zakaryah, Shulmu moaned in his sleep.

What had wakened him? Nothing seemed amiss, but here he was, eyes wide open. *Might as well use the chamber pot.* He wrapped himself in the blanket and stood. Where had he left his sandals? He felt around with his foot. There! He slipped the foot into it, then the other. He would have to be more careful in a month, when the nights would be warm enough for scorpions to move around.

As he groped after the chamber pot, he crossed the open doorway to the rest of the house. He could hear Danna's breathing.

Frowning, he stepped through into the small courtyard and across to the side room where the girls slept. Danna's pallet was in shadow, but the silver light from the courtyard splashed across the other half of the room.

Hannah's pallet was empty.

Before he could shout, the outside door swung silently open. A small figure stood there, silhouetted against the moonlight. "If you shout," the boy whispered, "he'll kill her."

CHAPTER 39

"WHAT? WHAT?" Zakaryah came out of his dream.

The shaking resumed. "Zakaryah! Up! Now!"

He opened his eyes.

Gimillu was kneeling by his side, reaching to shake him again.

"I'm awake." He rubbed his eyes, stomach clenching. Something was wrong, that was clear from Gimillu's desperate whisper, from his trembling voice.

Next to him, Shulmu scrambled to his feet. His eyes glistened in the faint moonlight that penetrated into the back room. The dog whined, swinging his head from Gimillu to Zakaryah and back again.

"It's Kudurru. He has Hannah. Quick!"

Zakaryah bolted upright, his breath rasping in his throat.

Gimillu's hand clamped hard over his mouth. "Quiet! If we shout, he'll kill her. Get dressed."

Zakaryah scrambled up from under the blanket. He pulled on a second robe and belted it tight, but it did nothing to stop the tremors racking his body.

He slid his feet into his sandals and followed Gimillu into the moonlit interior courtyard, Shulmu at his heels.

Danna turned toward Gimillu, her eyes grim and black in the darkness of her face. "Grab your bow," she ordered him.

"No!" The boy at the door was almost dancing, shifting his weight from foot to foot. "No," he repeated. "He said no weapons. If you bring weapons he'll kill her right away." He pointed to Danna. "Th-that includes your sling. You have to drop it, right now."

Danna slowly reached inside her robe and withdrew the sling. Without taking her eyes off the boy, she extended her arm in his direction, palm down. She opened her hand. The sling fell, pattering in the dust of the dirt floor. The boy shuddered and danced back into the street, though she never made a move toward him.

I would be terrified too, if she were looking at me that way.

But that voice. Where had Gimillu heard it? Then he had it. "You're that Neryah. I should have smashed you with the rock." He stepped toward the boy, fists already clenched tight.

Danna grabbed Gimillu's wrist. "No," she whispered. "We need him to take us to Hannah."

Neryah had jumped further back into the street, looking ready to bolt. "He made me come here! He'll kill my sister and brother if I don't do what he tells me. He said so. You have to come. Just the three of you. Hurry!"

The boy left at a run, Zakaryah and Danna taking off after him.

Gimillu shouted back over his shoulder, "Shulmu, stay!" The dog stopped short in the doorway, whining as Gimillu ran to catch up to the other two.

Neryah led them through the narrow streets, skidding around corners, speeding through the straight parts, never slowing, running as if wild beasts were after him. *And well they might be*, Gimillu thought, considering what he wanted to do to the boy right now.

But all four of them were slowing as the ground rose under their feet. Soon they were reduced to a fast, wheezing walk. Neryah kept throwing apprehensive glances behind at them.

Where was he taking them?

A hill loomed ahead. Circling the crest was a tumbled wall. The temple mount, that's what it was, with the ruined house of Yahweh on top. Gimillu had seen it from the other side when Hannah had led him and the priest to sacrifice on the broken-down altar.

Zakaryah stopped, bent over, trying to catch his breath.

Neryah bounced from foot to foot. "Hurry. He'll kill her. He'll kill my family."

KUDURRU WAS WAITING for them by the pile of rocks that had once been the house of Yahweh. He sat on a stone, looking relaxed, swinging a leg as he watched them approach. He was holding a knife in his right hand.

Before him was the altar, now rebuilt with stones both salvaged and newly hewn. Rising from each corner of the altar was a sort of square stone horn, about the size of a large man's hand.

Hannah lay on her side on top of the altar within the square defined by the horns. A cloth was wound tightly around her mouth. Her hands and feet were bound together in front of her.

Gimillu sank to his knees, unable to look away. She was staring straight at him, picking him out of the small exhausted group, just as she had back in the square in Al Yahudu.

He wrenched his eyes from her to Kudurru.

His brother was studying him, one eyebrow raised. "So, little brother," Kudurru remarked. "I've been expecting you. So nice to see you back from the dead. Our father would be so happy."

"Let her go," Gimillu got out, still struggling to breathe.

Behind Zakaryah, the boy Neryah was stepping back. Trying to slip away?

"You!" Kudurru shouted.

The boy froze in place.

Kudurru looked them over. "No weapons. Good." He pointed at Danna. "What about the Kushite?"

Neryah stammered, "Sh-she dropped it. On the floor. I saw her."

Kudurru told the boy, "Stay here. I want you to see this."

Neryah's shoulders slumped and he remained where he was.

Out of the corner of his eye, Gimillu saw Zakaryah pick up a stone.

Kudurru glanced at Zakaryah and stood. He leaned over

the edge of the altar, bringing the point of the knife to rest gently against Hannah's neck.

The stone dropped from Zakaryah's fingers.

Kudurru pulled the knife back but remained standing over her. He said nothing for a long while, a slight smile playing on his lips as he considered them.

The only sounds Gimillu could hear were the sleepy cooing of doves on their roosts and the scrabbling of a jackal or some other night hunter among the rocks behind them. What would a jackal think of this night scene?

"I've learned a lot about your history these last few months," Kudurru told them, addressing Danna and Zakaryah.

He switched his gaze to Gimillu. "And I guess it's your history, too, now. I don't know what you see in this backwater nation and their impotent little god."

He snorted, sweeping the knife around at the moonlit ruins. "Yahweh. He couldn't protect them from Bab-ili." He again poised the knife over Hannah's throat. "And now he can't protect them from *me*."

"She's just a girl," Gimillu said. "Let her go."

"Oh, she's more than just a girl," Kudurru responded. "She's the reason your exiles are all here. She's the reason they'll all go back, too. It's funny, though. I've been chasing this boy"— he glanced at Zakaryah—"and his Kushite lover for over half a year. I thought they were your enemies. But now here you are."

"We're not lovers!" Danna's teeth were bared, her jaw muscles standing out.

Don't argue with him! But Gimillu didn't say it out loud,

didn't even glance at her. He had to persuade Kudurru to let Hannah go. There had to be a way.

Their father!

"You think Mushezib-nabu will respect you for this, don't you?" Gimillu snarled. "You think he'll thank you, praise you. I went out to King Kurush. Father has his position because of me. What good did it do me? You think he'll thank you? The god of Yisra'el spoke to the king through the mouth of this girl. You'll be executed. Father will sharpen the ax personally and hand it to the headsman."

The knife wavered for a moment. But then Kudurru took a deep breath. "He doesn't respect you because you're worthless. But when all four thousand of you come whimpering back to Bab-ili, he'll thank me."

Gimillu's whole body slumped. It was the only argument that he could come up with, the only one that stood a chance. *He's going to kill her.* And it was all his fault. If he hadn't burned that barley field. . .

He looked back at Danna. Her eyes were locked on Hannah. Her hands clenched and unclenched. Tears streamed down her face. Danna had been right. He was stupid, stupid, stupid. Stupid to have wanted revenge on Zakaryah, stupid to have let his uncle push him into further evil.

Stupid to have believed his father could ever love him.

But there was one last thing he could do.

He straightened himself and stood, unable to suppress his trembling. "Take me. You hate me. Mother died because of me. Let Hannah go and kill me."

He heard gasps behind him. Two voices shouted, "Gimillu, no!" And someone was crying. It was Neryah. Gimillu had forgotten all about him. So strange. But he had no attention to spare for anyone except Kudurru.

His brother was holding the knife at his side now. His head was tilted, his eyebrows raised. He was studying Gimillu as if seeing him for the first time.

"Tempting, little brother," he said after a long pause.

Hannah had turned her head and was now gazing at Kudurru without emotion, her silver eyes gleaming with more than the light of the moon.

Kudurru swallowed once, looking uncertain for the first time. Then his lips thinned into a tight line. "It's tempting, but I have to tell you a story. There was a king of Yahudu, Yoshiyahu. He decided the Yahudu god was angry at the other gods. The land was polluted with them, that's what he said. He slaughtered the priests on their own altars, desecrating them for all time."

He twisted his hand in Hannah's long black hair. He pulled her head back, exposing the soft skin of her throat. He looked at each of them in turn. "And it turns out that this is the only altar in all the world where you Yahudus can sacrifice to your god." He stared hard at Gimillu. "I think it's better to leave you alive. You can think about how you caused all of this. And you're wrong about Mushezib-nabu. Father will thank me."

He raised the knife.

There was a scrabbling noise behind them. Shulmu dashed from the rocks, blurring into a dark streak and snarling as he fastened his teeth in the soft flesh of the man's lower leg, jerking

and tearing as if it were a large rabbit. Kudurru cursed, screaming in pain. He spun around, stabbing down with the knife. The
dog screeched—a high, horrific sound—then staggered off a
few paces and collapsed.

Kudurru rubbed his calf and straightened, the knife now
covered in blood. He turned back toward the altar, but before
he could lift the blade, he staggered and fell over backward, his
whole length stretched out on the ground. His eyes were open
to the sky, seeing nothing.

A bowman! He could be hiding anywhere in these ruins. Gimillu scrambled onto the altar and stretched out to cover Hannah with his body. But where were the arrows coming
from? He looked more closely at Kudurru.

There was no arrow.

Instead, blood seeped from a deep indentation in the side
of his head, staining the dirt black in the pale white light.

Danna stood, rigid in the moonlight, the empty sling dangling from her right hand.

"I made a second one two weeks ago," she whispered as
they stared at her. "I was going to teach Hannah."

She sank to the ground and sat, eyes focused on nothing.

THEY TOOK TURNS carrying Shulmu's lifeless body
down from the temple mount. When they got back to the
house, they washed him and wrapped him in linen.

Gimillu sat on the floor of the house, curled over Shulmu.
He rocked back and forth, beyond the reach of words of sym-

pathy and caring. Danna, Zakaryah and Hannah sat with him in silent vigil. Their tired, drawn faces reflected his own grief.

That did offer some consolation.

The morning dawned clear and beautiful, promising a warm and lovely day. Zakaryah was the first to move. He stretched, then stood and stretched some more.

"I need to tell Zerubavel what happened," he announced, his voice subdued. "Someone will have to collect Kudurru's body."

When he returned, the four of them ate a brief morning meal, then headed toward the northern gate.

Gimillu refused their offers of help. He carried Shulmu's body, not willing to share the burden with anyone else.

The place he chose was the hill to the north of the temple mount. He had climbed it with Hannah when she had led him, the priest, and yes, Shulmu, to the altar of the house of Yahweh for that first sacrifice.

They accompanied him to the hilltop. Zakaryah carried Hannah, who was in pain from the cords that had bound her. Danna walked on behind. From there they could see into the temple compound.

The house of Yahweh would be rebuilt, Zerubavel had promised. When it was, it would block the view of the altar. For now, though, this hilltop was a fitting place, Gimillu decided, the most fitting he could find.

He dug the grave by himself, a partial atonement, in his mind, for the evils he had brought upon Shulmu, upon his friends, and even upon his brother.

After he spread the last of the earth on top of the small grave, first Zakaryah, then Danna, clasped him in a tight embrace.

Hannah pressed his two hands between hers. "I'll be here," she told him.

Now what did she mean by that? But it helped lighten by just a bit the devastation that was crushing him.

The three of them headed down the hill, leaving him alone with his thoughts, his sorrow and his regrets.

He stayed there the rest of the day.

CHAPTER 40

THE TRADE CARAVAN ARRIVED six days later, just before the start of Shabbat.

Zakaryah first heard about it from children who ran screaming through the streets.

Their excitement was catching. He decided he deserved a break from rebuilding walls and houses, so he went to find Danna, Gimillu and Hannah. The four of them hiked up the main street to the northern gate where they had first entered the city.

Zakaryah looked back over his shoulder and sighed. The boy Neryah was following about fifteen paces behind. He had been hovering around them for the past several days, not talking to them, still looking like a frightened animal, but hovering all the same. When Zakaryah had mentioned it to Danna, all she said was, "We saved his family." And maybe that was it. At some point he would try to get the boy to hold still so he could ask.

Along the way, he looked with a critical eye at the progress of the reconstruction efforts. The streets were now uncluttered, the stones all having been moved to the side or repurposed for the buildings along the way. The houses they passed all had roofs, and most of the walls seemed intact. He had worked on many of them himself and had the muscles and callouses to prove it.

It was a shame about the house of Yahweh, though. He had expected to start working on that, but there always seemed to be some other project that desperately needed to be done. Zerubavel had told him not to worry, that they'd be able to start work soon. Of course, the man had been saying that for the past four weeks. Zakaryah had begun hearing rumors lately that a man named Haggai, who some were calling a prophet, had been complaining about the lack of progress. Zakaryah wished him well with the complaints, but it was silly to think of him as a prophet just because he didn't like the pace of the building efforts. As far as he was concerned, there was only one prophet of Yahweh in Yerushalayim, and she was holding his hand right now, bouncing with excitement and tugging him along because she wanted him, Danna and Gimillu to go faster.

They passed through the north gate. It was cleared now. The massive doors still lay on the ground, but they had been moved off so that they didn't interfere with foot and cart traffic. The walls that stretched away on either side were still the same piles of jumbled stone that they had been when he first saw them. There simply hadn't been time or men enough to begin rebuilding them. That would come, he knew. For now, though, the need didn't seem very urgent. Mushezib-nabu, the man ultimately behind the danger, was far away. There had been no more attacks since Kudurru's death. The people from the countryside who had been so violently opposed to the return of the exiles were beginning to realize that the new inhabitants of the city constituted a huge nearby market for their produce, wool, and pottery.

It seemed that the peace of King Koresh lay over the land.

The trading caravan was encamped on the plain outside the gate, the same plain where the returning exiles had set up their camp. Zakaryah saw donkey carts laden with provisions and trade goods. Tents were being raised and there was a general feeling of intense, purposeful activity.

Here and there camels were tethered or kneeling on the ground. Ugly, lazy beasts. Smelly too. That's what he had always thought of them.

Children had already swarmed into the camp like a plague of locusts, settling in clusters, surrounding the carts and peppering the traders with demands for toys, treats and games. Parents and other relatives shouted and chased after them in a futile effort to bring some order and restraint to the scene.

As they approached the edge of the encampment, a man who had been pounding a tent pin into the hard ground stood and stretched, wiping the sweat from his forehead with the sleeve of his robe. He turned toward them. Danna stopped in her tracks and the two of them stared at each other for an endless moment. Then they ran together with a shout. The man scooped her up and swung her around.

By this time Zakaryah had recognized him.

When he had set her down, Danna motioned to the three of them to come closer, her face shining.

"You remember Hannah and Zakaryah, don't you?"

The man smiled and nodded.

She grabbed Gimillu's hand and pulled him forward. "And this is Gemalyahu. You might know of him by his birth name. Gimillu."

The man's eyes widened.

Danna looked the three of them over, still smiling as widely as Zakaryah could remember.

"Gimillu," she said, "this is my cousin from Bavel. Immeru."

"I WAS HOPING I would find you here," Immeru told Danna. He had joined them in their house to share refreshments and family news, and to catch up on events. "Tell me about the journey, about Yerushalayim. And tell me about our former corpse here." He smiled at Gimillu.

Danna took the lead, the others jumping in from time to time. They told him about everything that had happened since Bab-ili, starting with their nighttime flight to Abir-ilu's farm and ending with the death of Kudurru six days before.

"Danna saved Hannah's life," Zakaryah said.

Danna shook her head. "It was really Shulmu. I miss him." Her eyes misted. "We all do."

"But why was he after Hannah?" Immeru asked. "It doesn't make sense. She's six years old."

"I'll be seven in one more month!"

For a moment, nobody spoke. Then Gimillu answered. "He decided she was responsible for the exiles coming back to Yehudah. He wanted to prove to our father that he wasn't a failure."

"Your father! I forgot. The king imprisoned him. The rumors are that he was enriching himself an unseemly amount from the king's treasury. Some embezzlement is expected, you know, but in his case the king apparently judged it excessive. The speculation is that he planned on fleeing and was accumulating silver to that end."

"Fleeing?" Gimillu exclaimed. "Why would he flee?"

"Supposedly it had something to do with the king's tax levies." He looked around at them. "So as I've just learned"— here he looked directly at Hannah—"it was because of you."

"And how's grandfather?" Danna asked, her voice quavering slightly. "He's well?"

"He's fine, though his knees are bothering him. He insisted that if I ran into you I was to tell you that he misses you terribly and that you should write. He was worried that you might have forgotten how." He reached into his bag and pulled out a papyrus sheet and a stylus. "He sent these along, in case you're having trouble remembering those expensive lessons he paid for."

Zakaryah laughed out loud at the blush that rose to darken her already dark forehead.

"Give half the sheet to Zakaryah," Hannah told her. "He has to write Abir-ilu too." She offered nothing further in response to the puzzled looks she got, but Zakaryah's face heated up like a pottery kiln.

"Oh," Immeru added. "He also sent this." He withdrew a beautiful colored scarf and held it out to Danna.

"My mother's scarf." Her hand trembled as she took it from him. "She wore it on festival days." She removed the plain scarf she was wearing and set it on the ground next to her. Her hair underneath was long and black, shiny with tight curls.

Zakaryah stared, unable to take his eyes off her. Gimillu and Immeru exchanged glances, something that Zakaryah only became aware of when he noticed Hannah's smug look. He shook himself, turning red again.

Danna looked around at the sudden silence. "What?" she demanded. When there was no answer, she shrugged and covered her hair with the new scarf.

Hannah jabbed Zakaryah in the ribs with her elbow. Why did she have to keep doing that? Prophet or not, couldn't she just talk to him like a normal child? But he leaned toward her.

She whispered into his ear. "The mirror."

He stared at her without understanding. Then he got it. He scrambled to his feet and ran into the back room where he kept his things. He came out holding his mother's copper mirror. He wiped it on his robe to restore the shine and handed it to Danna. She accepted with a wide smile and held it up, moving it around to see the scarf from as many angles as she could.

She sighed finally and handed the mirror back to Zakaryah.

"Why did you join the caravan?" she asked Immeru. "You used to invest in them but I don't remember you actually going out with one."

"I felt like a chicken in a pen," Immeru recounted. "I was pecking around for goods and profits with too many other chickens. When the organizers of this caravan came to me about making an investment, I said yes but that I would need to come along. It's high risk but the profit potential is enormous."

"Profits?" Zakaryah's face fell. He liked this man, this cousin of Danna's. "You won't find much here, I'm afraid. We're just getting started. We barely have anything ourselves."

"Oh, this is just a stop along the way. We'll be moving out tomorrow. There's trading to be done along the coast, spices and other goods that will be worth a lot of silver back in Bavel. But the real profits will come from what we pick up further on. We're going to Mitzrayim, maybe as far as Kush."

He locked eyes with Danna, his expression suddenly serious. "Perhaps you want to come with us?"

She swept her gaze around, lingering on each of their faces in turn; Gimillu first, then Hannah, then longest of all, Zakaryah. Tears filled the corners of her eyes, welling out to leave wet trails down her cheeks before beading on her jaw and dropping to the dirt of the floor.

Slowly, very slowly, she nodded.

THE CARAVAN BEGAN MOVING OUT just after dawn, before the sun had crested the mountains to the east that separated Yerushalayim from the deep valley that was the wilderness of Yehudah.

Zakaryah felt that wilderness pulling at him now. He

could get lost there, in that wasteland, wandering among the great dry cliffs. Maybe he would go to Ein Gedi, where cool water flowed from the stone. He could live there. Hadn't David hidden in the caves of Ein Gedi when he was fleeing from mad King Saul?

He shook off the thought with an effort. He would never do it, would never leave Hannah, even if Danna was leaving him. But then, he didn't have a claim on her, did he? Maybe if he had written to Abir-ilu when Hannah told him to. But no, it would have taken five or six months for a letter to get all the way to Bavel and back again. And what if he had asked, and her grandfather had said yes? Danna would still do what she wanted, and what she wanted was clear enough. She cared for him, he knew she did, but it wasn't enough to hold her here, to keep her from going off forever, searching for a father she might never find.

And Gimillu. Gimillu, who was looking now as distraught as he himself felt. Gimillu, who he had first thought of as his enemy, lately as his friend, and in between as his opponent in a rivalry for Danna that even now he had trouble admitting to himself. When had he stopped worrying about that?

Danna was releasing Gimillu now, holding him at arm's length, studying his face as if trying to memorize it.

And what about Hannah? Danna was a big sister to Hannah, a sister that Hannah never had. How could she leave, how could she devastate Hannah that way?

But Hannah didn't look devastated. No, in fact it was Danna who was crying in great gulping sobs, crying so hard her nose was running. Hannah was smiling and hugging her, telling her that it would be good, that she would see.

And then Danna turned to him. She was in front of him, less than an arm's length away, but it felt like there was a chasm between them. She reached toward him, let her arms fall back. He opened his mouth, shut it again. He wanted to tell her how much he would miss her, how sorry he was for the mean things he had said to her, thought about her.

He couldn't find the words. All he could do was stand there looking at her, helpless.

They stared silently at each other for a long moment. She reached out suddenly, touched his cheek, then spun on her heels and ran off after Immeru.

Zakaryah raised his hand to the spot she had touched and stood watching until she disappeared around a bend in the road.

There was a tug on his sleeve. He wrenched his gaze from the distance to Hannah's small figure.

"Look," she commanded, pulling him around to face the ruins. For a moment he saw before him a beautiful city, shattered no longer, its walls and buildings glowing golden in the morning light.

As the vision faded, Hannah took his hand and led him back into the waiting city.

EPILOGUE

Three Years Later

The Lord thrust forth His hand and touched my
mouth, and the Lord said to me: Behold, I put My
words in your mouth.

JEREMIAH 1:9

THE LIGHT IN MY HEAD hasn't been there, not as
much. Sometimes there are months in between. I think maybe
He feels bad about His prophet Yirmeyahu, how the only thing
he wanted was a wife, children, a chance to live a life like ordinary people. He's letting me go, so I don't have to be like that
sad old man. That's what I think.

When the light's gone I don't *know* things. I love that,
not *knowing*. It's like I'm ordinary. *Pretend* ordinary, anyway.
I'll never really be ordinary. But maybe I can be partly ordinary,
partly like everyone else.

My poor brother has been sad ever since Danna left. He doesn't talk about it, but I know. That's know, not *know*.

The work helps. He's been building the foundation of His house. It keeps him busy, and that's good. Neryah has become his apprentice. He's that boy who led them up to the temple mount to save me from Kudurru.

The other men working on His house look up to Zakaryah. He knows how to build things. That's *knows*, not knows. At least I think so.

The work is going to stop soon. Some people around here are angry. They're going to write to the king. One of his ministers will make the men stop building. I *know* this. But then after many years, a new king will say they can do it, they can start building His house again. When he says that, it will be Zakaryah who will lead the building.

I haven't told him.

Instead, I just tell him things will be fine. He smiles but he doesn't believe me. He doesn't think things will be fine ever again.

Zakaryah is sixteen and handsome. He has strong arms from lifting all that stone. The girls stare at him but he doesn't notice. He can only think about Danna.

Yesterday I told him he needs to get married. He asked was it me talking, or Him? I didn't say, but it was me, *sort of*. I didn't answer him because there's something I *know*. Danna is coming back.

See? Not ordinary.

She told him once that he was dumb as a clay jug. Well,

that goes for her too. They should have just talked to each other. That's something I know, not *know*.

I'm going to help them.

Since Danna's been gone I've learned how to write. She tried to teach me, but He had other plans then. Now I've learned and I think He must have helped, because I'm very, very good.

Not ordinary, not ordinary at all.

I'll write a poem. In the poem they'll talk to each other.

Danna will say *I am dark and beautiful, dark like the tents of Kedar, like the bed curtains of King Shlomo.*

Zakaryah will answer, *Arise my beloved, and come out to me. The season of the songbirds has arrived, and the voice of the dove is heard in our land.*

Danna will answer, *Let us go early to the vineyards; let us see if the vine has flowered, if the pomegranates are in bloom.*

Then Zakaryah will say, *You have stolen my heart, my sister, my love; you have stolen my heart, with one glance of your eyes.*

They'll be *so* embarrassed. Even He will smile. Those other girls will never stand a chance.

It's a pretty poem, isn't it? I put the words down on the papyrus but I'm not sure I really wrote them. Maybe there's something He wants to do with it that I don't know about. It's exciting! I have to wait and find out like everyone else.

And Gimillu? We never call him that anymore. He's Gemalyahu. He went back to Bavel a year ago. He wanted to see to his sister, Nidintu, who had no one to look after her. That's what he said.

He believed it, too.

That wasn't it, though. He went back to find his mother. Not the one who died. Michal. Michal will heal his shattered heart, and he will fill the emptiness in hers.

When I'm fourteen and all grown up, he'll come back. It will be spring. The hills will be covered in flowers, songbirds will be singing, figs will be growing on the fig trees, the air will be filled with the fragrance of grape vines.

And me?

I'll be adding verses to the poem for two new lovers.

Sometimes it's good to be a prophet.

THE END

HISTORICAL NOTE

IN 586 BCE, the Babylonian king Nebuchadnezzar conquered Jerusalem, deported most of its people to Babylonia and then destroyed the city and the temple of the Israelite god Yahweh.

This was the second deportation. The first took place in 597 BCE and included the then-king, his family, many of his ministers, and other members of the elite.

Some scholars also argue for a third deportation in 582 BCE, though there is some controversy over that.

In any case, in the early sixth century (BCE) there was a relatively large community of exiles from Judah living in Babylonia. Nebuchadnezzar settled them in communities of their own ethnic background along waterways, where they farmed and participated in the Babylonian economy in many ways.

In 539 BCE, Babylonia fell to King Cyrus II of Persia, who thereby inherited the entire Babylonian Empire. This he added to his possessions in Persia and adjacent lands before going on to conquer Anatolia and parts of what would later become Greece. The Persian Empire that he established in this way eventually reached from the Indus Valley west to Europe, south through the Levant (including ancient Israel) and into Egypt. It was the largest empire in the world to that time.

The details of how Cyrus (*Kurush* in Babylonian; *Koresh* in Hebrew) conquered Babylonia are anything but clear. The most detailed sources come from Greek historians writing hundreds of years after the fact. Scholars continue to argue over which elements of their histories are factual and which are mythological.

There are two roughly contemporaneous accounts, the Cyrus Cylinder and the Nabonidus Chronicle, which appear to have many factual details but also include what is clearly royal propaganda from the time of Cyrus or his successors.

The version I've pieced together for the novel goes roughly like this: Cyrus conquered the Babylonian border city of Opis (*Upi* in Babylonian) with considerable bloodshed. He moved on to the city of Babylon itself, where his conquest was aided by the collusion of the priests of Marduk, Babylon's patron god and principal deity. The priesthood was angry at the then-king, Nabonidus (*Nabu-na'id* in Babylonian), because he honored the moon god Sin to the detriment of Marduk. This meant a loss of influence and wealth by the Marduk-oriented establishment.

Because of the inside help he received, the city fell without a fight. You'll have to read the novel to understand how this happened, at least in my version. Cyrus became king and inherited the administrative infrastructure of the Babylonian Empire. This made it easier for him to leave behind a sort of care-taker government so he could go off and conquer more lands.

Babylonian dates were based on the day, the lunar month and the regnal year (the number of the year of the king's reign). Based on the dates indicated in the two texts mentioned above, as converted to modern reckoning, Cyrus' conquest of Babylonia took place in October 539 BCE. In the novel I've moved this date forward to the early summer of the same year.

Scholarship in recent years inclines to the view that things were more nuanced than my version would suggest and that the notion that Nabonidus was hated by the priesthood is mostly the result of Cyrus' after-the-fact propaganda. Nevertheless, the contemporaneous information is sufficiently obscure that this conclusion is not entirely certain.

In any case, one of the policies that Cyrus established was that peoples brought to Babylonia against their will by previous kings were free to return to their lands of origin and rebuild the temples of their gods. Again, endless arguments by scholars over how and why he did this, and how broadly it applied. The Cyrus Cylinder identifies only certain captive peoples from Mesopotamia itself who were allowed to return. It's clear, though, that this right of return extended to other populations as well, because over the next hundred years many peoples did return. Among them were some of the descendants of the exiles from Judah.

The biblical books of Ezra and Nehemiah deal with the return of the Judahites and their building of the Second Temple. These books include the only documentary evidence to date that Cyrus' policies (and those of his successors) did specifically permit and encourage the return of the exiles from Judah. Not surprisingly, it's unclear whether Cyrus did indeed single out the people from Judah for the right of return, as the biblical story asserts, or whether in fact they simply benefited from a broader policy of the empire.

Either way, the return to Zion led to some of the most consequential events in the history of the western world, including the establishment of Yahweh, the God of Israel, as a (and in fact *the*) universal god; the writing and/or finalization of the Bible; its transformation into a sacred canon; and, during the following centuries, the transformation of the Israelite cult into Judaism. Further down the road, the land and culture that the returnees created led to the establishment of Christianity and Islam, which, together with Judaism, constitute the religions of well over three billion people living in the world today.

For a writer of historical fiction, the paucity of authoritative sources from the period and the scholarly arguments over them constitute both a disadvantage and an advantage.

The disadvantage is that it's impossible to know exactly what happened. Anything I put in the story will be rejected by some specialists in the field.

The advantage is that I have a certain freedom to stretch what's known to its limits, and even beyond. This is fiction, after all. I do try not to abuse this freedom, so most of what you'll read in the novel is either factual or reasonably extrapolated from contemporaneous documents and scholarly papers.

One liberty that some readers may notice concerns a number of persons mentioned in the books of Ezra and Nehemiah. The fact is that the timing of the events mentioned in these books is unclear. One reason for this is that these events are dated in the texts to the regnal years of a number of Persian kings, but several of these kings had the same names. Another reason is that the narrative of Ezra/Nehemiah isn't always chronological, so it's sometimes not possible to say in what order things happened, or even when. For the purposes of the story I've brought some of the events and people mentioned in Ezra/Nehemiah forward to the time of the original return— around 539-538 BCE.

One other liberty that specialists may view with suspicion concerns the young people who are at the center of the story. In the novel, they sometimes travel through the countryside without adult chaperones. Were young people who were not yet of marriageable age allowed to do this in the culture of ancient Babylonia? Evidence from both ancient sources and modern scholarship is obscure. Even so, at least one expert I consulted felt this is dubious. My rationale, though, is that the period of the transition from Nabonidus to Cyrus was one of great societal upheaval, even though in the end the conquest was mostly bloodless. But did the inhabitants of Babylonia realize this at first? Surely there would have been large movements of people trying to escape what they would have seen as a massive impending conflict, just as there are today. And if some of these people were orphan children, then. . .

Well, you'll decide whether the story justifies this particular extrapolation.

GUIDE TO LANGUAGES
AND PRONUNCIATION

ABOUT THE LANGUAGES

Although the Hebrew scriptures are written in Hebrew, the language is not referred to by that name in the Bible itself. Instead, the term "Hebrew" is used to designate the people—that is, the Israelite descendants of Abraham. In 2 Kings 18:26, the ministers of King Hezekiah refer to their language as *Yehudit* ("Judean," roughly) when speaking with an envoy of the king of Assyria. For this section I'll refer to the language as Hebrew, although in the novel itself you will see it referred to as *Yehudit*.

The precise original pronunciation of ancient Hebrew is uncertain. Given this I've used the pronunciation of modern Hebrew, the language of the state of Israel, to render biblical words and names. Many of these have more familiar English equivalents (e.g., "Yerushalayim"—Jerusalem) and these I list here with the more authentic pronunciations of the modern language.

The other language that features prominently in the story is Babylonian, referred to in the text as "Chaldean" following the biblical usage. This was a dialect of Ancient Akkadian. Akkadian was a written language with a literary tradition that was already more than two thousand years old at the time the events of the novel take place. It used the cuneiform writing system, a system characterized by word and sound symbols that were pressed into wet clay with a wooden stylus. Akkadian was a Semitic language distantly related to Hebrew. The sound system was considerably different from that of Hebrew, though, so when Hebrew names were captured in Babylonian texts by Babylonian scribes (and hundreds of such texts have been found) they were rendered according to the Babylonian system. As a result they look rather different from the Hebrew versions of the same names, but not so different that their Hebrew provenance can't be recognized.

The other major language in use at the time was Aramaic. This was another Semitic language, one that was much closer to Hebrew than Akkadian was. In fact, some passages in the Bible are written in it, and it is the principal language of the Midrashic commentaries on the Torah. There's general agreement among scholars that in the period during which the story takes place Aramaic had displaced Akkadian as the language of diplomacy and trade throughout the ancient Near East. In the centuries following the events of the novel it in fact became the everyday language of people throughout the region. What is less clear in the scholarly literature is how widespread the use of Aramaic was among ordinary people during the time of the story.

In Jeremiah 5:15 God tells the people of Judah through the prophet that they will be attacked by a far-off nation whose language they do not know. Partly to avoid cluttering the narrative with a third language and partly because it seems to make the most sense, I have taken God's warning to refer to Babylonian and have therefore largely ignored Aramaic for the purposes of the novel.

You will notice that some terms will appear in different languages depending on the context in which the dialog or passage is taking place. For example, when people in the story are speaking Hebrew (*Yehudit*) the name for the biblical kingdom Judah is written as *Yehudah*. However, when the characters are speaking Babylonian it is written as *Yahudu*. Not to panic—the meanings will be clear from context, and naturally the story itself is entirely in English.

ABOUT THE BABYLONIAN NAMES

They're taken from actual Babylonian texts of the period, though they've been repurposed here for the novel.

FINAL NOTES ON PRONUNCIATION

The symbol ' (apostrophe) represents the Hebrew consonants *alef (א)* and *ayyin (ע)*, pronounced in modern Hebrew as the sound in the middle of the English expression "uh oh." Using this convention that expression would be written "uh'oh."

The letter combination "ch" is pronounced like the ch in the name "Bach," not like the normal English ch as in "church."

PRONUNCIATIONS (AND SOME MEANINGS)

Abir-ilu – ah-beer-EE-loo (Babylonian). Name of a Babylonian guard.

Achiyah - AH-chee-yah (Hebrew). Neighbor of Zakaryah in Nar Kabara.

Akkadu – ah-KAH-doo (Babylonian). The name of the Babylonian language in that language. A dialect of Ancient Akkadian, a language distantly related to Hebrew.

Aqara - AH-kah-rah (Babylonian). Tenant farmer on Zakaryah's farm.

Bab-ili – bahb-EE-lee (Babylonian). Babylon. Literally, "gate of the gods."

Banayahu - bah-nah-YAH-hoo (Hebrew). A wealthy Judahite.

Bana-yama - bah-nah-YAH-mah (Babylonian). Babylonian form of Banayahu.

Bavel - bah-VEHL (Hebrew). "Babylon" in Hebrew.

Bel-shar-utsur - bel-shar-OOT-soor (Babylonian). Son of Nabonidus; crown prince of Babylonia. *Belshazzar* in English.

Bel-shunu - bel-SHOO-noo (Babylonian). A Babylonian judge.

Chaldea(n) - kahl-DEE-a(n) (English / Hebrew). The term used in the Bible for the region of Babylonia ("Chaldea") and Babylonian ("Chaldean").

Esagila - eh-sah-GHEE-lah (Babylonian). Temple in Babylon next to the ziggurat of Marduk. A major power center in its own right.

Enuma Elish - eh-NOO-mah-eh-LEESH (Babylonian / Sumerian). The name (first two words) of the Mesopotamian Creation epic. A standard text used in teaching the cuneiform writing system.

E-temen-anki - eh-teh-men-AHN-kee (Babylonian). The ziggurat (stepped pyramid) of Marduk in Babylon. Literally, "the foundation of heaven and earth."

Gemalyahu - geh-mahl-YAH-hoo (Hebrew). Hebrew version of Gimillu's name.

Gimillu - gih-MEEL-loo (Babylonian). One of the main characters in the book. A boy.

Ginat - ghee-NAHT (Hebrew). An old lady in the town of Al Yahudu.

Guzannu - goo-ZAH-noo (Babylonian). Uncle of Gimillu.

Halabu – CHAH-lah-boo (Babylonian). Modern Aleppo. A city that was a way-station on the road to the Euphrates river in what is today Syria.

Hizkiyahu – cheez-kee-YAH-hoo (Hebrew). Hezekiah, formerly king of Judah. Built the famous water tunnel in Jerusalem in preparation for the siege of the Assyrian king Sennacherib.

Immeru - EE-meh-roo (Babylonian). Danna's Judahite cousin. He has a Babylonian name.

Koresh - KOH-resh (Hebrew). Cyrus the Great in Hebrew.

Kudurru - koo-DOO-roo (Babylonian). Gimillu's brother.

Kurush - KOO-roosh (Babylonian). Cyrus the Great, in Babylonian.

Marduk - mar-DOOK (Babylonian). Chief god of Babylon.

Misha'el - MEE-shah-ehl (Hebrew). Zerubavel's wife.

Mitzrayim – meets-RAH-yeem (Hebrew). Egypt.

Moshe – moh-SHAY (Hebrew). Moses.

Mushezib-nabu - moo-SHEH-zeeb-nah-BOO (Babylonian). Father of Gimillu, Kudurru and Nidintu.

Nabu - nah-BOO (Babylonian). Babylonian god; son of Marduk.

Nabu-kuduri-utsur – nah-boo-koo-doo-ree-OOT-soor (Babylonian). Nebuchadnezzar / Nebuchadrezzar, king of Babylonia.

Nabu-na'id - nah-boo-nah-EED (Babylonian). Babylonian king at the time of the Persian conquest.

Nabu-ushabshi - nah-boo-oo-SHAHB-shee. Master of the tablet-house where Gimillu and Zakaryah study cuneiform writing.

Nar Kabara - nahr-kah-BAHR-ah (Babylonia). Judahite agricultural village in Babylonia. Lit. "River Kabara."

Neriyah - NEH-ree-yah (Hebrew). Neighbor of Zakaryah in Nar Kabara.

Neryah - NEHR-yah (Hebrew). Boy in Jerusalem.

Nevuchadnetsar - neh-vu-chahd-NETS-ar. Judahite version of the Babylonian name of the king of Babylon, Nabu-kuduri-utsur. In English, Nebuchadnezzar or Nebuchadrezzar.

Nidintu - nee-DEEN-too (Babylonian). Gimillu's sister.

Ovadyah - oh-VAHD-yah. (Hebrew). A character in the novel.

357

LIGHT OF EXILE

Parsaya - par-SAH-yah (Babylonian). The Persian language.

Parsu - PAR-soo (Babylonian). Persia.

Pazuzu - pah-ZOO-zoo (Babylonian). A Babylonian demon, often represented on amulets to ward off evil.

Shillemyah - shee-LEM-yah (Hebrew). Zakaryah's father.

Shillim-yama - shee-leem-YAH-mah (Babylonian). Babylonian form of name Shillemyah.

Shulmu - SHOOL-moo (Babylonian). A dog.

Upi - OOH-pee (Babylonian). Border town of Babylonia conquered by Cyrus.

Uqupu - ooh-KOO-poo. A character in the book; a boy.

Ya'el - yah-EHL (Hebrew). Zakaryah's grandmother. Heroine of *By the Waters of Babylon.* "Jael" in most English translations of the Bible.

Yahudu – yah-HOO-doo (Babylonian). The kingdom of Judah; Judahitc (Judean).

Yarden - yahr-DEHN (Hebrew). The Jordan river.

Yehezkel - yeh-HEHZ-kehl (Hebrew). The prophet Ezekiel.

Yehoyachin - yeh-HOH-yah-chin (Hebrew). Jehoiachin in English. King of Judah before Zedekiah.

Yehudah – yeh-hu-DAH (Hebrew). The kingdom of Judah.

Yehudim – yeh-hu-DEEM (Hebrew). Judahites, people of the kingdom of Judah. The meaning in modern Hebrew: Jews.

Yehudit – yeh-hu-DEET (Hebrew). The language of Judah, i.e. Hebrew.

Yericho - YEH-ree-cho (Hebrew). Jericho.

Yerushalayim - yeh-roo-shah-LAH-yeem (Hebrew). Jerusalem.

Yirmeyahu - yeer-meh-YAH-hoo (Hebrew). Jeremiah.

Yisra'el - YEES-rah-ehl (Hebrew). Israel.

Yoshiyahu – yoh-shee-YAH-hoo (Hebrew) Josiah, formerly king of Judah. During his reign a scroll of the law was found. Later it would be included in the Bible as the book of Deuteronomy, the last of the five books of Moses.

Zakaryah - zah-KAR-yah (Hebrew). One of the main characters in the novel; a boy.

Zakar-yama - zah-kar-YAH-mah (Babylonian). Babylonian form of name Zakaryah.

Zerubavel - zeh-ROOH-bah-vehl (Hebrew). Zerubbabel, leader of the return to Judah after the fall of Babylon (or the governor of Judah several years later - the Bible gives him both roles).

Zidkiyahu – tseed-kee-YAH-hoo (Hebrew). Zedekiah, king of Judah at the time of the Babylonian conquest.

Ziqqurat - TSEE-koo-raht (Babylonian). Babylonian word for "ziggurat," a sort of stepped pyramid used in Mesopotamia for the temples of the Mesopotamian gods.

ACKNOWLEDGMENTS

WRITING NOVELS IS HARD! Think about it. Every page is blank until you fill it with words. Remember that statistics course in college that you hated? Well, how many degrees of freedom do you think there are on a blank screen? I can tell you, there are an infinite number. It's a fact. You can construct an infinite number of sentences in English (I'm a linguist—I know these things), and each one of them is a potential candidate for that empty page. A daunting thought, believe me.

What made it possible for me was the help I received from friends, family and disinterested bystanders. They read bits and pieces as I wrote. They told me what was working and what wasn't—with the characters, with the plot, with the logic, and with the language.

And let's not forget continuity. Paul Kramer didn't: *Hey Chris, why does the door of the school swing inward in one scene and outward a hundred pages later?*

So in addition to Paul (may his memory be for a blessing), I owe a deep debt of thanks to my wonderful readers: friends Jay Babbitt, Lisa Norris, Tom Geers, Brünhilda Albers, Pam Tumler, Rabbi Gary Huber, and Janis Carter. Similarly, I need to thank my sister Kim Houser, my brother Jon Farrar and my wife Rhonda Moskowitz. All of these delightful people devoted time and energy to helping me bring this novel to completion.

I also owe special thanks to my friend Dr. Steven Fink. He served as my literary consultant on the project. I called him that tongue-in-cheek, but in fact it was his deep background in English literature that gave me the confidence I needed to get over the rough spots where the story seemed to have stalled. Steve, always a glutton for punishment, also drew the maps and pictures that introduce the different sections of the book.

Thanks also to the scholars who helped me with factual information and insights from their own research: Dr. Tero Alstola, Prof. Kevin Burrell, Prof. Geoffrey Emberling, Prof. Laurie Pearce, and Prof. Jason Radine. None of them would agree with every historical detail that I included in the novel, but I'm hoping they'll enjoy the story anyway. And as Dr. Alstola told me when I was obsessing over some such details, "It's fiction after all!"

Finally, I've leaned heavily on the professional expertise of Columbus Publishing Lab in Newark, Ohio. If you think this book looks professionally executed, if the story flows, if the pacing is right, if you like the cover art, if it feels good in your hand as you hold it; you can thank me a little bit and them a lot.

FROM THE AUTHOR

Who were the ancient Israelites, and how did they come to produce the Bible? How can archaeology help us to understand them and the times they lived in?

There's a deep hunger in our culture for insight into the world of the Bible. In the best case this leads people to explore reputable and authoritative sources of insight. In the worst case it creates a space for pseudo-archaeologists to pander silly ideas that have no basis in responsible research.

I'm in the first camp. Scholarly works, popular books, TV programs, trips to Israel with tours of Biblical sites, learning Hebrew, attending archaeology conferences and taking university courses: these have been the stepping stones from which I've built my path.

But scholarly works are not intended to feed the broad popular desire for understanding the Bible. How can people like you and me get a feeling for life in Biblical times, for how the people who lived then saw their world and how, out of that world the Bible emerged?

That's where fiction comes in.

I bring the period of the Bible alive with stories of ordinary people caught up In the world-shaping events of the Hebrew scriptures (Old Testament).

I hope you enjoyed *Light of Exile*. If you did, please join me in exploring the world of ancient Israel through my blogs, books and stories via my website. You may be surprised at who you meet.

www.ChristopherFarrar.com
Facebook: @christopherfarrar

Printed in the USA
CPSIA information can be obtained
at www.ICGtesting.com
CBHW020822251023
1444CB00007B/15